PENGUIN INTERNAT

THE GENERAL IN

Gabriel García Márquez was born in Aracataca, Colombia, in 1928. He studied at the University of Bogotá and later worked as a reporter for the Colombian newspaper *El Espectador* and as a foreign correspondent in Rome, Paris, Barcelona, Caracas and New York. He is the author of several novels and collections of stories, including *No One Writes to the Colonel and Other Stories*, *The Autumn of the Patriarch*, *Innocent Eréndira and Other Stories*, *In Evil Hour*, *Leaf Storm and Other Stories*, *Chronicle of a Death Foretold*, *Love in the Time of Cholera* and the internationally bestselling *One Hundred Years of Solitude*. Gabriel García Márquez was awarded the Nobel Prize for Literature in 1982. He lives in Mexico City.

GABRIEL GARCÍA MÁRQUEZ

The General in His Labyrinth

PENGUIN BOOKS

PENGUIN BOOKS

Published by the Penguin Group
Penguin Books Ltd, 27 Wrights Lane, London W8 5TZ, England
Penguin Books USA Inc., 375 Hudson Street, New York, New York 10014, USA
Penguin Books Australia Ltd, Ringwood, Victoria, Australia
Penguin Books Canada Ltd, 10 Alcorn Avenue, Toronto, Ontario, Canada M4V 3B2
Penguin Books (NZ) Ltd, 182–190 Wairau Road, Auckland 10, New Zealand

Penguin Books Ltd, Registered Offices: Harmondsworth, Middlesex, England

First published in Spain, under the title *El General en Su Laberinto*, by
Mondadori Espana, Madrid, 1989
This translation first published in Great Britain by Jonathan Cape 1990
Published in Penguin Books 1991
3 5 7 9 10 8 6 4 2

A portion of this work was previously published in the *New Yorker*

Printed in England by Clays Ltd, St Ives plc

FOR ALVARO MUTIS,

who gave me the idea for writing this book

It seems that the devil controls the business of my life.

(LETTER TO SANTANDER, AUGUST 4, 1823)

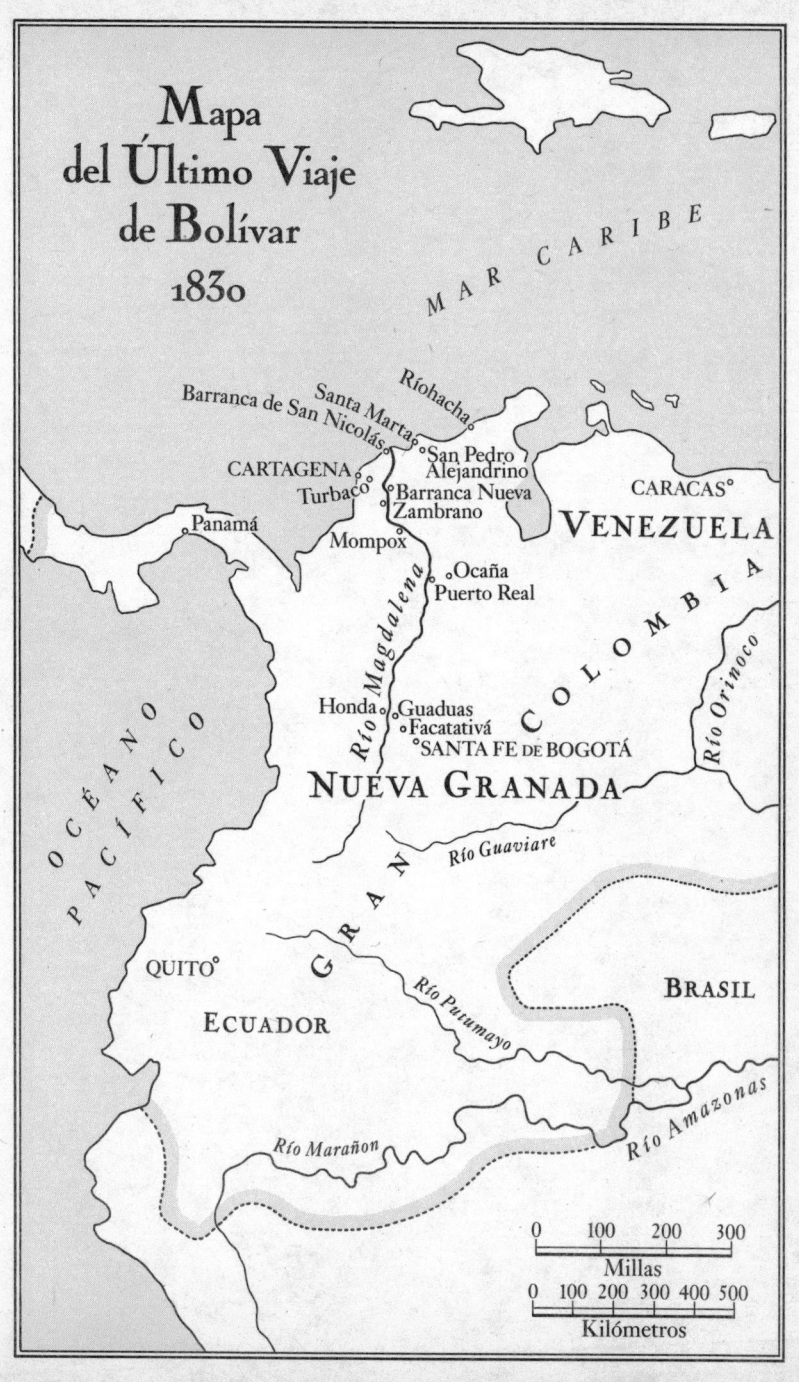

Mapa
del Último Viaje
de Bolívar
1830

MAR CARIBE

Ríohacha

Barranca de San Nicolás
Santa Marta
San Pedro
Alejandrino
CARTAGENA
Turbaco
Barranca Nueva
Zambrano

CARACAS°

VENEZUELA

Panamá

Mompox

Ocaña
Puerto Real

COLOMBIA

OCÉANO
PACÍFICO

Honda
Guaduas
Facatativá
SANTA FE DE BOGOTÁ

Río Magdalena

Río Orinoco

NUEVA GRANADA

GRAN

Río Guaviare

QUITO°

ECUADOR

Río Putumayo

BRASIL

Río Marañón

Río Amazonas

0   100   200   300
Millas
0   100 200 300 400 500
Kilómetros

JOSÉ PALACIOS, his oldest servant, found him floating naked with his eyes open in the purifying waters of his bath and thought he had drowned. He knew this was one of the many ways the General meditated, but the ecstasy in which he lay drifting seemed that of a man no longer of this world. He did not dare come closer but called to him in a hushed voice, complying with the order to awaken him before five so they could leave at dawn. The General came out of his trance and saw in the half-light the clear blue eyes, the curly squirrel-colored hair, the impassive dignity of the steward who attended him every day and who held in his hand a cup of the curative infusion of poppies and gum arabic. The General's hands lacked strength when he grasped the handles of the tub, but he rose up from the medicinal waters in a dolphin-like rush that was surprising in so wasted a body.

"Let's go," he said, "as fast as we can. No one loves us here."

José Palacios had heard him say this so many times and

on so many different occasions that he still did not believe it was true, even though the pack animals were ready in the stables and the members of the official delegation were beginning to assemble. In any event, he helped him to dry and draped the square poncho from the uplands over his naked body because the trembling of his hands made the cup rattle. Months before, while putting on a pair of chamois trousers he had not worn since his Babylonian nights in Lima, the General discovered he was losing height as well as weight. Even his nakedness was distinctive, for his body was pale and his face and hands seemed scorched by exposure to the weather. He had turned forty-six this past July, but his rough Caribbean curls were already ashen, his bones were twisted by premature old age, and he had deteriorated so much he did not seem capable of lasting until the following July. Yet his resolute gestures appeared to be those of a man less damaged by life, and he strode without stopping in a circle around nothing. He drank the tea in five scorching swallows that almost blistered his tongue, avoiding his own watery trail along the frayed rush mats on the floor, and it was as if he had drunk the magic potion of resurrection. But he did not say a word until five o'clock had sounded in the bell tower of the nearby cathedral.

"Saturday, May 8, 1830, the Day of the Blessed Virgin, Mediatrix of all Grace," announced the steward. "It has been raining since three o'clock in the morning."

"Since three o'clock in the morning of the seventeenth century," said the General, his voice still shaken by the bitter breath of insomnia. And he added, in all seriousness: "I didn't hear the roosters."

"There are no roosters here," said José Palacios.

"There's nothing here," said the General. "It's the land of the infidel."

For they were in Santa Fe de Bogotá, city of the Holy Faith, two thousand six hundred meters above the level of the distant sea, and the cavernous bedroom with its bare walls, exposed to the icy winds that filtered through ill-fitting windows, was not the most favorable for anyone's health. José Palacios placed the basin of lather on the marble top of the dressing table, along with the red velvet case that held the shaving implements, all of golden metal. He put the small candleholder with its candle on a ledge near the mirror so the General would have enough light, and he brought the brazier to warm his feet. Then he handed him the spectacles with squared lenses and thin silver frames that he always carried for him in his jacket pocket. The General put them on and began to shave, guiding the razor with as much skill in his left hand as in his right, for his ambidexterity was natural to him, and he showed astonishing control of the same wrist that minutes before could not hold a cup. He finished shaving by touch, still walking around the room, for he tried to see himself in the mirror as little as possible so he would not have to look into his own eyes. Then he plucked the hairs in his nose and ears, polished his perfect teeth with charcoal powder on a silver-handled silk brush, trimmed and buffed the nails on his fingers and toes, and at last took off the poncho and poured a large vial of cologne over his entire body, rubbing it in with both hands until the flask was empty. That dawn he officiated at the daily mass of his ablutions with more frenetic severity than usual, trying to purge his body and spirit of twenty years of fruitless wars and the disillusionments of power.

The last visitor he received the night before was Manuela Sáenz, the bold Quiteña who loved him but was not going to follow him to his death. As always she would remain behind, charged with keeping the General informed of everything that happened in his absence, since for some time he had trusted no one but her. He left in her care some articles whose only value was that they had belonged to him, as well as some of his most prized books and two chests containing his personal archives. The previous day, during their brief formal farewell, he had said to her: "I love you a great deal, but I will love you even more if you show more judgment now than ever before." She understood this as another of the many homages he had paid to her in their eight years of ardent love. Of all the people he knew, she was the only one who believed him: this time it was true that he was leaving. But she was also the only person who had at least one telling reason for expecting him to return.

They had not intended to see each other again before the journey. Nevertheless, the lady of the house wanted to present them with the gift of a final, secret farewell, and she had Manuela, dressed in a cavalry uniform, enter through the main stable doors in order to sidestep the prejudices of the overpious local community. Not because they were clandestine lovers, for they were lovers in the full light of day and with great public scandal, but to preserve at all costs the good name of the house. He was even more careful, for he ordered José Palacios not to close the door to the adjoining room that was a necessary passageway for the household servants and where the aides-de-camp on guard duty played cards until long after the visit was over.

Manuela read to him for two hours. She had been young until a short time before, when her flesh began to overtake her age. She smoked a sailor's pipe, used the verbena water favored by the military as her perfume, dressed in men's clothing, and spent time with soldiers, but her husky voice still suited the penumbra of love. She read by the scant light of the candle, sitting in an armchair that bore the last viceroy's coat of arms, and he listened to her in bed, lying on his back, dressed in the civilian clothes he wore at home and covered by the vicuña poncho. Only the rhythm of his breathing indicated that he was not asleep. The book, by the Peruvian Noé Calzadillas, was entitled *A Reading of News and Gossip Circulating in Lima in the Year of Our Lord 1826*, and she read with a theatrical emphasis that matched the author's style very well.

For the next hour her voice was all that could be heard in the sleeping house. But after the last watch a sudden chorus of men's laughter erupted, rousing all the dogs in the courtyard. He opened his eyes, more intrigued than disturbed, and she closed the book in her lap, marking the page with her thumb.

"Those are your friends," she said to him.

"I have no friends," he said. "And if I do have any left it won't be for long."

"Well, there they are outside, standing guard so you won't be killed," she said.

That was how the General learned what the whole city already knew: not one but several assassination plots against him were brewing, and his last supporters were in the house to try to thwart them. The entrance and the corridors around the interior garden were held by hussars and grenadiers, the Venezuelans who would accompany him to the port of Cartagena de Indias, where he was to board a sailing ship to Europe. Two of them had placed their sleeping mats across the main doorway to the bedroom, and the aides-de-camp would continue playing cards in the adjoining room after Manuela finished reading, but surrounded by so many soldiers of uncertain origin and diverse character, this was not the time for feeling safe about anything. He showed no reaction to the bad news, and with a wave of his hand he ordered Manuela to continue reading.

He always considered death an unavoidable professional hazard. He had fought all his wars in the front lines, without suffering a scratch, and he had moved through enemy fire with such thoughtless serenity that even his officers accepted the easy explanation that he believed himself invulnerable. He had emerged unharmed from every assassination plot against him, and on several occasions his life had been saved because he was not sleeping in his own bed. He did not use an escort, and he ate and drank with no concern for what was offered him, or where. Only Manuela knew that his disinterest was not lack of awareness or fatalism, but rather the melancholy certainty that he would die in his bed, poor and naked and without the consolation of public gratitude.

The only noteworthy change he made that night in the ritual of his insomnia was that he did not take a hot bath before getting into bed. José Palacios had prepared it early, with water steeped in medicinal leaves to heal the General's body and facilitate expectoration, and had kept it at a good temperature for whenever he might want it. But he did not want it. He took two laxative pills for his chronic constipation and settled down to doze to the soothing murmur of Lima's gallant gossip. Then, without warning or apparent cause, he was overcome by an attack of coughing that seemed to shake the very foundations of the house. The officers gambling in the adjacent room were stunned. One of them, the Irishman Belford Hinton Wilson, came to the door in case he was needed, and he saw the General lying face down on the bed, trying to vomit up his insides. Manuela was holding his head over the basin. José Palacios, the only man authorized to enter his bedroom without knocking, stood on the alert, next to the bed, until the crisis passed. Then, with his eyes full of tears, the General took a deep breath and pointed to the dressing table.

"Those graveyard flowers are to blame," he said.

As always, for he always found some unpredictable cause for his misfortunes. Manuela, who knew him better than anyone, made a sign to José Palacios to take away the vase with the morning's withered spikenards. The General stretched out again on the bed and closed his eyes, and she resumed reading in the same tone as before. Only when it seemed to her that he had fallen asleep did she place the book on the night table, kiss his forehead, seared with fever, and whisper to José Palacios that after six o'clock that morning she would be waiting for a last goodbye at Cuatro Esquinas, where the King's Highway to Honda began. She wrapped herself in a battle cloak and tiptoed out of the bedroom. Then the General opened his eyes and said to José Palacios in a thin voice:

"Tell Wilson to take her home."

The order was carried out against Manuela's will, for she thought she could protect herself better than a squadron of lancers. José Palacios lit their way to the stables, around an interior garden with a stone fountain, where the first spikenards of the dawn were beginning to open. The rain had stopped and the wind no longer whistled through the trees, but there was not a single star in the frozen sky. Colonel Belford Wilson repeated the password as he walked in order to quiet the sentries lying on straw mats in the corridor. When he passed the window of the principal reception room, José Palacios saw the master of the house serving coffee to the group of friends, military and civilian, who had volunteered to stand watch until the moment of departure.

When he returned to the bedroom he found the General in the clutches of delirium. He heard him utter disconnected phrases that all fit together into one: "Nobody understood anything." His body burned in a bonfire of fever, and he was farting stony, foul-smelling gas. The next day not even the General would be able to tell if he had been talking in his sleep or raving while awake, and he would not remember anything he said. These were what he called "my crises of dementia." They no longer alarmed anyone, since he had suffered them for over four years without any doctor risking a scientific explanation, and the following day would find him risen from the ashes with his reason intact. José Palacios wrapped him in a blanket, left the candle burning on the marble top of the dressing table, and went out without closing the door so he could continue watching from the adjoining room. He knew he would recover sometime at daybreak and immerse himself in the icy waters of the bath in an effort to restore the strength that had been ravaged by the horror of his nightmares.

It was the end of a clamorous day. A garrison of seven hundred eighty-nine hussars and grenadiers had rebelled on the pretext of demanding payment of wages they had not received for the past three months. But the real reason was this: most of them were from Venezuela, and many had fought wars for the liberation of four different nations, but in recent weeks they had been the victims of so much vituperation and provocation on the streets that they had cause to fear for their safety after the General left the country. The conflict was settled by payment of their travel expenses and a thousand gold pesos instead of the seventy thousand the insurgents had asked for, and at dusk they had marched away to their native land, followed by a pack of women with their baggage and all their children and domestic animals. The din of the bass drums and the military brass band could not drown out the tumultuous shouting of the mobs that set their dogs on them and hurled strings of firecrackers at their feet to make them break step, actions they had never taken against enemy troops. Eleven years earlier, after three long centuries of Spanish domination, the brutal Viceroy Don Juan Sámano had fled through those same streets disguised as a pilgrim, but his trunks were full of gold statues and uncut emeralds, sacred toucans and brilliant stained-glass butterflies from Muzo, and there was no lack of people to weep for him from their balconies and throw flowers in his path and offer him heartfelt wishes for a calm sea and a prosperous voyage.

Without moving from the house that had been lent to him by the Minister of the Army and Navy, the General had played a secret part in negotiating the conflict, and in the end he had ordered General José Laurencio Silva, his nephew by marriage and a trusted aide, to leave with the rebellious troops as a guarantee that there would be no new disturbances before they reached the Venezuelan border. He did not see the parade under his balcony, but he had heard the bugles and the drumrolls, and the raucous yells of the throngs in the street, whose shouts he could not understand. He attributed so little importance to them that he reviewed back correspondence with his secretaries and dictated a letter to Grand Marshal Don Andrés de Santa Cruz, the President of Bolivia, in which he announced his withdrawal from power but was not very certain whether he would travel abroad. "I won't write another letter for the rest of my life," he said when he had finished. Later, while he was sweating his siesta fever, the sound of distant disturbances penetrated his sleep, and he was startled awake by a series of explosions that could just as well have been insurgency as fireworks. But when he asked about it he was told it was a fiesta. That was all: "It's a fiesta, General." And no one, not even José Palacios, would have dared to explain just what fiesta it was.

Only when Manuela told him that night during her visit did he learn that it was the followers of his political enemies, the demagogue party as he called them, who, with the compliance of the police, were roaming the streets and inciting the artisans' guilds against him. It was Friday, market day, which made it easier to create disorder in the main square. A heavier rain than usual, accompanied by thunder and lightning, dispersed the rioters at nightfall. But the damage was done. Students from the Academy of San Bartolomé had assaulted and seized the offices of the Supreme Court in order to force a public trial of the General, and they had slashed with bayonets and then hurled down from the balcony his life-size portrait painted in oils by a veteran of the liberating army. The mobs, drunk on corn liquor, had looted the shops along the Calle Real as well as the bars in the poor suburbs that had not closed down in time, and in the main square they shot a general stuffed with sawdust, which did not need the long blue tunic with gold buttons for everyone to know who it was. They accused him of being the secret instigator of the military uprising in a belated effort to regain the power he had exercised for twelve uninterrupted years and that the Congress had taken away from him by unanimous vote. They accused him of wanting to be president for life so he could appoint a European prince as his successor. They accused him of pretending to travel abroad when in reality he was going to the Venezuelan border and planned to return at the head of the insurgent troops in order to seize power. Public walls were plastered with *papeluchas*, the popular name for the abusive broadsides printed against him, and his best-known followers remained in hiding in other people's houses until passions cooled. The press devoted to General Francisco de Paula Santander, his principal enemy, had taken to its bosom the rumor that the General's mysterious and very well publicized illness, and the tiresome, ostentatious show he made of leaving, were mere political ruses to make people beg him to stay. That night, while Manuela Sáenz recounted details of the perilous day, the soldiers of the Interim President were trying to wipe away a sentence scrawled in charcoal on the wall of the Episcopal Palace: "He won't leave and he won't die." The General sighed.

"Things must be very bad," he said, "and getting even worse for me if this could happen only a block from here and they could make me think it was a fiesta."

The truth was that even his most intimate friends did not believe he was abandoning either power or the country. The city was too small and his own people too punctilious not to know the two great flaws in his dubious departure: he did not have enough money to go anywhere with such a large entourage, and having been President of the Republic, he could not leave the country before a year had passed without the permission of the government, and he had not even had the guile to request it. The order to pack, which he gave in an obvious manner so that anyone who wanted to could hear it, was not taken as decisive proof even by José Palacios, for on other occasions he had gone to the extreme of leaving a house empty in order to feign his departure, and it had always been a clever political maneuver. His military aides felt that the symptoms of disillusionment had been too evident during the last year. Nevertheless, the same thing had occurred before, and when they least expected it they had seen him awaken with new spirit and take up again the thread of his life with more enthusiasm than ever. José Palacios, who always followed these unpredictable changes at close range, said it in his own way: "Only my master knows what my master is thinking."

His repeated renunciations of power had been incorporated into popular song, beginning with the first one, an ambiguous statement in the very speech with which he had assumed the presidency: "My first day of peace will be my last one in power." In the years that followed, his renunciations were reiterated so many times, and in such dissimilar circumstances, that no one ever knew again which to believe. The most sensational of all had occurred two years earlier, on the night of September 25, when he escaped unharmed from an attempt to assassinate him right in the bedroom of Government House. The congressional delegation that visited him at dawn, after he had spent six hours under a bridge, exposed to the weather, found him wrapped in a woolen blanket with his feet in a basin of hot water, but not as shaken by fever as by disillusion. He announced that the conspiracy would not be investigated, that no one would be prosecuted, and that the Congress designated for the coming year would meet without delay to elect another President of the Republic.

"After that," he concluded, "I will leave Colombia forever."

Nevertheless, the investigation took place, the guilty were judged with an iron hand, and fourteen were shot in the main square. The Constituent Congress of January 2 did not meet for another sixteen months, and no one spoke again of his resignation. But during that time there was no foreign visitor, or chance companion, or casual acquaintance, to whom he did not say: "I will go where I am wanted."

The public announcements of his fatal disease were also not taken as valid evidence of his departure. No one doubted he was ill. On the contrary, since his last return from the southern wars everyone who had seen him pass beneath the floral arches was struck by the astounding idea that he had returned only to die. Instead of Palomo Blanco, his historic horse, he came back riding a poor bald mule with trappings of straw, his hair had turned gray and his forehead was furrowed by passing storm clouds, and he wore a dirty tunic with a torn sleeve. The glory had left his body. At the gloomy reception held for him that night at Government House he was morose and uncommunicative, and no one ever knew if it was political perversity or simple distraction that made him greet one of his ministers by another's name.

Not even his moribund appearance was enough to make anyone believe he was leaving—for six years they had said he was dying, and still he preserved intact his desire to rule. The first report had been brought by a British naval officer who chanced to see him in the Pativilca Desert north of Lima at the height of the war for the liberation of the south. He found him lying on the floor of a miserable hut that served as an improvised head-quarters, wrapped in a barracan cloak, with a rag tied around his head because he could not bear the cold in his bones during the hellish noonday heat, and too weak even to chase away the hens pecking the ground around him. After an awkward conversation interrupted by outbursts of dementia, he said goodbye to his visitor with dramatic pathos:

"Go and tell the world how you saw me die covered with chicken shit on these inhospitable sands."

They said his illness was a kind of madness caused by the mercurial desert sun. Then they said he was dying in Guayaquil, and later in Quito, of a gastric fever whose most alarming symptom was lack of interest in the world and absolute spiritual calm. No one ever learned the scientific basis for these reports, for he had always been opposed to medical science, and he diagnosed and treated himself according to Donostierre's *La médecine à votre manière*, a French manual of home remedies that José Palacios carried wherever he went as an oracle for understanding and curing any disturbance of body or soul.

In any case, there had never been a death agony more fruitful than his. For while they thought he was dying in Pativilca he crossed the Andean peaks again, conquered at Junín, completed the liberation of all of Spanish America with the final victory at Ayacucho, created the Republic of Bolivia, and was happier in Lima and more intoxicated with glory than he had ever been before or would ever be again. As a consequence, the repeated announcements that he at last was leaving power and country because of illness, and the formal public ceremonies that seemed to confirm them, were no more than idle repetitions of a drama too often seen to be believed.

A few days after his return, at the end of a bitter meeting of the Council of State, he took Field Marshal Antonio José de Sucre by the arm. "Stay with me," he said. He led him to his private office, where he received only a select few, and he almost forced him to sit in his personal armchair.

"That place is more yours now than mine," he said.

The Field Marshal of Ayacucho, his intimate friend, was well aware of the state of the nation, but the General gave him a detailed accounting before he came to the point. In a few days the Constituent Congress would meet to elect the President of the Republic and approve a new constitution in a belated effort to save the golden dream of continental unity. Perú, dominated by a reactionary aristocracy, seemed irretrievable. General Andrés de Santa Cruz was leading Bolivia by the nose down a path of his own making. Venezuela, under the imperi-

ous rule of General José Antonio Páez, had just proclaimed its autonomy. General Juan José Flores, Prefect
General in the south, had united Guayaquil and Quito to
create the independent Republic of Ecuador. The Republic of Colombia, the embryo of an immense, unified
nation, had been reduced to the size of the former Viceregency of New Granada. Sixteen million Americans
who had just begun their life of freedom were at the
mercy of local tyrants.

"In short," the General concluded, "everything we
created with our hands is being trampled on by others."

"It's destiny's joke," said Field Marshal Sucre. "It
seems we planted the ideal of independence so deep that
now these countries are trying to win their independence
from each other."

The General's response was spirited.

"Don't repeat the enemy's vile remarks," he said, "even
when they're as accurate as that one."

Field Marshal Sucre apologized. He was intelligent,
methodical, shy, and superstitious, and he had a sweetness
in his face that old smallpox scars could not diminish. The
General, who loved him so well, had said of him that he
feigned a modesty he did not possess. He was a hero at
Pichincha, Tumusla, and Tarqui, and not long after his
twenty-ninth birthday he had commanded the glorious
battle of Ayacucho, which destroyed the last Spanish
stronghold in South America. But more than for these
achievements he was notable for the goodness of his heart
in victory and for his talent as a statesman. At that moment he had renounced his offices, used no military mark-
ings of any kind, and wore a black wool greatcoat that

reached down to his ankles and always had its collar turned up to protect him against the stabbing glacial winds from the nearby hills. His only involvement with the nation, and he desired it to be his last, was to participate in the Constituent Congress as a deputy from Quito. He was thirty-five years old, as healthy as a rock, and mad with love for Doña Mariana Carcelén, the Marquise of Solanda, a beautiful and vivacious Quiteña just out of adolescence whom he had married by proxy two years earlier and with whom he had a six-month-old daughter.

The General could not imagine anyone better qualified to succeed him as President of the Republic. He knew he was five years too young for the office, according to a constitutional limitation imposed by General Rafael Urdaneta in order to block Sucre's way. Nevertheless, the General was taking secret steps to amend the amendment.

"Accept," he said to him, "and I will stay on as Generalissimo, circling the government like a bull round a herd of cows."

His appearance was feeble but his determination was powerful. Nevertheless, the Field Marshal had known for some time that the General's seat would never be his. A short while before, when the possibility of becoming president was first suggested to him, he had said he would never govern a nation whose structure and future direction were growing more and more hazardous. In his opinion, the first step toward correction was to distance the military from power, and he wanted to propose to the Congress that no general could become president for the next four years, perhaps with the intention of blocking Urdaneta's way. But the strongest opponents of this amendment would be the strongest men of all: the generals themselves.

"I am too tired to work without a compass," said Sucre. "Besides, Your Excellency knows as well as I do that what will be needed here is not a president but a breaker of insurrections."

He would attend the Constituent Congress, of course, and he would even accept the honor of presiding if it was offered to him. But nothing more. Fourteen years of wars had taught him there was no greater victory than being alive. The presidency of Bolivia, that vast, unexplored country which he had founded and governed with a wise hand, had taught him the capriciousness of power. The wisdom of his heart had taught him the vanity of glory. "And therefore no, Excellency," he concluded. On June 13, the Feast of Saint Anthony, he would be in Quito with his wife and daughter to celebrate with them not only that saint's day but all the others the future might hold in store for him. His determination to live for them, and only for them, in the joy of love, had been made this past Christmas.

"It is all I ask of life," he said.

The General was livid. "I thought nothing could surprise me anymore," he said. And he looked into his eyes.

"Is this your last word?"

"The next to last," said Sucre. "My last word is my eternal gratitude for all Your Excellency's kindness."

The General slapped his own thigh to wake himself out of an irredeemable dream.

"Good," he said. "You have just made the last decision of my life for me."

That night he composed his resignation under the demoralizing effect of an emetic prescribed by a chance physician to calm his biliousness. On January 20 he opened the Constituent Congress with a farewell address in which he praised its president, Field Marshal Sucre, as the worthiest of generals. The praise drew an ovation from the Congress, but a deputy who was near Urdaneta whispered in his ear: "That means there's a general worthier than you." The General's remark and the deputy's malice were like two burning nails in the heart of General Rafael Urdaneta.

And with reason. Even if Urdaneta did not enjoy Sucre's immense military achievements or his great powers to charm, there was no reason to think he was any less worthy. His presence of mind and his constancy had been extolled by the General himself, his fidelity and his love for him had been proved many times over, and he was one of the few men in this world who dared tell him to his face the truths he was afraid to hear. Conscious of his mistake, the General tried to make amends in the galley proofs, and in his own hand he changed "the worthiest of generals" to read "one of the worthiest." The correction did not mitigate Urdaneta's rancor.

Days later, at a meeting between the General and loyal deputies, Urdaneta accused him of pretending to leave while secretly trying to be reelected. Three years earlier General José Antonio Páez had seized power in the Department of Venezuela in a first attempt at separation from Colombia. The General went to Caracas and effected a reconciliation with Páez in a public embrace amid hymns of jubilation and ringing bells, and he created a special made-to-measure regime for Páez that allowed him to rule however he pleased. "That's where the disaster began," said Urdaneta. For the accommodation had not only led to poisoned relations with the New Granadans but also infected them with the germ of separatism. Now, Urdaneta concluded, the greatest service the General could render the nation would be to renounce without delay the habit of command and leave the country. The General replied with comparable vehemence. But Urdaneta was an upright man who spoke with skill and passion, and he left everyone with the impression that they had witnessed the ruin of a deep, long-standing friendship.

The General repeated his resignation and designated Don Domingo Caycedo as Interim President until Congress elected a permanent leader. On March 1 he left Government House by the service entrance in order to avoid the guests who were toasting his successor with champagne, and he drove in a borrowed carriage to Fucha Manor, an idyllic retreat on the outskirts of the city which the provisional President had lent to him. The simple knowledge that he was no more than an ordinary citizen intensified the devastating effects of the emetic. He was half awake when he asked José Palacios to prepare the materials he would need to write his memoirs. José Palacios brought him ink and enough paper for forty years of memories, and he advised Fernando, the General's nephew and secretary, so that he would be ready to offer his services on the following Monday at four o'clock in the morning, which was the General's best time for thinking, with all his rancor fresh and raw. According to what he had often told his nephew, he wanted to begin with his oldest memory, a dream he had on the

Hacienda San Mateo, in Venezuela, not long after his third birthday. He dreamed that a black mule with gold teeth had come inside and gone through the house from the principal reception room to the pantries, eating without haste everything in its path while the family and slaves were taking their siestas, until at last it had eaten the curtains, the rugs, the lamps, the vases, the table service and linen in the dining room, the saints in the altars, the wardrobes and chests with all their contents, the pots in the kitchens, the doors and windows with their hinges and bolts, and all the furniture from the portico to the bedrooms, and the only thing left intact was the oval of his mother's dressing table mirror, floating in its own space.

But he felt so content in the house at Fucha, and the air was so soft under a sky of hurrying clouds, that he did not mention his memoirs again but used the dawns to walk the fragrant paths of the savanna. Those who visited him in the days that followed had the impression he had recuperated, and the officers above all, his most loyal friends, urged him to remain in the presidency even if it was by military coup. He discouraged them with the argument that power by force was unworthy of his glory, but he did not seem to reject altogether the hope of being confirmed by a legitimate decision of Congress. José Palacios repeated: "Only my master knows what my master is thinking."

Manuela continued to live a few steps from San Carlos Palace, the presidential residence, with her ear tuned to the talk in the streets. She came to Fucha two or three times a week, more often if she had urgent news, bringing marzipan and sweets fresh from the convents, and bars of chocolate with cinnamon for their four o'clock tea. She almost never brought the newspapers, because the General had become so susceptible to criticism that any trivial misgiving could unhinge him. On the other hand, she reported intrigues in infinite detail, the betrayals in the salons and the prognostications of the rumor mills, and he had to listen to these with his guts in a knot even when they were critical of him, because she was the only person permitted to tell him the truth. When they did not have a great deal to say to each other they reviewed his correspondence, or she read to him, or they played cards with the aides-de-camp, but they always had lunch alone.

They had met in Quito eight years before at a gala ball to celebrate the liberation, when she was still the wife of Dr. James Thorne, an English gentleman who had become established among the aristocrats of Lima during the final days of the viceregency. In addition to being the last woman with whom the General maintained a long-term liaison after the death of his wife, twenty-seven years earlier, she was also his confidante, the guardian of his archives, his most impassioned reader, and a member of his staff with the rank of colonel. The days were long past when she had been ready to bite off his ear during a jealous quarrel, but their most trivial conversations still tended to end with the explosions of hatred and the tender reconciliations of a great love affair. Manuela did not sleep at the manor house. She left early enough so that darkness would not take her by surprise en route, above all during that season of brief twilights.

In contrast to what had occurred at La Magdalena Manor in Lima, where he had to invent pretexts for keeping her at a distance while he took his pleasure with ladies who were highborn and with others who were less so, at Fucha Manor he showed signs of not being able to live without her. He would watch the road she had to travel, he plagued José Palacios, asking him the time every few seconds, requesting that he change the placement of his armchair, that he stir up the fire, that he put it out, that he light it again, and he was impatient and ill-humored until he saw her coach appear from behind the hills and light up his life. But he showed signs of the same agitation when her visit lasted longer than expected. When it was time for siesta they would get into bed without closing the door, without undressing, without sleeping, and more than once they made the mistake of attempting one final lovemaking, for he refused to admit he no longer had enough bodily substance to gratify her soul.

During this time his tenacious insomnia showed signs of disruption. He would fall asleep at any hour, in the middle of a sentence while dictating a letter, or during a card game, and even he was not really certain if they were sudden bursts of sleep or brief fainting spells, but as soon as he lay down he felt overcome by a crisis of lucidity. He would just slip into a mire of half-sleep at daybreak, until he was awakened again by the wind of peace in the trees. Then he did not resist the temptation to put off dictating his memoirs for yet another morning in order to take a solitary walk that sometimes lasted until lunchtime.

He would go without an escort, without the two faithful dogs that had accompanied him even on the battlefield, without any of his epic horses, which had already been sold to the battalion of hussars to increase his travel funds. He would walk to the nearby river over the blanket of decayed leaves on the interminable tree-lined paths, protected from the icy savanna winds by the vicuña poncho, the boots lined with raw wool, and the green silk cap he used to wear only for sleeping. He would sit for a long while to meditate in the shade of the weeping willows, facing the narrow bridge made of loose planks, absorbed in the river currents he had once compared to the destiny of men, in a rhetorical simile worthy of his childhood tutor, Don Simón Rodríguez. One of his guards would follow him, unseen, until he returned soaked with dew and with a thread of breath almost too thin for him to climb the steps to the portico, haggard and dazed but with the eyes of a happy madman. He felt so content during those evasive walks that the hidden guards would hear him through the trees, singing the soldiers' songs he used to sing in the years of his legendary glories and his Homeric defeats. Those who knew him best asked themselves the reason for his high spirits when Manuela herself doubted he would be confirmed another time as President of the Republic by a Constituent Congress even he had described as admirable.

On the day of the election, during his morning walk, he saw a greyhound without its owner chasing quail through the hedges. He called to it with a street-corner whistle, and the animal made an abrupt stop, looked for him with ears erect, and found him with his poncho almost dragging on the ground, his cap worthy of a Florentine pontiff, forsaken by God between the swift-moving clouds and the immense plain. It smelled him with painstaking care while he caressed its coat with his fingertips, but then the dog leaped away in a sudden rush, looked into his eyes with its golden eyes, growled with suspicion, and fled in fear. He followed along an unfamiliar path that ended in a poor suburb of muddy narrow streets and red-roofed adobe houses from whose patios rose the smell of milking. He heard the sudden shout:

"Skinny Shanks!"

He did not have time to dodge the cow manure that was hurled at him from a stable, smashed into the middle of his chest, and spattered his face. But it was the words more than the explosion of dung that woke him from the stupor in which he had lived since leaving the presidential residence. He knew the nickname the New Granadans had given him: it was the name of a madman famous for his theatrical uniforms. Even one of the senators who called themselves liberals had used the name in Congress in his absence, and only two men had stood up to protest. But he had never heard it in person. He began to wipe his face with the edge of the poncho, and had not yet finished when the unseen guard who was following him ran out from between the trees with his sword drawn to punish the insult. He turned on him in a burning flash of anger.

"And what the hell are you doing here?" he asked.

The officer snapped to attention.

"I'm following orders, Excellency."

"I'm not your excellency," he replied.

He stripped him of his ranks and titles with so much rage that the officer considered himself fortunate that the General no longer had the strength for a more savage reprisal. Even José Palacios, who understood him so well, found it difficult to understand his severity.

It was a disastrous day. He spent the morning walking

around the house as distraught as when he was waiting for Manuela, but he concealed from no one that this time his longing was not for her but for news from the Congress. Minute by minute he attempted to calculate the detailed progress of the session. When José Palacios answered that it was ten o'clock, he said: "No matter how the demagogues want to go on braying, they must have begun voting by now." Then, after a long period of reflection, he wondered aloud: "Who can know what a man like Urdaneta is thinking?" José Palacios knew that the General knew, because Urdaneta was still proclaiming far and wide the cause and extent of his resentment. Once, as José Palacios happened to be walking past, the General asked in an offhand manner: "Whom do you think Sucre will vote for?" José Palacios knew as well as he that Field Marshal Sucre could not vote because he was on a congressional mission to Venezuela with the Bishop of Santa Marta, Monsignor José María Estévez, to negotiate the terms of that country's separation. And so he did not stop when he answered: "You know that better than anyone, Señor." The General smiled for the first time since he had returned from his abominable walk.

Despite his erratic appetite he almost always sat at the table before eleven o'clock to eat a boiled egg with a glass of port, or to pick at a wedge of cheese, but that day he watched the road from the terrace while the others had lunch, and he was so absorbed not even José Palacios dared to disturb him. It was past three o'clock when he heard the sound of the mules' hooves before he saw Manuela's carriage coming over the hills, and he leaped from the chair. He ran to receive her, he opened the door to help her down, and from the moment he saw her face he knew. Don Joaquín Mosquera, the oldest son of an illustrious family from Popayán, had been elected President of the Republic by unanimous vote.

His reaction was not so much anger or disillusion as astonishment, for he himself had suggested the name of Don Joaquín Mosquera to the Congress in the certainty he would not accept. He sank into deep thought, and he did not speak again until tea. "Not a single vote for me?" he asked. Not a single one. Nevertheless, the official delegation of devoted deputies who visited him later explained that his followers had agreed to make the vote unanimous so he would not appear to be the loser in a bitter contest. He was so irritated, he did not seem to appreciate the subtlety of that gallant maneuver. He thought, instead, it would have been worthier of his glory if they had accepted his resignation the first time he offered it.

"The long and short of it is," he sighed, "that the demagogues have won again, and twice over."

Nevertheless, he was very careful to hide his consternation until he said goodbye to them on the portico. But their coaches had not been lost from view when he was struck down by a crisis of coughing that kept the manor house in a state of alarm until nightfall. One of the members of the official delegation had said that the decision of the Congress had been so prudent it had saved the Republic. He ignored the remark, but that night, while Manuela was obliging him to drink a cup of broth, he said to her: "No congress ever saved a republic." Before going to bed he assembled his aides and servants, and with the solemnity that was customary in his dubious renunciations he announced:

"Tomorrow I leave the country."

It was not tomorrow, but four days later. In the meantime he recovered his lost equanimity, dictated a farewell proclamation in which he did not betray the wounds to his heart, and returned to the city to prepare for the journey. General Pedro Alcántara Herrán, Minister of the Army and Navy in the new government, brought him to his house on Calle La Enseñanza, not so much to offer hospitality as to protect him from the death threats that were becoming more and more alarming.

Before leaving Santa Fe de Bogotá he liquidated the little of value he still owned in order to increase his treasury. In addition to the horses, he sold a silver service dating back to the lavish days of Potosí, which was appraised at two thousand five hundred pesos by the Mint for the simple value of the metal, without taking into account the beauty of its workmanship or its historic importance. When the final reckoning was made, he had seventeen thousand six hundred pesos and sixty centavos in cash, a draft for eight thousand pesos drawn on the public treasury of Cartagena, a pension for life granted him by the Congress, and a little over six hundred ounces of gold distributed among various trunks. This was the woeful remnant of a personal fortune that on the day of his birth had been considered among the greatest in the Americas.

On the morning of their departure, in the bags that José Palacios packed without haste while the General finished dressing, there were only two well-worn sets of underclothing, two changes of shirt, the battle tunic with a double row of buttons that were supposed to have been made from the gold of Atahualpa, the silk cap for sleeping, and a red hood that Field Marshal Sucre had brought him from Bolivia. His footwear consisted of his house slippers and the patent-leather boots he would be wearing. In his personal trunks José Palacios was carrying, along with the chest of medicines and a few other articles of value, Rousseau's *Social Contract* and *The Art of War* by the Italian general Raimundo Montecuccoli, two bibliographical treasures that had belonged to Napoleon Bonaparte and had been given to him by Sir Robert Wilson, the father of his aide-de-camp. There was so little that it all fit into a soldier's knapsack. When he saw it as he was about to go to the room where the official delegation was waiting, he said:

"We never would have believed, my dear José, that so much glory could fit into a shoe."

His seven pack mules, however, were carrying chests full of medals and gold tableware and numerous objects of a certain value, ten trunks of private papers, two of books he had read and at least five of clothing, and several chests with all manner of good and bad things that no one had the patience to tally. All of this, however, was not even a shadow of the baggage he had brought with him on his return from Lima three years earlier, when he was invested with triple power as President of Bolivia and Colombia and Dictator of Perú: a drove of pack animals carrying seventy-two trunks and over four hundred chests with countless objects whose value had not been established. On that occasion he had left in Quito more than six hundred books, which he never attempted to recover.

It was almost six o'clock. The millenarian drizzle had stopped for a moment, but the world was still cloudy and cold, and the house, taken over by the troops, had begun to emit a foul barracks smell. The hussars and the grenadiers scrambled to their feet when they saw the taciturn General approaching from the end of the corridor, surrounded by his aides-de-camp and looking green in the light of dawn, his poncho thrown across his shoulder and his broad-brimmed hat making the shadows of his face even deeper. Following an old Andean superstition he covered his mouth with a handkerchief soaked in cologne as protection against harmful drafts caused by abrupt exposure to the weather. He did not wear any insignia of his rank, and there was no trace left of the immense authority he had once possessed, but the magic halo of power distinguished him from the noisy retinue of officers. He walked toward the drawing room at an unhurried pace along the corridor, lined with straw matting, that encircled the interior garden, indifferent to the soldiers of the guard who snapped to attention as he passed. Before entering the drawing room he tucked the handkerchief into his cuff, as only clerics did now, and handed his hat to one of the aides-de-camp.

In addition to those who had kept watch in the house, other civilians and soldiers had been arriving since dawn. They were drinking coffee in scattered groups, and their somber clothing and hushed voices had rarefied the atmosphere with a mournful solemnity. The sudden sharp voice of a diplomat rose above the whispers:

"This looks like a funeral."

No sooner had he spoken than he sensed the cloud of cologne saturating the air in the room behind him. Then he turned, holding a cup of steaming coffee between his thumb and forefinger, and he was disturbed by the thought that the phantom who had just walked in might have heard his impertinence. But no: although the General's last visit to Europe had been twenty-four years earlier, when he was very young, his fond European memories were sharper than his resentment. And so the diplomat was the first he approached, in order to greet him with the extreme courtesy he believed the English deserved.

"I hope there is not much fog this fall in Hyde Park," he said.

The diplomat experienced a moment's hesitation, for in recent days he had heard that the General was going to three different places, and none of them was London. But he recovered in an instant.

"We will try to have the sun shining night and day for Your Excellency," he said.

The new President was not there, for the Congress had elected him in absentia and he would need more than a month to arrive from Popayán. In his stead was General Domingo Caycedo, the Vice-President-elect, of whom it had been said that any office in the Republic was too restrictive for him because he had the bearing and distinction of a king. The General greeted him with great deference and said in jest:

"Do you know I don't have permission to leave the country?"

Everyone greeted his statement with laughter, although everyone knew it was not a joke. General Caycedo promised he would send a valid passport to Honda by the next post.

The official delegation was composed of the Archbishop of the city and other notable men and high-ranking officials with their wives. The civilians wore chaps and the military wore riding boots, for their intention was to accompany the illustrious exile for several leagues. The General kissed the Archbishop's ring and the ladies' hands, and shook the gentlemen's hands without effusiveness, an absolute master of well-bred ceremony but a total stranger to the kind favored in that ambiguous city, about which he had said on more than one occasion: "This isn't my theater." He greeted them all in turn as he walked through the room, and for each he had a phrase learned with all due deliberation in the manuals of etiquette, but he looked no one in the eye. His voice was metallic and cracked with fever, and his Caribbean accent, which so many years of travels and the tribulations of war had not softened, sounded even harsher compared to the lush diction of the Andeans.

When he completed his greetings, the Interim President handed him a paper signed by numerous distinguished New Granadans expressing the nation's gratitude for so many years of service. In yet another tribute to local formality he pretended to read it before the silent company, for he could not have seen it without spectacles and unless the handwriting were larger. And yet when he pretended to have finished, he directed a few brief words of gratitude to the delegation, which were so appropriate to the occasion that no one could have said he had not read the document. Then he looked around the room, and without hiding a certain amount of concern, he asked:

"Didn't Urdaneta come?"

The Interim President informed him that General Rafael Urdaneta had left with the rebel troops in support of General José Laurencio Silva's precautionary mission.

Then someone let his voice be heard above the others:

"Sucre didn't come either."

He could not ignore the malicious intention of that unsolicited report. His eyes, which had been dimmed and aloof until that moment, flashed with feverish intensity and he replied, not knowing to whom:

"The Field Marshal of Ayacucho was not informed of the time of our departure, so as not to interfere with his mission."

It was apparent he did not know that Field Marshal Sucre had returned two days earlier from his failed mission to Venezuela, where he had not been allowed to enter his own country. No one had told him the General was leaving, perhaps because it had not occurred to anyone that he was not the first to know. José Palacios learned this at a difficult moment, and then he forgot it in the confusion of their final days. He did not discount, of course, the dreadful idea that Field Marshal Sucre might feel resentful at not being informed.

In the adjoining dining room the table was laid with a splendid American breakfast: tamales in corn husks, blood sausage with rice, eggs scrambled in casserole, a rich variety of pastries on lace cloths, and pots of hot chocolate as thick as perfumed paste. The hosts had delayed breakfast in the event he agreed to preside over the table, although they knew that in the morning he took nothing but the infusion of poppies and gum arabic. In any case, the lady of the house fulfilled her obligations by inviting him to sit in the armchair reserved for him at the head of the table, but he declined the honor and addressed everyone with a formal smile.

"My road is a long one," he said. "Enjoy your meal."

He stood on tiptoe to take his leave of the Interim President, who responded with an enormous embrace that allowed everyone to see how small the General's body was, how forsaken and defenseless he looked when it was time for farewells. Then he shook all the gentlemen's hands again and kissed the ladies' hands. Someone attempted to detain him until the weather cleared, although both of them knew it would not clear for the rest of the century. Moreover, his desire to leave without delay was so evident that attempting to keep him seemed an impertinence. The master of the house walked with him to the stables through the invisible drizzle in the garden. He had tried to assist the General by holding his arm with his fingertips, as if it were made of glass, and he was amazed at the tension of the energy coursing beneath his skin like a secret torrent that bore no relationship to the impoverishment of his body. Representatives of the government, the diplomatic corps, and the armed forces, with mud up to their ankles and their cloaks soaked with rain, were waiting to accompany him on the first stage of his journey. No one was certain, however, who was there for the sake of friendship, who in order to protect him, and who to be sure that in fact he was leaving.

The mule reserved for him was the best of a pack of one hundred presented to the government by a Spanish merchant in exchange for canceling his indictment as a horse thief. The General already had his boot in the stirrup that the groom was holding for him when the Minister of the Army and Navy called to him: "Excellency." He stood motionless, his foot still in the stirrup and both hands holding the saddle.

"Stay," said the Minister, "and make one final sacrifice to save our country."

"No, Herrán," he replied. "I no longer have a country to sacrifice for."

It was the end. General Simón José Antonio de la Santísima Trinidad Bolívar y Palacios was leaving forever. He had wrested from Spanish domination an empire five times more vast than all of Europe, he had led twenty years of wars to keep it free and united, and he had governed it with a firm hand until the week before, but when it was time to leave he did not even take away with him the consolation that anyone believed in his departure. The only man with enough lucidity to know he really was going, and where he was going to, was the English diplomat, who wrote in an official report to his government: "The time he has left will hardly be enough for him to reach his grave."

THE FIRST DAY'S travel had been the most trying, and would have been even for someone less ill than he, for his mood had been twisted by the larval antagonism he sensed in the streets of Santa Fe de Bogotá on the morning of his departure. The light was just beginning to penetrate the drizzle, and he encountered only a few stray cows along the way, but the rancor of his enemies hung heavy in the air. Despite the government's precautionary order that he be escorted through the quieter streets, the General still saw the insults painted on convent walls.

Beside him rode José Palacios, who wore what he always wore, even in the heat of battle: the sacramental frock coat, the topaz pin in his silk tie, the kidskin gloves, and the brocade vest crossed by the chains of his two identical watches. The trimmings on his saddle were of Potosí silver and his spurs were made of gold, and for this reason he had been mistaken for the President in more than one Andean village. Nevertheless, the diligence with which he attended to even the slightest whim of his master made any such confusion unthinkable. José Palacios knew and loved him so well he could feel in his own flesh the pain of this furtive departure from a city that at one time had made the mere announcement of his arrival reason enough for patriotic fiestas. Less than three years earlier, when he had returned from the arid southern wars weighted down by more glory than any American, living or dead, had ever won before, he had been greeted by a history-making spontaneous reception. Those were still the days when people would grasp his horse by the halter and stop him in the street to complain about public services or taxes, or to ask him for favors, or simply to feel themselves close to the radiance of greatness. He would pay as much attention to petitioners in the street as he did to the most serious matters of state, demonstrating a surprising knowledge of each one's domestic troubles, or the condition of his business, or the state of his health, and every man who spoke to him was left with the impression that he had shared for a moment in the joys of power.

No one would have believed he was the same man, or that this taciturn place he was leaving forever, with all the wariness of an outlaw, was the same city. Nowhere had he felt so much a stranger as in those stiff, narrow streets, the identical houses with dark roofs and private gardens filled with sweet-smelling flowers, where, over a slow flame, a village community simmered whose affected manners and crafty speech hid more than they told. And nevertheless, although it might have seemed to him then a trick of the imagination, this was the same city of fog and icy winds he had selected long before he saw it as the place to build his glory, the same city he had loved more than any other and had idealized as the center and reason of his life and the capital of half the world.

When the final reckoning came he seemed more surprised than anyone at the loss of his prestige. The government had posted hidden guards even at the least dangerous locations, and this prevented a confrontation with the choleric gangs of hoodlums who had shot him in effigy the previous afternoon, but all along the route he could hear the same distant shout: "Skinny Shaaaaanks!" The one soul who took pity on him was a beggar woman, who said as he passed by:

"Go with God, phantom."

No one showed any sign of hearing her. The General sank into a brooding gloom and rode on, lost to the world, until they came out onto the grandeur of the savanna. At Cuatro Esquinas, where the paved road began, Manuela Sáenz, alone and on horseback, was waiting for the entourage to pass, and she kept her distance as she waved a last goodbye to the General. He waved back and continued on his way. They never saw each other again.

The drizzle stopped a short while later, the sky turned radiant blue, and two snow-covered volcanoes remained at the same spot on the horizon for the rest of the day. But this time he displayed none of his passion for nature, he took no notice of either the villages they passed through at a steady trot or the greetings of the people who did not recognize them. And yet what seemed most extraordinary to his companions was that he did not have so much as a tender glance for the magnificent herds of horses on the numerous breeding farms in the savanna —the sight, as he had often said, that he loved best in the world.

In Facatativá, the village where they slept the first

night, the General said goodbye to his spontaneous companions and continued the journey with his permanent entourage. There were five men in addition to José Palacios: General José María Carreño, whose right arm had been amputated as the result of a wound received in combat; his Irish aide-de-camp, Colonel Belford Hinton Wilson, the son of Sir Robert Wilson, a general who had fought in almost all the wars of Europe; Fernando, his nephew, aide-de-camp, and clerk, who held the rank of lieutenant and was the son of his older brother, who had died in a shipwreck during the First Republic; his kinsman and aide-de-camp Captain Andrés Ibarra, whose right arm had been disabled by a saber cut during the assault of September 25 two years before; and Colonel José de la Cruz Paredes, who had proven himself in countless campaigns for independence. The honor guard was composed of one hundred hussars and grenadiers selected from the best of the Venezuelan contingent.

José Palacios took special care of two dogs that had been taken as booty in Alto Perú. They were beautiful and brave and had served as watchdogs at Government House in Santa Fe de Bogotá until two of their companions had been slashed to death on the night of the attempted assassination. On the interminable journeys from Lima to Quito, from Quito to Santa Fe de Bogotá, from Santa Fe de Bogotá to Caracas, and back again to Quito and Guayaquil, the two dogs had watched over the cargo, walking alongside the pack animals. They did the same on the final journey from Santa Fe de Bogotá to Cartagena, although this time there was less cargo, and it was guarded by the troops.

The General awoke in Facatativá in a bad temper, but

his mood improved as they descended from the upland plateau through rolling hills and the climate grew more temperate and the light less harsh. They invited him several times to rest, for his physical condition was cause for concern, but he preferred to go on, not stopping for lunch, until they reached the hotlands. He often said that the motion of his horse helped him to think, and he would travel for days and nights on end, changing mounts several times so as not to ride them to death. He had the bowed legs of old cavalrymen and the gait of those who sleep with their spurs on, and a callus as hard as a barber's leather strop had formed on his buttocks, earning him the honorable nickname Iron Ass. Since the beginning of the wars for independence he had ridden eighteen thousand leagues: more than twice the distance around the world. No one had ever disproved the legend that he slept in the saddle.

After midday, when they were already beginning to feel the hot breath rising up from the ravines, they agreed to rest in the cloister of a mission. The Mother Superior attended them in person, and a group of indigenous novices gave them marzipan fresh from the oven and a grainy corn *masato* to drink that was about to ferment. When she saw the column of sweating soldiers in their haphazard uniforms, the Mother Superior must have thought Colonel Wilson was the highest-ranking officer, perhaps because he was good-looking and blond and wore the uniform with the best trimmings, and she concerned herself only with him, displaying a very feminine deference that provoked evil-minded comments.

José Palacios did not disabuse her of her mistake so that his master, wrapped in a wool blanket to sweat out his fever, could rest in the shade of the ceiba trees in the cloister. There he remained, not eating or sleeping, listening through a fog to New World love songs sung by the novices to the harp accompaniment of an older nun. When they finished, one of them walked through the cloister with a hat, begging alms for the mission. The nun with the harp said to her as she passed: "Don't ask the sick one for anything." But the novice took no notice. The General, without even looking at her, said with a bitter smile: "I'm the one who needs charity, my girl." Wilson gave from his own purse with so much generosity that he earned a cordial jest from his superior: "Now, Colonel, you see the price of glory." Wilson himself later expressed his surprise that no one at the mission, or anywhere else along their route, had recognized the best-known man in the new republics. No doubt this was an unexpected lesson for the General as well.

"I am no longer myself," he said.

They spent the second night in an old tobacco factory that had been converted into lodgings for travelers near the village of Guaduas, where they were expected for a formal ceremony of regretful farewells which he refused to attend. The building was immense and gloomy, and its very location caused a peculiar malaise because of its untamed vegetation and the black precipitous waters of the river that hurtled in a thundering explosion down to the banana plantations in the hotlands. The General knew the spot, and his first time there he had said: "If I had to ambush someone to assassinate him, this is the place I would choose." He had shunned it on other occasions only because it reminded him of Berruecos, a sinister stretch on the road to Quito that even the most fearless travelers preferred to avoid. Once, against the judgment of all his men, he had made camp two leagues away because he did not think he could bear so much sorrow. But this time, despite his fatigue and fever, it seemed in every way more tolerable than the love feast of condolences his troubled friends in Guaduas had prepared for him. When the innkeeper saw him arrive in so grievous a state, he proposed sending for a local Indian who could cure a sick man, regardless of distance, and sight unseen, just by smelling a shirt he had sweated into. The General laughed at his credulity and forbade his men to attempt any kind of dealings with the miracle-working Indian. If he had no faith in doctors, whom he called traffickers in other people's pain, he could not be expected to entrust his fate to a backwater spiritualist. And then, as further affirmation of his contempt for medical science, he refused the decent bedroom they had prepared for him because it was the one most appropriate for the state of his health, and he ordered his hammock hung in the broad open gallery that faced the ravine, where he would be exposed to the dangers of the night air.

Nothing had passed his lips that day except the infusion he drank at dawn, but he joined his officers at the table only for the sake of courtesy. Although he adapted better than anyone to the rigors of life in the field, and was almost ascetic in his eating and drinking, he knew and appreciated the arts of the wine cellar and the kitchen as if he were a refined European, and beginning with his first trip abroad he had learned from the French the custom of talking about food while he ate. That night he drank only half a glass of red wine and tasted the venison stew out of curiosity, to see if what the innkeeper claimed and his officers confirmed was true: that the phosphorescent meat had the flavor of jasmines. He said no more than two sentences during the meal, and he did not say them with any more animation than the very few he had said during the journey, but they all held in high esteem his effort to sweeten the vinegar of his public misfortunes and poor health with a spoonful of good manners. A man who could not overcome the bitter gall of a grudge for years after the offense, he had not said another word about politics or alluded to any of Saturday's events.

Before they finished eating he asked to be excused, and shivering with fever, he put on his nightshirt and sleeping cap and collapsed into his hammock. The night was cool, and an enormous orange moon was beginning to rise between the hills, but he was in no frame of mind to look at it. The soldiers of his escort began to sing popular songs a few steps from the gallery. Following a standing order of his, they always encamped close to where he slept, like the legions of Julius Caesar, so he could learn from their conversations at night what they were thinking and feeling. His insomniac's wanderings had often taken him to where they slept in the field, and not a few dawns had found him and the soldiers singing barracks songs with the stanzas of praise or mockery they improvised in the heat of the fiesta. But that night he could not tolerate their singing, and he ordered them to be still. The eternal crashing of the river among the rocks was magnified by his fever and became part of his delirium.

"The fucking water!" he shouted. "If we could just stop it for a minute!"

But no: he could no longer stop the flow of rivers. José Palacios tried to calm him with one of the many palliatives they carried in the chest of medicines, but he refused it. That was the first time he was heard to say his recurrent phrase: "I've just renounced power because of an emetic that should not have been prescribed, and I'm not prepared to renounce life as well." Years before, he had said the same thing, when another physician cured him of tertian fever with an arsenical mixture that almost killed him with dysentery. From that time on, the only medicines he accepted were the purgative pills he took without hesitation several times a week for his persistent constipation, and a senna enema for the most critical bouts of sluggishness. A short while after midnight, exhausted by his master's delirium, José Palacios stretched out on the bare brick floor and fell asleep. When he awoke, the General was not in his hammock, and his nightshirt, drenched with perspiration, lay on the floor. This was nothing out of the ordinary. When there was no one else in the house he would leave his bed and wander naked until dawn, whiling away his insomnia. But that night there were more reasons than usual to fear for him: he had been ill all day, and the cool, damp weather was not the most propitious for his walking about unclothed. José Palacios took a blanket and looked for him in the house that was lit by a lunar green, and he found him lying like a funerary statue on a stone bench built into the corridor wall. The General turned to him with a lucid gaze in which no trace of fever remained.

"This is another night like the one in San Juan de Payara," he said. "Without Queen María Luisa, sad to say."

José Palacios understood the allusion all too well. It referred to a January night in the year 1820 when the

General and two thousand troops had come to a remote spot on the upland plateaus of the Apure in Venezuela. He had already liberated eighteen provinces from Spanish domination. He had created the Republic of Colombia out of the former territories of the Viceregency of New Granada, the Captaincy General of Venezuela, and the Presidency of Quito, and he was at the same time its first president and the commander in chief of its armies. His ultimate hope was to extend the war into the south in order to realize the fantastic dream of creating the largest country in the world: one nation, free and unified, from Mexico to Cape Horn.

Nevertheless, his military situation that night was not the most favorable for dreaming. A sudden plague that struck down the animals in midstride had left behind a pestilential trail fourteen leagues long of dead horses on the Llano plain. Many demoralized officers consoled themselves with rapine and reveled in their disobedience, and some even laughed when he threatened to have the guilty shot. Two thousand ragged and barefoot soldiers without weapons, without food, without blankets to defy the bleak upland plains, weary of wars and disease, had begun to desert in droves. For lack of a rational solution, he had ordered a reward of ten pesos for any patrol that captured and turned in a deserter, who would be shot with no questions asked.

Life had already given him sufficient reasons for knowing that no defeat was the final one. Less than two years before, when he was lost with his troops in the not too distant jungles of the Orinoco, he had been obliged to give orders to eat the horses for fear the soldiers would eat each other. At that time, according to the testimony of an officer in the British Legion, he had the outlandish appearance of an exotic vagabond guerrilla. He wore the helmet of a Russian dragoon, a mule driver's espadrilles, a blue tunic with red trim and gold buttons, and he carried the black banner of a privateer hoisted on a plainsman's lance, the skull and crossbones superimposed on a motto in letters of blood: "Liberty or death."

On the night in San Juan de Payara his costume was less disreputable, but his situation was no better. And this reflected not only the momentary condition of his troops but the entire drama of the liberating army, which often reemerged triumphant from the worst defeats and was nevertheless about to collapse under the weight of its many victories. On the other hand, the Spanish general Don Pablo Morillo, with all the resources to crush the patriots and restore the colonial order, still controlled large areas of western Venezuela and was entrenched in the mountains.

Faced with this state of the world, the General tended to his insomnia by walking naked through the deserted rooms of the old hacienda mansion, which was transfigured by brilliant moonlight. Most of the horses that died the day before had been burned at a good distance from the house, but the stench of decay was still intolerable. The troops had not sung again after the death-ridden marches of the past week, and even he felt incapable of preventing the sentries from falling asleep with hunger. Then all at once, at the end of a gallery open to the vast blue plains, he saw Queen María Luisa sitting on the floor. A beautiful mulatta in the flower of her youth and with the profile of an idol, she was wrapped in a flower-embroidered shawl that reached down to her feet and was smoking a long cigar. The sight of him frightened her, and she made a cross with her index finger and thumb and pointed it in his direction.

"Whether you come from God or the devil," she said, "what do you want?"

"You," he said.

He smiled, and she was to remember the flash of his teeth in the moonlight. He embraced her with all his strength, holding her so she could not move while he nibbled with soft kisses at her forehead, her eyes, her cheeks, her neck, until he had quieted her. Then he removed the shawl, and it took his breath away. She too was naked, for her grandmother, who slept in the same room, took her clothes to keep her from going out to smoke, not realizing that at dawn she would escape wrapped in the shawl. The General carried her to the hammock, giving her no respite from his soothing kisses, and she gave herself to him not out of desire or love but out of fear. She was a virgin. Only after she regained her courage did she say:

"I'm a slave, sir."

"Not anymore," he said. "Love has made you free."

In the morning he bought her from the owner of the hacienda for one hundred pesos taken from his impoverished treasury and granted her unconditional freedom. Before he left he could not resist the temptation of presenting her with a public dilemma. He was in the back patio of the house with a group of officers who sat any way they could on the backs of pack animals, the only survivors of the slaughter. Another body of troops, under the command of Brigadier General José Antonio Páez, who had arrived the night before, was assembled to see them off.

The General gave a brief farewell speech in which he underplayed the drama of the situation, and he was preparing to leave when he saw Queen María Luisa in her new condition as a free and well-wooed woman. She had just bathed, and under the Llano sky she looked beautiful and radiant, dressed all in starched white with the lace petticoats and skimpy blouse of a slavewoman. He asked her with good humor:

"Are you staying or coming with us?"

She answered with an enchanting smile:

"I'm staying, sir."

Unanimous laughter greeted her reply. The master of the house, a Spaniard who was an early convert to the cause of independence and an old acquaintance, was helpless with laughter as he tossed him the little leather purse with the hundred pesos. He caught it in midair.

"Keep them for the cause, Excellency," the Spaniard said. "The girl is free in any case."

General José Antonio Páez, whose faunlike expression harmonized with his shirt patched in many colors, burst into expansive laughter.

"Now you see, General," he said. "This is what we get for acting like liberators."

He assented to what they said and took his leave of everyone with a wide circle of his hand. Then he said a sportsmanlike goodbye to Queen María Luisa, and that was the last he heard of her. As far as José Palacios could remember, before a year of full moons had gone by, the General claimed he was reliving that night, without the miraculous appearance of Queen María Luisa, sad to say. And always on a night of defeat.

At five o'clock, when José Palacios brought him his first tisane, he found him resting with his eyes open. But the General tried to stand up with such force that he almost fell on his face and suffered a severe attack of coughing. He sat on the hammock, holding his head in his hands and coughing until the crisis passed. Then he began to drink the steaming infusion, and his humor improved with the first sip.

"I was dreaming about Cassandro all night," he said.

It was his secret name for the New Granadan, General Francisco de Paula Santander, who had been his great friend at one time and his greatest gainsayer of all time, his chief of staff from the very beginning of the war and the man he appointed President of Colombia during the cruel campaigns for the liberation of Quito and Perú and the founding of Bolivia. More for reasons of historical necessity than of vocation, Santander was an effective and brave soldier, with a rare fondness for cruelty, but his civic virtues and his excellent academic training were the mainstays of his glory. He was without a doubt the second man in the movement for independence and the first in the legal codification of the Republic, on which he imprinted forever the stamp of his formalist, conservative spirit.

On one of the many occasions when the General planned to resign, he had said to Santander that he was abandoning the presidency with confidence because "I am leaving you here, my other self, and perhaps my better self." He had never, either by reasoned intention or by force of circumstance, placed so much confidence in any man. It was he who distinguished Santander with the title The Man of Law. Nevertheless, the person who had merited all this had been living in exile in Paris for the past two years because of his unproved complicity in a plot to assassinate the General.

This is what happened. On September 25, 1828, at the stroke of midnight, twelve civilians and twenty-six soldiers forced the great door of Government House in Santa Fe de Bogotá, cut the throats of two of the President's bloodhounds, wounded several sentries, slashed the arm of Captain Andrés Ibarra with a saber, shot to death the Scotsman Colonel William Fergusson, a member of the British Legion and an aide-de-camp to the President, who had called him as valiant as Caesar, and reached the presidential bedroom, shouting "Long live liberty!" and "Death to the tyrant!"

The rebels would justify the attempt by referring to the extraordinary powers of obvious dictatorial intent that the General had assumed three months before in order to thwart the Santanderist victory at the Ocaña Convention. The vice-presidency of the Republic, which Santander had occupied for seven years, was abolished. Santander told a friend about it in a sentence typical of his personal style: "I have had the pleasure of being buried under the ruins of the Constitution of 1821." He was then thirty-six years old. He had been named Plenipotentiary Minister to Washington but had postponed his departure several times, perhaps in anticipation of the conspiracy's success.

The General and Manuela Sáenz were just beginning a night of reconciliation. They had spent the weekend in the village of Soacha, two and a half leagues away, and had returned on Monday in separate coaches after a lovers' quarrel that was more virulent than usual because he remained deaf to her warnings of a plot to kill him, something everyone was talking about and only he refused to believe. She had not accepted the insistent messages he sent to her house that night from San Carlos Palace across the street, but at nine o'clock, after three very urgent messages, she put waterproof boots over her shoes, covered her head with a shawl, and crossed the street flooded by rain. She found him floating face up in the fragrant waters of the bath, unattended by José Palacios, and if she did not believe he was dead it was because she had often seen him meditating in that state of grace. He recognized her footsteps and spoke without opening his eyes.

"There is going to be an insurrection," he said.

Irony did not disguise her anger.

"Congratulations," she said. "There could be ten, since you give such a cordial welcome to warnings."

"I only believe in portents," he said.

He permitted himself the joke because his chief of staff, who had already told the conspirators the password for the night so they could deceive the palace guard, had given him his word that the conspiracy had failed. And therefore he was in good humor as he rose from the tub.

"Don't worry," he said. "It seems the little fairies got cold feet."

He was naked and she was half dressed, and they were just beginning their love play in bed when they heard the first shouts, the first shots, and the cannons thundering against loyal barracks. Manuela helped him to dress as quickly as possible, put her waterproof boots on his feet since the General had sent his only pair of boots to be polished, and helped him to escape out the balcony with a saber and a pistol but no protection against the eternal rain. As soon as he reached the street he pointed his cocked pistol at an approaching shadow: "Who goes there?" It was his steward returning home, grief-stricken by the news that they had killed his master. Resolved to share his fate to the end, José Palacios hid with him under Carmen Bridge in the brambles along the San Agustín River until loyal troops quelled the uprising.

With the same shrewdness and courage she had already demonstrated during other historic emergencies, Manuela Sáenz received the attackers who forced the bedroom door. They asked for the President, and she replied that he was in the council room. They asked why the door to the balcony was open on a wintry night, and she said she had opened it to see what the noises were in the street. They asked why the bed was warm, and she said she had lain down without undressing to wait for the President. As she played for time with her parsimonious replies, she puffed great clouds of smoke from the cheapest kind of wagon driver's cigar to cover the fresh scent of cologne that still lingered in the room.

A tribunal presided over by General Rafael Urdaneta established that General Santander was the secret intelligence behind the conspiracy and condemned him to death. His enemies would say that the sentence was more than fair, not so much for Santander's culpability in the assassination attempt as for his cynicism in being the first to appear in the main square to embrace and congratulate the President, who sat on horseback in the drizzling rain, without a shirt and with his tunic ripped and soaked through, surrounded by the cheers of the troops and the common people who arrived en masse from the poor suburbs clamoring for the death of the assassins. "All the conspirators will be punished to some degree," the General said in a letter to Field Marshal Sucre. "Santander is the principal one, but also the most fortunate, because my generosity protects him." And in fact, exercising his absolute powers, he commuted the death sentence to exile in Paris. On the other hand, Admiral José Prudencio Padilla, imprisoned in Santa Fe de Bogotá for a failed rebellion in Cartagena de Indias, was shot on insufficient evidence.

José Palacios did not know when his master's dreams about General Santander were real and when they were imaginary. Once, in Guayaquil, he said he dreamed about Santander's holding an open book on his round belly, but instead of reading he tore out the pages and ate them one by one, taking great delight in chomping them with as much noise as if he were a goat. Another time, in Cúcuta, he dreamed he saw him covered with cockroaches. Another time, on the country estate of Monserrate in Santa Fe de Bogotá, he woke up screaming because he dreamed that while they were having lunch together General Santander plucked out his own eyeballs because they interfered with his eating and placed them on the table. And so at dawn near Guaduas, when the General said he had dreamed once again about Santander, José Palacios did not even ask for the plot of the dream but tried instead to console him with reality.

"There's a whole ocean between him and us," he said.

But the General cut him off with a sharp glance.

"Not anymore," he said. "I'm certain that stupid bastard Joaquín Mosquera will let him come back."

That thought had tormented him since his last return to the country, when his definitive renunciation of power presented itself as a question of honor. "I prefer exile or death to the dishonor of leaving my glory in the hands of the Academy of San Bartolomé," he had said to José Palacios. Nevertheless, the antidote contained its own poison, for the closer he came to the final decision, the more certain he grew that as soon as he was gone, General Santander, the most eminent graduate of that den of quibbling lawyers, would be called home from exile.

"That one's really a slippery bastard," he said.

He had no trace of fever, and he felt so strong he asked José Palacios for pen and paper, put on his spectacles, and wrote six lines to Manuela Sáenz in his own hand. This was bound to seem strange even to someone who was as accustomed as José Palacios to his impulsive actions, and could be understood only as a portent or an attack of unendurable inspiration. For it not only contradicted his decision on the previous Friday never to write another letter for the rest of his life, but it was also contrary to his custom of waking his secretaries at any hour to attend to back correspondence, or to dictate a proclamation, or to put in order the ideas that occurred to him in the ruminations of his insomnia. It seemed even stranger since the letter was of no apparent urgency, and he added only a rather cryptic sentence to his parting advice: "Be careful what you do, for if you're not, your ruination will be the ruination of us both." He wrote it in his slapdash way, as if he had given it no thought, and when he finished he continued to sway in his hammock, engrossed, holding the letter in his hand.

"There is great power in the irresistible force of love," he sighed without warning. "Who said that?"

"Nobody," said José Palacios.

He did not know how to read or write, and he had refused to learn, with the simple argument that there was no greater wisdom than a donkey's. But on the other hand, he could remember any sentence he had ever heard, and he did not remember that one.

"Then I said it myself," said the General, "but let's say it was Field Marshal Sucre."

No one was better suited than Fernando for those times of crisis. He was the most willing and patient of the General's many clerks, although not the most brilliant, and he bore with stoicism the arbitrariness of his schedule or the irritability of his insomnia. The General would wake Fernando at any hour to have him read aloud from a dull book or take notes on urgent extemporizations, which ended in the trash the next morning. The General had fathered no children during his countless nights of love (although he said he had proofs he was not sterile), and on the death of his brother he had taken charge of Fernando. He had sent him with outstanding letters of introduction to the Military Academy at Georgetown, where General Lafayette expressed the sentiments of admiration and respect his uncle inspired in him. Later he attended the University of Virginia in Charlottesville. He was not the successor the General perhaps had dreamed of, for academic subjects bored him, and he was delighted to exchange them for life in the open air and the sedentary arts of gardening. When he completed his studies the

General called him back to Santa Fe de Bogotá and soon discovered his virtues as a secretary, not only because of his beautiful handwriting and his command of spoken and written English, but also because he was unique in his ability to invent the kinds of devices used in serialized novels to keep the reader in suspense, and when he read aloud he would improvise audacious episodes to add spice to soporific paragraphs. Like everyone in the service of the General, Fernando had suffered his moment of misfortune, when he attributed to Cicero a sentence by Demosthenes that his uncle later cited in a speech. He was more severe with his nephew than with the others, since he was who he was, but he pardoned him before he had completed his punishment.

Colonel Joaquín Posada Gutiérrez, the governor of the province, had ridden out two days ahead of the traveling party, to announce their arrival in the towns where they would spend the night and to caution the authorities regarding the serious state of the General's health. But those who saw him arrive in Guaduas on Monday afternoon accepted as true the persistent rumor that the Governor's reports, and even the journey itself, were nothing more than a political ruse.

The General was invincible once more. He rode into town on the main street, his shirt unbuttoned and a Gypsy bandanna tied around his head to absorb the perspiration, waving his hat amid the cheers and the fireworks and the church bell that drowned out the music, sitting on a nimble-footed mule that once and for all stripped the parade of any pretension to solemnity. The only house where the windows stayed closed was the nuns' academy, and in the afternoon the rumor would fly that they had forbidden the girls to participate in the welcome, but he advised those who told him the story not to believe convent gossip.

On the previous night José Palacios had given the shirt the General wore when he sweat out his fever to an orderly for laundering. He in turn gave it to the soldiers who went down to the river at dawn to wash clothes, but when it was time to leave, no one knew anything about it. During the trip to Guaduas, and even while the fiesta was going on, José Palacios had succeeded in establishing that the innkeeper had taken the unwashed shirt so that the miracle-working Indian could demonstrate his powers. And when the General returned, José Palacios informed him of the innkeeper's breach of faith, reminding him that he had no shirts other than the one he was wearing. He took the news with a certain philosophical resignation.

"Superstitions are harder to uproot than love," he said.

"The strange thing is we haven't had a fever since last night," said José Palacios. "What if the witch doctor is a real magician?"

He found no immediate reply, and he allowed himself to be carried away by deep reflection as he swayed in the hammock to the rhythm of his thoughts. "The truth is I haven't had another headache," he said. "My mouth doesn't taste bitter, and I don't feel as if I were about to fall off a tower." But in the end he slapped his knees and sat up with a resolute movement.

"Don't put any more confusion in my head," he said.

Two servants carried a large pot of boiling water with aromatic leaves into the bedroom, and José Palacios prepared the evening bath, confident the General would soon go to bed because of his weariness after a day of traveling. But the bath grew cold while he dictated a letter to Gabriel Camacho, the husband of his niece Valentina Palacios, and his agent in Caracas for the sale of the Aroa Mines, a copper deposit he had inherited from his parents. Even he did not seem to have a clear idea of his destination, for in one sentence he said he was going to Curaçao while Camacho brought this piece of business to a successful conclusion, and in another he asked that he write to him in London in care of Sir Robert Wilson, with a copy for Mr. Maxwell Hyslop in Jamaica, to be sure he received one of the letters even if the other was lost.

For many people, above all his secretaries and copyists, the Aroa Mines were another of his feverish ravings. He had shown so little interest in them that for years they had been worked by casual operators. He remembered the mines toward the end of his life when money began to grow scarce, but he could not sell them to an English company because his titles were not clear. That was the beginning of a legendary legal imbroglio that would go on for two years after his death. In the midst of wars, political conflicts, personal hatreds, everyone knew what he meant when the General said "my case." In his opinion the Aroa Mines were the only case. The letter he dictated in Guaduas to Don Gabriel Camacho left his nephew with the mistaken impression that they would not leave for Europe until the dispute was settled, and Fernando mentioned this later when he was playing cards with the other officers.

"Then we will never leave," said Colonel Wilson. "My father has reached the point where he wonders if that copper exists in the real world."

"The fact that no one's seen them doesn't mean the mines don't exist," replied Captain Andrés Ibarra.

"They exist," said General Carreño. "In the Department of Venezuela."

Wilson replied in disgust:

"At this stage I even wonder if Venezuela exists."

He could not hide his vexation. Wilson had come to believe the General was not fond of him and kept him in his entourage only out of consideration for his father, to whom he was forever grateful for his defense of American emancipation in the English Parliament. Through the disloyalty of a former aide-de-camp, a Frenchman, he learned that the General had said: "Wilson needs to spend some time in the school of difficulties, not to mention adversity and misery." Colonel Wilson had not been able to determine if that was in fact what the General had said, but in any case he believed that just one of his battles would qualify him as a graduate of all three schools. He was twenty-six years old, and eight years earlier, when he finished his studies at Westminster and Sandhurst, his father had sent him to serve the General. He had been his aide-de-camp at the battle of Junín, and he was the man who carried the first draft of the Bolivian Constitution on muleback from Chuquisaca to La Paz along three hundred sixty leagues of narrow precipice. When he said goodbye the General told him he had to be in La Paz in twenty-one days at the latest. Wilson snapped to attention: "I'll be there in twenty, Excellency." It took him nineteen.

He had decided to return to Europe with the General, but each day increased his certainty that he would always find another reason for deferring the trip. His mention of the Aroa Mines after more than two years of not even using them as a pretext for anything was a disheartening sign for Wilson.

José Palacios reheated the water after the letter had been dictated, but the General did not take a bath and continued his aimless walking, declaiming poetry in a voice that resounded throughout the house. He went on to poems he had written that only José Palacios knew about. Several times he passed the gallery where his officers were playing *ropilla*, the American name for Galician lansquenet, which he too had once played. He would stop for a moment to watch over each officer's shoulder, draw conclusions regarding their progress, and continue walking.

"I don't know how you can waste your time on such a boring game," he said.

Nevertheless, on one of his many turns around the house he could not resist the temptation of asking Captain Ibarra to allow him to take his place at the table. He did not possess the patience good gamblers have, he was aggressive and a poor loser, but he was also astute and fast and knew how to put himself on equal footing with his subordinates. On that occasion, with General Carreño as his partner, he played six games and lost all of them. He threw the cards on the table.

"This game is shit," he said. "Who's brave enough to try ombre?"

They all were. He won three games in a row, his humor improved, and he tried to ridicule the way Colonel Wilson played. Wilson took it well but made use of the General's enthusiasm to gain an advantage, and he did not lose again. The General became tense, his lips hardened and turned pale, and the eyes set deep under bushy eyebrows burned with the savage brilliance of other times. He did not speak again, and a pernicious cough interfered with his concentration. It was past twelve o'clock when he stopped the game.

"The wind's been blowing on me all night," he said.

They carried the table to a more sheltered spot, but he continued losing. He asked them to quiet the fifes that could be heard playing at some nearby fiesta, but the fifes continued to sound over the din of the crickets. He changed his seat, he put a pillow on his chair so he could sit higher and be more comfortable, he drank an infusion of linden blossoms to relieve his cough, he played several games while walking from one end of the gallery to the other, but he continued losing. Wilson kept his clear, embittered eyes on him, but he did not deign to look back.

"This deck is marked," he said.

"The deck is yours, General," said Wilson.

It was in fact one of his, but still he examined it card by card, and at last he had it changed. Wilson gave him no rest. The crickets stopped, there was a long silence shaken by a humid breeze that brought the first scent of the burning valleys to the gallery, and a rooster crowed three times. "That rooster's crazy," said Ibarra. "It can't be later than two o'clock." Without taking his eyes off the cards, the General ordered in a surly voice:

"Nobody moves from here, damn it!"

No one breathed. General Carreño, who was following the game with more apprehension than interest, remembered the longest night of his life, two years before, when they were waiting in Bucaramanga for the results of the Ocaña Convention. They had begun to play at nine o'clock and did not finish until eleven the next morning, when his companions agreed to let the General win three games in a row. Fearing another test of endurance that night in Guaduas, General Carreño signaled Colonel Wilson to begin to lose. Wilson ignored him. Then, when he asked for a five-minute break, General Carreño followed him along the terrace and found him pissing his ammoniacal bitterness into the pots of geraniums.

"Colonel Wilson," General Carreño ordered. "Attention!"

Wilson replied without turning his head:

"Wait until I finish."

He finished with absolute serenity and turned around as he adjusted his trousers.

"Begin to lose," General Carreño told him, "if only as an act of kindness to a friend in trouble."

"I refuse to pay anyone such an insult," said Wilson with a touch of irony.

"That's an order!" said Carreño.

Wilson, standing at attention, looked down at him from his full height with imperial contempt. Then he returned to the table and began to lose. The General understood.

"It isn't necessary for you to do it so badly, my dear Wilson," he said. "When all is said and done, it's time we went to sleep."

He took his leave of everyone with a firm handshake, as he always did when he got up from the card table, in order to show that the game had not altered his feelings, and he returned to the bedroom. José Palacios had fallen asleep on the floor, but he stood up when he saw him come in. The General stripped off all his clothes in a rush and began to sway in his hammock, his thoughts in a whirl, his respiration growing louder and harsher the more he thought. When he sank into the tub he was shaking down to the marrow of his bones, but this time it was not fever or cold, but rage.

"Wilson's a slippery bastard," he said.

It was one of his worst nights. José Palacios disobeyed orders and warned the officers in case it proved necessary to call a doctor, and he kept him wrapped in sheets so he could sweat out the fever. He soaked through several of them, with momentary respites that only hurled him back into hallucinatory crises. Several times he shouted: "Make those damn fifes be quiet!" But no one could help him this time, because the fifes had been silent since midnight. Later he discovered who was responsible for his prostration.

"I was feeling fine," he said, "until I let all of you talk me into that fucking Indian with the shirt."

The last stage of the journey to Honda was along a heartstopping precipice through air like molten glass that only physical stamina and willpower like his could have endured after a night of agony. After the first few leagues he had moved back from his usual position to ride beside Colonel Wilson, who knew to interpret the gesture as an invitation to forget the grievances of the gaming table and who offered his arm, as if he were a falconer, for the General to rest his hand on. In that way they made the descent together, Colonel Wilson moved by his courtesy and the General using his last strength to struggle for breath but sitting unbowed in the saddle. When the steepest stretch was over he asked with a voice from another century:

"What do you suppose London is like now?"

Colonel Wilson looked at the sun, which was almost in the center of the sky, and said:

"Very bad, General."

He showed no surprise but asked another question in the same voice:

"And why is that?"

"Because there it's six in the evening, the worst time in London," said Wilson. "And a rain as filthy and dead as toad water must be falling, because spring is our sinister season."

"Don't tell me you've conquered nostalgia," he said.

"On the contrary: nostalgia has conquered me," said Wilson. "I no longer put up the slightest resistance to it."

"Then do you or don't you want to go back?"

"I don't know anything anymore, General," said Wilson. "I'm at the mercy of a destiny that isn't mine."

The General looked straight into his eyes and said in amazement:

"That's what I should be saying."

When he spoke again, his voice and mood had changed. "Don't worry," he said. "Whatever happens, we will go to Europe, if for no other reason than to not deprive your father of the pleasure of seeing you." Then, after long reflection, he concluded:

"And let me tell you one last thing, my dear Wilson: they can call you anything they like except a slippery bastard."

Accustomed to his gallant repentances, above all after a stormy card game or a victory in battle, Colonel Wilson yielded to him one more time. He continued to ride at a slow pace with the feverish hand of the most glorious invalid in the Americas clutching like a hunting falcon at his forearm, while the air began to boil and funereal birds circling above their heads had to be driven away like flies.

On the most difficult part of the slope they crossed paths with a crew of Indians carrying a party of European travelers in sedan chairs. Then, when they had almost completed the descent, a demented horseman passed them at full gallop, riding in the same direction they were taking. He wore a red hood that almost covered his face, and his haste was so disordered that Captain Ibarra's mule almost plunged over the edge in fright. The General just had time to shout "Watch where you're going, damn you!" He stared after him until he disappeared around the first bend but was still watching for him each time he reappeared on the lower curves of the precipice.

At two o'clock in the afternoon they rode the crest of the last hill, and the horizon opened into a brilliant plain at the end of which the celebrated city of Honda lay dozing, with its bridge of Castilian stone spanning the great marshy river, with its walls in ruins and its church tower destroyed by an earthquake. The General contemplated the burning valley but betrayed no emotion except when he saw the rider in the red hood crossing the bridge at his unending gallop. Then the light he had seen in his dreams was rekindled.

"Merciful God," he said. "The only explanation for that kind of speed is that he's carrying a letter for Cassandro with the news that we've left."

DESPITE THE WARNING against any public demonstrations to mark his arrival, a high-spirited troop of horsemen rode out to welcome him in the port, and Governor Posada Gutiérrez arranged three days of bands and fireworks. But rain ruined the fiesta before they even reached the streets of the commercial district. It was an inopportune downpour of devastating violence, which tore up the cobbles in the streets and sent water flooding through the poor neighborhoods, but the heat remained imperturbable. In the welter of greetings someone repeated the eternal cliché: "It's so hot here the hens lay fried eggs." For the next three days this same disaster was repeated without any variation. During the torpor of siesta a black cloud descended from the mountains, settled over the city, and burst open in an instant deluge. Then the sun shone again in a diaphanous sky, as merciless as before, while the civic brigades cleared the streets of the debris left by the flood, and the next day's black cloud began to form on the crests of the hills. At any hour of the day or night, indoors or out, one heard the panting of the heat.

Prostrate with fever, the General could scarcely endure the official welcoming ceremony. The air was at a rolling boil in the salon of the town hall, but he managed a sermon worthy of a cautious bishop, which he spoke very slowly in an unwilling voice without getting up from the armchair. A ten-year-old girl wearing angel wings and a dress of ruffled organza choked with haste as she recited from memory an ode to the glories of the General. But she made a mistake, began again at the wrong place, became lost beyond all hope, and not knowing what else to do, stared at him in panic. The General gave her a smile of complicity and reminded her of the lines in a low voice:

> *The brilliance of his saber*
> *is the living reflection of his glory.*

In the early years of his power, the General missed no opportunity to give splendid banquets for a multitude of guests, whom he would urge to eat and to drink to the point of inebriation. From that sumptuous past he still had his personal monogrammed place setting, which José Palacios would bring to dinner parties. At the reception in Honda he agreed to sit in the place of honor, but he drank only a glass of port and just tasted the river turtle soup, which left an unpleasant flavor in his mouth.

He withdrew early to the sanctuary Governor Posada Gutiérrez had readied for him in his house, but the news that the mail from Santa Fe de Bogotá was expected the next day drove away the little sleep that was left to him. Prey to apprehension after the three-day respite, he began to think again about his misfortunes, and again he tormented José Palacios with idle questions. He wanted to know what had happened since he left, what the city would be like with a government different from his own, what life would be like without him. On one gloomy occasion he had said: "America is half a world gone mad." That first night in Honda he had even more reason to believe this was so.

He spent the night in suspense, plagued by mosquitoes because he refused to sleep with netting. At times he walked around and around the room talking to himself, at times he swayed with great lurching swings in the hammock, at times he rolled himself in a blanket and succumbed to his fever, almost shouting with delirium in a marshland of sweat. José Palacios stayed with him, answering his questions, telling him the exact hour and minute every few seconds without having to consult the two watches he wore on chains fastened to the buttonholes of his vest. He rocked the hammock when the General did not have the strength to do it himself and drove away the mosquitoes with a cloth until at last he lulled him into a sleep that lasted over an hour. But he awoke with a start just before dawn when he heard the sound of animals and men's voices in the patio, and he went out in his nightshirt to receive the mail.

His young Mexican aide-de-camp, Captain Agustín de Iturbide, who had been detained in Santa Fe de Bogotá by a last-minute emergency, arrived with the mail carriers. He had with him a letter from Field Marshal Sucre, a heartfelt lament at not having arrived in time to say goodbye. There also arrived in the mail a letter written two days earlier by President Caycedo. Governor Posada Gutiérrez came into the bedroom a short while later with clippings from the Sunday papers, and the General asked that he read the letters to him since the light was still too dim for his eyes.

The news was that on Sunday the weather had cleared in Santa Fe de Bogotá, and numerous families with their children invaded the horse-breeding farms with baskets of roast suckling pig, baked brisket, blood sausage with rice, potatoes with melted cheese, and ate their lunch on the grass under a radiant sun that had not been seen in the city for ages. This May miracle had dissipated Saturday's tension. The students from the Academy of San Bartolomé had taken to the streets once more with the all too familiar farce of symbolic executions, but to no effect. They dispersed in boredom before nightfall, and on Sunday they exchanged rifles for treble guitars and could be seen on the breeding farms singing *bambucos* among the crowds of people warming themselves in the sun, until it rained again without warning at five o'clock in the afternoon and the fiesta was over.

Posada Gutiérrez interrupted his reading of the letter.

"Nothing in this world can stain your glory," he said to the General. "No matter what they say, Your Excellency will continue to be the greatest Colombian anywhere on earth."

"I don't doubt it," said the General, "if all I had to do was leave to make the sun shine again."

The only item in Caycedo's letter to provoke him was that even the Interim President of the Republic committed the abuse of calling Santander's followers liberals, as if it were official terminology. "I don't know where the demagogues got the right to call themselves liberals," he said. "They stole the word, pure and simple, just as they steal everything they lay their hands on." He leaped from the hammock and continued to vent his anger to the Governor as he paced off the room from one end to the other with his soldier's strides.

"The truth is, the only two parties here are those who are with me and those who are against me, and you know that better than anyone," he concluded. "And although they may not believe it, no one is more liberal than I am."

Later a personal emissary from the Governor brought him the verbal message that Manuela Sáenz had not written to him because the mail carriers had categorical instructions not to accept her letters. The message came from Manuela herself, who on the same date had sent the Interim President a letter to protest the prohibition, which was the origin of a series of mutual provocations that would end in her exile and oblivion. Nevertheless, contrary to the expectations of Posada Gutiérrez, who had firsthand knowledge of the stormy quarrels in that tormented love affair, the General smiled at the bad news.

"These conflicts are the natural state of my amiable madwoman," he said.

José Palacios did not hide his vexation at the lack of consideration shown in the programming of the three days in Honda. The most surprising invitation was to visit the silver mines at Santa Ana, six leagues away, but more surprising was that the General accepted, and much more surprising was that he went down to a subterranean gallery. Even worse: on the way back, despite his high fever and a head about to explode with migraine, he went swimming in a backwater of the river. The days were long gone when he would wager that he could cross a rushing torrent on the plains with one hand tied and still

beat the most skillful swimmer. In any case, this time he
swam for half an hour without tiring, but those who saw
his scrawny ribs and rachitic legs did not understand how
he stayed alive with so little body.

On the last night, the municipal government held a
gala ball in his honor, which he declined to attend because of fatigue after his excursion. Secluded in the bedroom with Fernando since five o'clock that afternoon,
he dictated the reply to General Domingo Caycedo and
had his nephew read aloud several more pages of Lima's
gallant adventures, in some of which he had been the
protagonist. Then he took a lukewarm bath and lay motionless in the hammock, listening to the strains of music wafting in from the ball in his honor. José Palacios
thought he was asleep, when he heard him say:

"Do you remember that waltz?"

He whistled several measures to remind the steward
of the music, but he could not identify it. "It was the
waltz they played the night we arrived in Lima from
Chuquisaca," said the General. José Palacios did not remember it, but he would never forget the glorious night
of February 8, 1826. That morning Lima had given them
an imperial reception, and the General responded with
a sentence he repeated without fail at every toast: "There
is not a single Spaniard left in the vast territory of Perú."
That day confirmed the independence of the huge continent which he proposed to turn, according to his own
words, into the most immense, or most extraordinary,
or most invincible league of nations the world had ever
seen. For him the emotions of the fiesta were associated
with the waltz he had asked them to repeat as many times
as necessary so that every lady in Lima would have the

opportunity to dance to it with him. His officers, who wore the most dazzling uniforms the city had ever seen, did their best to follow his example, for they all waltzed admirably—a memory that endured in the hearts of their partners much longer than any glories of war.

On the last night in Honda they opened the fiesta with the victory waltz, and he waited in the hammock for them to repeat it. But when it was clear they would not, he leaped up, put on the same riding clothes he had worn on the excursion to the mines, and presented himself at the ball without being announced. He danced for almost three hours and had them repeat the piece each time he changed partners, attempting perhaps to reconstitute the splendor of long ago out of the ashes of his memories. Gone were the years of illusion when everyone dropped with exhaustion and only he and his last partner were left to dance until dawn in the deserted ballroom. Dancing was for him so dominant a passion that he would dance without a partner when one was not at hand, or he would dance alone to music he whistled himself, and he would express his moments of great jubilation by dancing on the dining room table. On the last night in Honda his strength was so diminished that during intermissions he had to inhale the fumes from the handkerchief soaked with cologne in order to revive, but he danced with so much enthusiasm and such youthful skill that without intending to, he confounded the tales of his fatal illness.

Not long after midnight, when he returned to the house, they reported that a woman was waiting for him in the reception room. Elegant and haughty, emitting the fragrance of spring, she wore a long-sleeved velvet dress, riding boots of the finest cordovan leather, and the silk-veiled hat of a medieval lady. The General made her a formal bow, intrigued by the nature and hour of the visit. Without saying a word she held up a reliquary hanging around her neck on a long chain, and he recognized it in astonishment.

"Miranda Lyndsay!" he said.

"It's me," she said, "although I'm no longer the same."

The grave, warm voice like a cello, rippled by just the slightest trace of her native English, must have awakened unrepeatable memories in him. With a wave of his hand he dismissed the sentry standing guard at the door, and he sat down facing her, so close their knees almost touched, and took both her hands in his.

They had met fifteen years earlier in Kingston, during his second exile, at an informal luncheon in the home of the English merchant Maxwell Hyslop. She was the only child of Sir London Lyndsay, an English diplomat who had retired to a sugar plantation in Jamaica to write the six volumes of memoirs that nobody read. Despite the unquestionable beauty of Miranda and the susceptible heart of the young exile, at that time he was too immersed in his dreams and too involved with another woman to notice anyone else.

She would always remember him as a bony, pale man who seemed much older than his thirty-two years, who had the coarse sideburns and mustache of a mulatto and hair that hung down to his shoulders. Like all the young men of the native aristocracy, he was dressed in the English style: a white cravat, a jacket too heavy for the climate, and the Romantics' gardenia in his lapel. Dressed in this fashion on a libertine night in 1810, he was mistaken by a gallant whore in a London brothel for a Greek pederast.

For better or worse, what was most memorable about him were his dazzling eyes and his endless, exhausting talk in the strident voice of a bird of prey. Strangest of all, he kept his eyes lowered and held the attention of his table companions without looking straight at them. He spoke with the cadence and diction of the Canary Islands and in the educated forms of Madrid, which he alternated that day with an elementary but comprehensible English in honor of two guests who did not understand Spanish.

During the luncheon he paid attention to no one except his own phantoms. He spoke without pause in an erudite, declamatory style, delivering raw prophetic sentences, many of which would appear in an epic proclamation published some days later in a Kingston newspaper, which history would consecrate as *The Jamaica Letter*. "It is not the Spaniards but our own lack of unity that has brought us again to slavery," he said. Speaking of the greatness, the resources, and the talents of America, he repeated several times: "We are the human race in miniature." When she returned home her father asked Miranda about the conspirator who so disquieted Spanish agents on the island, and she summed him up in a single sentence: "He feels he's Bonaparte."

Some days later he received an unexpected message with detailed instructions for meeting her in a deserted spot, alone and on foot, the following Saturday night at nine o'clock. That challenge endangered not only his own life but the fate of the Americas as well, for at that time he was the last resort of a shattered insurrection.

The General in His Labyrinth

After five years of troubled independence, Spain had just reconquered the Viceregency of New Granada and the Captaincy General of Venezuela, territories that did not offer resistance to the ferocious onslaught of General Pablo Morillo, called The Pacifier. The supreme command of the patriots had been eliminated by the simple formula of hanging every man who could read and write.

Of all the generation of enlightened Americans who sowed the seeds of independence from Mexico to Río de la Plata, he was the most convinced, the most tenacious, the most farseeing, the one who best reconciled the ingenuity of politics and the intuition of warfare. He lived in a rented two-bedroom house with his military aides, two adolescent former slaves who continued to serve him after their emancipation, and José Palacios. Going off at night, on foot and without an escort, to meet a stranger was a senseless risk and historical folly as well. But despite all the value he placed on his life and his cause, nothing tempted him more than the enigma of a beautiful woman.

Miranda was waiting for him on horseback in the pre-arranged place, she too was alone, and he sat behind her on the horse as she rode along an invisible path. Lightning and thunder far out to sea threatened rain. A pack of dark-colored dogs, barking in the shadows, ran between the feet of the horse, but she kept them at bay with the soft words she whispered to them in English. They passed very close to the sugar plantation where Sir London Lyndsay was writing the memories that no one but him would remember, they forded a rocky stream, and when they were on the other side they entered a pine forest at the end of which lay an abandoned hermitage. There they dismounted, and she led him by the hand through the dark oratory to the ruined sacristy, dimly lit by a torch set in the wall and containing no other furniture but two rough-hewn logs. Only then did each see the other's face. He was in shirtsleeves, his hair was tied back at the nape of the neck in a pigtail, and Miranda found him more youthful and attractive than at the luncheon.

He took no initiative, for his method of seduction did not follow a set pattern, but each case, above all the first move, was distinctive. "In the preambles to love no error can be rectified," he had said. On this occasion he must have been convinced that all obstacles had been surmounted ahead of time, since the decision had been hers.

He was wrong. Along with her beauty Miranda possessed a dignity difficult to ignore, so that a fair amount of time went by before he realized he had to take the initiative on this occasion too. She had invited him to sit down, and just as they were to do fifteen years later in Honda, they faced each other, sitting so close on the rough-hewn trunks that their knees almost touched. He took her by the hands, pulled her toward him, and tried to kiss her. She allowed him to draw near until she felt the warmth of his breath, and then she moved her face away.

"All in good time," she said.

The same words cut off his many subsequent attempts. At midnight, when the rain began to filter in through the cracks in the roof, they were still sitting opposite each other, holding hands while he recited a poem he had recently been composing in his mind. The lines were metrical, well-rhymed royal octaves combining the flattery of love and the bluster of war. She was moved, and she mentioned three names in an effort to guess the author.

"It's by a soldier," he said.

"A fighting soldier or a salon soldier?" she asked.

"Both," he said. "The greatest and most solitary soldier who ever lived."

She remembered what she had said to her father after Mr. Hyslop's luncheon.

"That can only be Bonaparte," she said.

"Close," said the General, "but the moral difference is enormous, because the author of the poem did not allow himself to be crowned."

As the years passed and news of him reached her, she would ask herself with growing amazement if he had been aware that his clever sally was the prefiguration of his own life. But that night she did not even suspect it, involved as she was in the almost impossible task of holding him off without offending him, of not giving in to the advances that grew more pressing as dawn approached. She went as far as allowing him a few casual kisses, but nothing more.

"All in good time," she said to him.

"At three o'clock this afternoon I am leaving forever on the packet boat to Haiti," he said.

She shattered his cunning with a charming laugh.

"In the first place, the packet boat doesn't leave until Friday," she said. "And besides, the cake you ordered yesterday from Señora Turner has to be brought to your supper tonight with the woman who hates me most in this world."

The woman who hated her most in this world was

named Julia Cobier, a beautiful and wealthy Dominican who was also an exile in Jamaica and in whose house, they said, he had spent more than one night. That evening just the two of them were going to celebrate her birthday.

"You're better informed than my spies," he said.

"And why not assume instead that I am one of your spies?" she said.

He did not understand her remark until six o'clock that morning, when he returned to his house and found the body of his friend Félix Amestoy, who had bled to death in the hammock where he would have been lying if it had not been for the counterfeit tryst. Sleep had overcome Amestoy as he waited for the General's return in order to give him an urgent message, and one of the former slaves, paid by the Spaniards, stabbed him eleven times in the belief he was the General. Miranda had learned of the planned assassination and could think of no more astute way to prevent it. He attempted to thank her in person, but she did not respond to his messages. Before leaving for Puerto Príncipe in a corsair's schooner, he sent José Palacios to her with the precious reliquary he had inherited from his mother, along with an unsigned note consisting of a single line:

"I am condemned to a theatrical destiny."

Miranda never forgot or understood that hermetic sentence of the young warrior who, in the years that followed, returned to his country with the help of General Alexandre Pétion, President of the Free Republic of Haiti, crossed the Andes with a mounted troop of barefoot plainsmen, defeated the royalists at Boyacá Bridge, and for the second time and forever liberated New Granada, and then his native Venezuela, and at last the rugged southern territories all the way to their borders with the Empire of Brazil. She followed his career, above all through the tales of travelers who never wearied of recounting his exploits. When the independence of the former Spanish colonies was established, Miranda married an English surveyor who changed professions and settled in New Granada to plant Jamaican sugarcane in the Honda Valley, where she had been the day before when she heard that her old friend, the Kingston exile, was only three leagues from her house. But she reached the mines when the General had already started on his way back to Honda, and she had to ride another half day to catch up with him.

She would not have recognized him on the street without the sideburns and mustache of his youth, with his white thinning hair and that look of final turmoil which gave her the terrifying impression she was talking to a dead man. Miranda had intended to raise her veil to speak with him once the danger of being recognized on the street was behind her, but she was held back by her horror that in her face he too would see the ravages of time. As soon as the preliminary courtesies were over, she went straight to the point:

"I've come to ask you a favor."

"I am at your service," he said.

"The father of my five children is serving a long prison term for killing a man," she said.

"With honor?"

"In an open duel," she said, and hurried to explain: "Because of jealousy."

"Unfounded, of course," he said.

"No, founded," she said.

But it was all in the past now, even him, and the only thing she asked for mercy's sake was that he exercise his power to put an end to her husband's imprisonment. All he could find to say was the truth:

"I am ill and destitute, as you can see, but there is nothing in this world I wouldn't do for you."

He had Captain Ibarra come in to take notes on the details of the case, and he promised to do everything in his waning power to obtain the pardon. That same night he exchanged ideas with Colonel Posada Gutiérrez, in absolute confidence and with nothing in writing, but everything was held in abeyance until they knew what the new government would be like. He accompanied Miranda to the portico of the house, where an escort of six emancipated slaves was waiting for her, and he kissed her hand in farewell.

"It was a happy night," she said.

He could not resist the temptation:

"This one or the other?"

"Both," she said.

She mounted a fresh horse, as handsome and well outfitted as a viceroy's, and she rode away at full gallop without a backward glance. He waited in the doorway until she was lost from view at the end of the street, but he was still seeing her in his dreams when José Palacios woke him at dawn for the start of their river journey.

Seven years before, he had granted special rights to a German, Commodore Johann B. Elbers, to initiate steam navigation. He himself had traveled in one of the vessels from Barranca Nueva to Puerto Real by way of Ocaña, and he had recognized it as a comfortable and safe form of transportation. Nevertheless, Commodore Elbers believed the business was not worth the effort if not backed by exclusive rights, and General Santander granted them without conditions when he occupied the presidency. Two years later, invested with absolute powers by the National Congress, the General broke the agreement with one of his prophetic statements: "If we leave the monopoly in the hands of the Germans, they will end up transferring it to the United States." Then he declared total freedom of river navigation throughout the country. And therefore when he attempted to obtain a steamship in the event he decided to make the journey, he encountered delays and circumlocutions that bore too close a resemblance to revenge, and when it was time to leave he had to settle for the traditional barges.

Since five o'clock that morning the port had been full of people on horseback and on foot, recruited by the Governor in great haste from the nearby streets to simulate a send-off like those of other times. Numerous launches sailed around the docks, loaded with lighthearted women shouting provocations at the soldiers of the guard, who responded with obscene compliments. The General arrived at six with the official delegation. He had left the Governor's house on foot, walking at a very slow pace, his mouth covered by a handkerchief soaked in cologne.

The day promised to be cloudy. The shops along the commercial street had been open since dawn, and some did business almost in the open air among the ruined shells of houses destroyed by an earthquake twenty years before. The General waved his handkerchief to those who greeted him from the windows, but they were the minority, because the majority watched him pass in silence, astounded by his deteriorated condition. He was in shirtsleeves, wearing his one pair of Wellington boots and a white straw hat. In the atrium of the church the priest had stood on a chair to deliver a speech, but General Carreño stopped him. The General walked up to him and shook his hand.

When they turned the corner one glance should have been enough for him to realize he would not survive the slope, but he began the ascent, clutching the arm of General Carreño, until it became apparent he could not go on. Then they tried to convince him to use the sedan chair that Posada Gutiérrez had ready in the event he needed it.

"No, General, I beg of you," he said in consternation. "Spare me this humiliation."

He reached the top of the incline, more by strength of will than of body, and he still had enough energy to descend to the dock without help. There he said goodbye with a pleasant remark for each member of the official delegation. And he did so with a feigned smile so they would not notice that on this May 15 with its ineluctable roses he was starting out on his return trip to the void. As a memento he gave Governor Posada Gutiérrez a gold medal engraved with his profile, thanked him for all his kindness in a voice strong enough to be heard by everyone, and embraced him with true emotion. Then he was in the stern of the barge waving goodbye with his hat, not looking at anyone in the clusters of people making their farewells from the shore, not seeing the disorder of the launches around the barges or the naked children swimming like shad under the water. He continued to wave the hat toward a fixed point, with a distant expression on his face, until all that could be seen was the stump of the church tower rising above the ruined walls. Then he went inside the shelter on the barge, sat on the hammock, and stretched his legs so that José Palacios could help him take off his boots.

"Now we'll see if they really believe we've gone," he said.

The flotilla was composed of eight barges of varying sizes, and a special barge for him and his entourage, with a helmsman in the stern and eight oarsmen who propelled it with poles made of guaiacum wood. Unlike ordinary barges, with a cargo shed of palm in the center, on this one they had set up a canvas tent so he could hang his hammock in the shade, lined it on the inside with printed cotton cloth and roofed it with rush matting, and cut four windows to increase the ventilation and light. It was furnished with a small table for writing or playing cards, a bookcase, and an earthen water jar with a stone filter. The man responsible for the flotilla, selected from among the best on the river, was Casildo Santos, a former captain in the battalion of the Marksmen of the Guard who had a voice like thunder, a pirate's patch over his left eye, and a somewhat undaunted notion of his authority.

May was the first of the good months for Commodore Elbers' ships, but the good months were not the best ones for barges. The mortal heat, the biblical storms, the treacherous currents, the menace of wild animals and predatory insects at night, all seemed to conspire against the comfort of the passengers. An additional torment for someone made sensitive by ill health was the pestilential stink of the strips of salted meat and smoked fish that had been hung by mistake on the overhead beams of the presidential barge, which he ordered removed as soon as he noticed them when he came on board. Having learned in this way that the General could not bear even the odor of food, Captain Santos had the provisioning barge with its pens of live chickens and pigs moved to last place in the flotilla, and from the very first day of navigation, when the General devoured two plates of cornmeal mush with great delight, it was established he would not eat anything else during the voyage.

"This seems to have been prepared by the magical hand of Fernanda the Seventh," he said.

And it was. His personal cook for the last few years, the Quiteña Fernanda Barriga, whom he called Fernanda the Seventh when she obliged him to eat something he did not like, was on board without his knowledge. She was an imperturbable, fat, sharp-tongued Indian whose greatest virtue was not good seasoning in the kitchen but an instinct for pleasing the General at the table. He had resolved that she would stay in Santa Fe de Bogotá with Manuela Sáenz, who made her part of her domestic staff, but in Guaduas General Carreño sent for her with great urgency after José Palacios announced to him in alarm that the General had not eaten a full meal since the eve of his departure. She had arrived in Honda in the early hours of the morning, and they hid her on the provisioning barge to wait for the right moment to make her appearance. This presented itself sooner than expected because of the pleasure the General felt when he ate the cornmeal mush, his favorite food since his health began to decline.

The first day of navigation might have been the last. Night fell at two o'clock in the afternoon, the water raged, thunder and lightning shook the earth, and the oarsmen seemed incapable of keeping the boats from breaking apart against the cliffs. From his tent the General observed the rescue operation directed at the top of his lungs by Captain Santos, whose naval ingenuity did not seem adequate to this kind of emergency. He observed first with curiosity and then with indomitable apprehension, and at the culminating moment of danger he realized that the Captain had given the wrong order. Allowing himself to be carried along by instinct, he made his way through the wind and the rain, and at the very edge of the abyss he countermanded the Captain's order.

"Not that way!" he shouted. "To the right, the right, damn it!"

The oarsmen responded to the shattered voice still full of an irresistible authority, and without realizing it he took over command until the crisis had passed. José Palacios hurried to cover him with a blanket. Wilson and Ibarra held him upright where he stood. Captain Santos moved to one side, conscious once again of having confused port and starboard, and waited with a soldier's humility until the General looked around for him and found him with a wavering glance.

"You'll forgive me, Captain," he said to him.

But he was not at peace with himself. That night, around the fires they lit on the wide beach where they pulled ashore for the first time to sleep, he told stories of memorable naval disasters. He told about his brother Juan Vicente, Fernando's father, who drowned in a shipwreck on his return from Washington, where he had purchased a shipment of arms and ammunition for the First Republic. He told about almost suffering the same fate when his horse died between his legs as he was crossing the swollen waters of the Arauca and he was pulled along head over heels with his boot caught in the stirrup until his guide managed to cut the straps. He told about finding a capsized boat in the rapids of the Orinoco on his way to Angostura, soon after he had assured the independence of New Granada, and seeing an officer he did not know swimming to shore. He was told it was General Sucre. He replied in indignation: "There is no General Sucre." But in fact it was Antonio José de Sucre, who had been promoted a short while before to the rank of general of the liberating army, and with whom he had maintained an intimate friendship ever since.

"I knew about that meeting," said General Carreño, "but not about the shipwreck."

"I may be confusing it with Sucre's first shipwreck, when he escaped from Cartagena with Morillo in pursuit and stayed afloat God knows how for almost twenty-four hours," he said. And he added, not quite to the point: "What I'm trying to do is to make Captain Santos understand somehow my impertinence this afternoon."

In the early hours of the morning, when everyone was sleeping, the entire jungle shuddered to an unaccompanied song that could only come straight from the soul. The General bolted upright in the hammock. "It's Iturbide," murmured José Palacios in the half-light. No sooner had he spoken than a brutal commanding voice interrupted the song.

Agustín de Iturbide was the oldest son of a Mexican general in the wars for independence who had proclaimed himself Emperor of his country but took over a year to reach office. The General had felt a distinct affection for him from the first time he saw him, standing at attention, trembling, unable to control the shaking of his hands at finding himself face-to-face with the idol of his youth. He was twenty-two years old at the time. Before he was seventeen his father had been shot in a dusty, hot village in the Mexican provinces a few hours after returning from exile unaware he had been tried in absentia and condemned to death for high treason.

Three things affected the General from the very beginning. One was that Agustín had the watch, made of gold and precious gems, sent to him by his father as he stood at the wall where they shot him, which he wore on a chain around his neck so that no one could doubt how much he honored him. Another was the candor with which he told him that his father, dressed in rags so he would not be recognized by the guards at the port, had been betrayed by the elegance with which he rode a horse. The third was how he sang.

The Mexican government had placed every kind of obstacle in the way of his joining the Army of Colombia, convinced that his training in the arts of war was part of a monarchist conspiracy, supported by the General, to crown him Emperor of Mexico with the pretender's rights of a hereditary prince. The General risked a serious diplomatic incident, not only by inducting young Agustín with his military titles but by making him his aide-de-camp. Agustín was worthy of his confidence, although he never enjoyed a day of happiness and only the habit of singing allowed him to survive his precarious position.

And therefore when someone silenced him in the jungles of the Magdalena the General, wrapped in a blanket, got up from the hammock, crossed the camp, lit by the fires of the guards, and went out to join him. He found him sitting on the bank watching the river go by.

"Continue singing, Captain," he said.

He sat next to him, and when he knew the words of the song he accompanied him in his thin voice. He had never heard anyone sing with so much love, and he could not remember anyone so sad who could still produce so much happiness around him. With Fernando and Andrés, who had been his classmates at the military school in George-town, Iturbide had formed a trio that brought a youthful air to the General's surroundings, so impoverished by the barrenness typical of barracks.

Agustín and the General continued singing until the clamor of the jungle animals startled the alligators sleeping on the shore, and the very heart of the water thrashed as if in cataclysm. The General remained seated on the ground, stunned by the awesome awakening of all of nature, until a ribbon of orange appeared on the horizon and it was light. Then he leaned on Iturbide's shoulder in order to stand up.

"Thank you, Captain," he said to him. "With ten men singing like you, we could save the world."

"Ah, General," sighed Iturbide. "What I wouldn't give if my mother could hear you say that."

On the second day of the voyage they saw well-kept haciendas with blue meadowlands and handsome horses running free, but then the jungle began, and everything became contiguous and unchanging. Earlier they had started to pass rafts made of enormous tree trunks that the woodcutters who lived on the riverbanks were taking to Cartagena de Indias to sell. They were so slow they seemed unmoving in the current, and entire families with their children and animals traveled on them with only the meager protection from the sun provided by simple lean-tos made of palm. At some bends in the jungle they could already see the first devastation caused by the steamship crews in order to feed the boilers.

"The fish will have to learn to walk on land because the water will disappear," he said.

The heat grew intolerable during the day and the raucous screams of the monkeys and birds became maddening, but the nights were silent and cool. On the broad beaches the alligators lay motionless for hours on end, their jaws open to catch butterflies. Next to the deserted settlements they could see corn plantings, and skeletal dogs that barked as the vessels passed by, and even in the uninhabited wilds there were tapir traps, and fishing nets drying in the sun, but there was no sign of any human being.

Idleness was painful after so many years of wars, bitter governments, and trivial loves. The little life with which the General began the day was spent meditating in the hammock. His immediate reply to President Caycedo had brought his correspondence up-to-date, but he passed the time dictating inconsequential letters. During the first few days Fernando finished reading aloud the gossip-laden chronicles of Lima, and could not interest him in anything else.

It was the last book he read in its entirety. He had been a reader of imperturbable voracity during the respites after battles and the rests after love, but a reader without order or method. He read at any hour, in whatever light was available, sometimes strolling under the trees, sometimes on horseback under the equatorial sun, sometimes in dim coaches rattling over cobbled pavements, sometimes swaying in the hammock as he dictated a letter. A bookseller in Lima had been surprised at the abundance and variety of works he selected from a general catalogue that listed everything from Greek philosophers to a treatise on chiromancy. In his youth he read the Romantics under the influence of his tutor, Simón Rodríguez, and he continued to devour them as if he were reading himself and his own idealistic, intense temperament. They were impassioned readings that marked him for the rest of his life. In the end he read everything that came his way, and he did not have a favorite author but rather many who had been favorites at different times. The bookcases in the various houses he lived in were always crammed full, and the bedrooms and hallways were turned into narrow passes between steep cliffs of books and mountains of errant documents that proliferated as he passed and pursued him without mercy in their quest for archival peace. He never was able to read all the books he owned. When he moved to another city he left them in the care of his most trustworthy friends, although he never heard anything about them again, and his life of fighting obliged him to leave behind a trail of books and papers stretching over four hundred leagues from Bolivia to Venezuela.

Even before his eyes began to fail he had his secretaries read to him, and then he read no other way because of the annoyance that eyeglasses caused him. But his interest in what he read was decreasing at the same time, and as always he attributed this to a cause beyond his control.

"The fact is there are fewer and fewer good books," he would say.

José Palacios was the only one who showed no signs of boredom in the torpor of the voyage, and the heat and discomfort in no way affected his elegant manners and dress or his meticulous service. He was six years younger than the General, in whose house he had been born a slave through the misadventure of an African woman and a Spaniard, from whom he had inherited his carrot-red hair, the freckles on his face and hands, and his light-blue eyes. In contrast to his natural sobriety, he owned the most complete and expensive wardrobe in the entire entourage. He had spent his entire life with the General—his two exiles, his campaigns from beginning to end, and all his battles in the front line—and always as a civilian, for he never acknowledged his right to wear a military uniform.

The worst part of the voyage was forced immobility. One afternoon the General was so desperate with pacing the narrow confines of the canvas tent that he had the boat stop so he could take a walk. In the hardened mud they saw tracks that seemed to be those of a bird as large as an ostrich and at least as heavy as an ox, but this seemed normal to the oarsmen, who said there were men roaming that desolate place who were as big as ceiba trees and had the crests and claws of roosters. He scoffed at the legend, as he scoffed at everything that had the slightest glimmer of the supernatural, but his walk took longer than expected and they had to make camp against the judgment of the captain and even his military aides, who considered the place dangerous and unhealthy. He spent a sleepless night, tortured by the heat and the clouds of mosquitoes that seemed to fly through the suffocating nets, unsettled by the fearful roars of a puma that kept them on the alert all night. At about two o'clock in the morning he went to chat with the groups standing watch around the bonfires. Only at dawn, as he contemplated the vast swamps gilded by the rising sun, did he renounce the dream that had kept him awake.

"All right," he said, "we'll have to leave without seeing our friends with the rooster claws."

Just as they weighed anchor a filthy, emaciated dog, suffering from mange and a paralyzed paw, leaped onto the barge. The General's two dogs attacked him, but the invalid defended himself with suicidal ferocity and refused to surrender even when he was covered with blood and his throat had been torn open. The General gave orders to keep him, and José Palacios took charge of him, as he had done so many times with so many other stray dogs.

That same day they rescued a German who had been abandoned on an island of sand for beating one of his oarsmen. When he came on board he represented himself as an astronomer and a botanist, but in conversation it became evident he knew nothing about either science. On the other hand, he had seen with his own eyes the men with rooster claws, and he was determined to capture one alive, put it in a cage, and exhibit it in Europe as a phenomenon comparable only to the Spider Woman of the Americas, who had caused such a sensation in the ports of Andalusia a century before.

"Take me instead," the General said to him. "I assure you you'll earn more money showing me in a cage as the biggest damn fool in history."

At first he had thought him an agreeable charlatan, but that changed when the German began to tell indecent jokes about the shameless pederasty of Baron Alexander von Humboldt. "We should leave him on the beach again," he said to José Palacios. In the afternoon they came across the mail launch sailing upstream, and the General used all his charm to have the mail agent open the sacks of official correspondence and give him his letters. And then he asked him to please take the German to the port of Nare, and the agent agreed even though the launch was overloaded. That night, while Fernando was reading the letters to him, the General growled:

"That motherfucker isn't worth a single hair on Humboldt's head."

He had been thinking about the Baron even before they rescued the German, for he could not imagine how he had survived in that untamed wild. He had met him during his years in Paris, after Humboldt's return from his trip through the equinoctial countries, and he had been as astonished by the splendor of his beauty, the likes of which he had never seen in any woman, as by his intelligence and erudition. On the other hand, what he had found least convincing was the Baron's certainty that the Spanish colonies in America were ripe for independence. He had said as much without a tremor in his voice, at a time when the thought had not occurred to the General even as an idle Sunday fantasy.

"All that's missing is the man," Humboldt said.

He told José Palacios about it many years later, in Cuzco, perhaps because he found himself at the top of the world at a moment when history had just demonstrated that he was the man. He did not tell anyone else, but each time the Baron was mentioned he took the opportunity to pay tribute to his prescience:

"Humboldt opened my eyes."

It was the fourth time he had traveled along the Magdalena, and he could not escape the impression that he was retracing the steps of his life. He had sailed its waters for the first time in 1813, when he was a colonel in the militia who had been defeated in his own country and had come to Cartagena de Indias from his exile in Curaçao in search of resources to continue the war. New Granada had been divided into autonomous fragments, the cause of independence was losing popular support in the face of savage repression by the Spaniards, and final victory seemed less and less certain. On the third voyage, aboard a paddleboat, as he called it, the work of liberation had been concluded but his almost maniacal dream of continental unity was beginning to crumble. On this, his final voyage, the dream was already destroyed, but it survived in a single sentence he never tired of repeating: "Our enemies will have all the advantages until we unify the government of America."

Of the countless memories he shared with José Palacios, one of the most moving was that first voyage, when they waged the war to liberate the river. He led two hundred men armed with whatever weapons they could find, and in some twenty days there was not a single monarchist Spaniard left in the Magdalena Basin. José Palacios himself realized how much things had changed when, on the fourth day of the voyage, they began to see the ranks of women along the riverbanks at every village, waiting for the barges to pass. "Those are the widows," he said. The General looked out and saw them, dressed in black, lined up on the bank like pensive crows under the burning sun, waiting for anything, even if it was only a charitable greeting. General Diego Ibarra, Andrés' brother, used to say the General never had a child but was, instead, father and mother to all the widows in the nation. They followed him everywhere, and he kept them alive with heartfelt words that were true proclamations of consolation. Nevertheless, he was thinking more of himself than of them when he saw the lines of funereal women in the villages along the river.

"Now we are the widows," he said. "We are the orphans, the wounded, the pariahs of independence."

They did not stop in any town before Mompox except Puerto Real, where the Ocaña emptied into the Magdalena River. There they met General José Laurencio Silva, the Venezuelan who had completed his mission of accompanying the rebel grenadiers to the border of their country and had come to join the cortege.

The General remained on board until nightfall, when he went ashore to sleep in an improvised encampment. While he was on the barge he received the ranks of the widows, the impoverished, the helpless of all the wars who wanted to see him. He remembered almost all of them with astounding accuracy. Those who had remained were dying of poverty, others had gone in search of new wars to survive or had become highwaymen, like countless veterans of the liberating army everywhere in the nation. One of them summed up their feelings in a phrase: "We have independence, General, so now tell us what to do with it." In the euphoria of victory he had taught them to speak to him this way, with the truth in their mouths. But now truth had changed masters.

"Independence was a simple question of winning the

war," he said to them. "The great sacrifices must come afterwards, to make a single nation out of all these countries."

"We've made nothing but sacrifices, General," they said.

He would not give an inch:

"More are needed," he said. "Unity has no price."

That night, as he wandered around the building where they had hung his hammock, he saw a woman who turned to look at him as he passed, and he was surprised by her lack of surprise at his nakedness. He even heard the words of the song she was singing under her breath: "*Tell me it's never too late to die of love.*" The watchman was awake under the portico.

"Is any woman here?" the General asked him.

The man was certain. "None worthy of Your Excellency," he said.

"And unworthy of my excellency?"

"None at all," said the watchman. "There's no woman within a league of here."

The General was so sure he had seen her that he looked for her everywhere in the house until it grew very late. He insisted that his aides-de-camp join the search, and the next day he delayed their departure for more than an hour until he was vanquished by the repeated reply: there was no one. The matter was not spoken of again. For the rest of the journey, each time he thought of it he insisted he had seen her. José Palacios would survive him by many years, with so much time to review his life with him that not even the most insignificant detail remained in shadow. The only matter he never clarified was whether the vision that night in Puerto Real had been a dream, a hallucination, or an apparition.

No one thought again about the stray dog, still with them recovering from his wounds, until the orderly in charge of the food realized he had no name. They had bathed him and perfumed him with baby powder, but they could not rid him of his dissolute appearance or the stench of mange. The General was taking the air in the stern when José Palacios pulled the dog over to him.

"What name shall we give him?" he asked.

The General did not even have to think about it.

"Bolívar," he said.

A GUNBOAT MOORED in port began to move as soon as it was informed that a flotilla of barges was approaching. José Palacios sighted it through the tent windows, and he leaned over the hammock where the General was lying with his eyes closed.

"Sir," he said, "we're in Mompox."

"God's country," said the General, without opening his eyes.

As they sailed down to the coast the river had grown more vast and solemn, like a swamp with no beginning or end, and the heat was so dense you could touch it with your hands. Without bitterness the General gave up the sudden dawns and piercing twilights that had kept him in the stern of the barge for the first few days, and he yielded to dejection. He did not dictate letters, or read, or ask his companions any question that might reveal a certain interest in life. Even during the hottest siestas he covered himself with the blanket and stayed in the hammock with his eyes closed. Thinking he had not heard him, José Palacios repeated the message, and again the General responded without opening his eyes.

"Mompox doesn't exist," he said. "Sometimes we dream about it, but it doesn't exist."

"At least I can testify to the existence of the Santa Bárbara Tower," said José Palacios. "I see it from here."

The General opened his tormented eyes, sat up in the hammock, and in the aluminum light of noon saw the first roofs of the very ancient and long-suffering city of Mompox that had been devastated by war, debased by the turmoil of the Republic, decimated by smallpox. This was the time when the river had begun to change course with an irreparable disdain that would become total abandonment by the end of the century. All that remained of the masonry dike that the colonial governors, with Peninsular obstinacy, had hastened to rebuild each time it was destroyed by flood was rubble scattered along a beach of fallen stones. The warship approached the barges, and a black officer who still wore the uniform of the old viceregal police aimed the cannon at them. Captain Casildo Santos managed to shout:

"Hey, black man, don't be an idiot!"

The oarsmen stopped rowing, and the barges were left to the mercy of the current. The grenadiers, waiting for orders, raised their rifles and took aim at the gunboat. The officer was unperturbed.

"Passports," he shouted. "In the name of the law."

Only then did he see the soul in torment who emerged from under the canvas, the exhausted hand that still held inexorable authority ordering the soldiers to lower their weapons. Then he said to the officer in a faint voice:

"Although you may not believe it, Captain, I have no passport."

The officer did not know who he was. But when Fernando told him he leaped into the water with his weapons and ran down the riverbank to inform everyone of the good news. The gunboat, its bell clanging, escorted the barges into port. Even before the entire city came into view at the last bend in the river, the bells of its eight churches were ringing out the tidings.

During the colonial period Santa Cruz de Mompox had been the commercial bridge between the Caribbean coast and the interior of the country, and this had been the origin of its wealth. When the windstorms of liberty began to blow, that stronghold of the American aristocracy was the first to proclaim independence. Reconquered by Spain, it was liberated again by the General himself. It consisted of only three wide, straight, and dusty streets running parallel to the river, with large-windowed, one-story houses where two counts and three marquises prospered. The fame of its craftsmanship in precious metals had survived the vicissitudes of the Republic.

On this occasion the General arrived so disillusioned with his glory and so disenchanted with the world that he was caught off guard by the crowd waiting for him in port. He threw on his velveteen trousers and high boots, wrapped himself in the blanket despite the heat, and changed his nightcap for the broad-brimmed hat he had used in Honda for waving farewell.

The funeral of a high dignitary was taking place in the Church of La Concepción. In attendance at the solemn Mass were all the civil and ecclesiastical authorities, the congregations and schools, and the leading citizens in their finest crepe, and the clamor of the bells made them lose their composure because they thought it was a fire alarm. But the same bailiff who had entered in great agitation and whispered the news into the Mayor's ear shouted for everyone to hear:

"The President is in the port!"

For many still did not know he was no longer President. On Monday a mail carrier had spread the rumors from Honda among the towns along the river but had clarified nothing. And so the ambiguity made the unexpected reception more effusive, and even the bereaved family understood that most of the mourners would leave the church to gather at the ruined wall. The funeral ended before it was over, and only an intimate group accompanied the coffin to the cemetery, in the midst of thundering rockets and bells.

The river was still low because of May's light rainfall, and as a consequence the General and his entourage had to scale cliffs of stone debris to reach the port. With bad grace the General refused someone's offer to carry him, and he climbed, leaning on Captain Ibarra's arm, staggering at each step and struggling to hold himself upright, but with his dignity intact.

He greeted the authorities in the port with energetic handshakes of incredible vigor, given the condition of his body and the smallness of his hands. Those who had seen him the last time he was there could not believe their memories. He seemed as old as his own father, but the little breath he had was enough to keep anyone from making special arrangements for him. He refused the platforms carried in Good Friday processions which they had prepared for him, and he said he would walk to the Church of La Concepción. In the end he had to ride the Mayor's mule that the official had saddled in great haste when he saw him disembark in so weakened a state.

José Palacios had noticed many faces in port tiger-striped with the red embers of smallpox, a stubborn illness endemic to the towns of the lower Magdalena. The patriots had come to fear it more than they feared the Spaniards after it decimated the liberating troops during the river campaign. Then, when the smallpox persisted, the General arranged for a visiting French naturalist to stay long enough to inoculate the people with the serous fluid that oozed from the smallpox of cattle. But this method of treatment caused so many deaths that in the end no one wanted to hear anything more about the cow cure, as they called it, and many mothers preferred that their children be exposed to the risks of contagion rather than the dangers of prevention. Nevertheless, official reports received by the General led him to believe that the scourge of smallpox was being conquered. And therefore when José Palacios pointed out to him the number of marked faces in the crowd, his reaction was not so much surprise as weary disgust.

"It will always be like this," he said, "as long as subordinates lie to make us happy."

He did not allow those who welcomed him in port to see his bitterness. He gave them a summary accounting of the events of his renunciation and the disorder that reigned in Santa Fe de Bogotá, exhorting them to give their unanimous support to the new government. "There is no other alternative," he said. "Either unity or anarchy." He said he was going and would not return, not so much to seek relief for the evident afflictions of his body, which were numerous and very grave, as to attempt to find respite from the untold sorrow that other people's suffering caused him. But he did not say when he was going, or where, and he repeated without real relevance that he had not yet received from the government the passport that would allow him to leave the country. He thanked them for the twenty years of glory that Mompox had bestowed upon him and begged them not to honor him with any title except Citizen.

The Church of La Concepción was still draped in mourning and the breath of funeral flowers and candles still floated through the air when the crowd trooped in for an improvised Te Deum. José Palacios, sitting with the rest of the entourage, realized that the General could find no comfort in his pew. Yet the Mayor, an immutable mestizo with a handsome leonine head, stayed next to him inside a closed circle. Fernanda, the Widow Benjumea, whose American beauty had created havoc at the court in Madrid, lent the General her sandalwood fan to help him defend himself against the stupefying ceremony. He moved it back and forth without hope, not even for the consolation of its little gusts of air, until the heat began to interfere with his breathing. Then he whispered in the Mayor's ear:

"Believe me, I don't deserve this punishment."

"The love of the people has its price, Excellency," said the Mayor.

"Sad to say, this isn't love, it's curiosity," he said.

When the Te Deum was over he said goodbye to the Widow Benjumea with a bow and returned her fan. She attempted to give it back to him.

"Do me the honor of keeping it as a remembrance of one who loves you well," she said to him.

"The sad thing, Señora, is that I do not have much time left for remembering," he said.

The priest insisted on protecting him from the suffocating heat with the Holy Week canopy as they walked from the Church of La Concepción to the Academy of San Pedro Apóstol, a two-story mansion with a monastic cloister of ferns and pinks, and a luminous orchard of fruit trees in the rear. The arcaded corridors were not habitable during those months because of unhealthy winds that blew in from the river even at night, but the rooms adjoining the large parlor were protected by thick masonry walls that kept them in autumnal shadow.

José Palacios had gone ahead to have everything ready. The bedroom, its rough walls covered by a fresh coat of whitewash, was dimly lit by a single green-shuttered window that looked out on the orchard. He had the position of the bed changed so that the window facing the orchard would be at the foot and not at the head of the bed, and in this way the General could see the yellow guavas on the trees and enjoy their perfume.

The General arrived on Fernando's arm and in the company of the priest from the Church of La Concepción, who was also the rector of the academy. As soon as he walked through the door he leaned his back against the wall, surprised by the scent of the guavas lying in a gourd on the windowsill, their luxuriant fragrance saturating the entire bedroom. He stood with his eyes closed, inhaling the heartbreaking aroma of days gone by until he lost his breath. Then he scrutinized the room with meticulous

attention as if each object were a revelation. In addition
to the canopied bed there was a mahogany chest of draw-
ers, a marble-topped night table, also of mahogany, and
an easy chair covered in red velvet. On the wall beside
the window was an octagonal clock with Roman numerals, which had stopped at seven minutes past one.

"At last, something's still the same!" said the General.
The priest was surprised.

"Excuse me, Excellency," he said, "but as far as I
know, you've never been here before."

José Palacios was also surprised, for they had never
visited this house, but the General persisted in his recol-
lections, with so many accurate references that he left
everyone perplexed. In the end, however, he attempted
to reassure them with his habitual irony.

"Perhaps it was during a previous incarnation," he said.
"After all, anything is possible in a city where we've just
seen an excommunicated man walking under a canopy."

A short while later a thunderstorm broke that left the
city shipwrecked. The General took advantage of it to
recover from his reception, enjoying the scent of the
guavas in the shadowy room while he pretended to sleep
on his back with all his clothes on, and then in fact did
fall asleep in the recuperative silence following the deluge. José Palacios knew this was true when he heard
him speaking with the good diction and sharp timbre of
his youth, which by this time he regained only in sleep.
He talked of Caracas, a city in ruins that was no longer his,
its walls papered with attacks against him and its streets
overflowing with a torrent of human shit. In a corner of
the room, almost invisible in the easy chair, José Palacios
watched to make certain that no one outside the entou-

rage could hear the secrets of his sleep. Through the half-opened door he signaled to Colonel Wilson, who sent away the soldiers of the guard wandering through the garden.

"Nobody wants us here, and in Caracas nobody obeys us," said the sleeping General. "It all evens out."

He continued with a psaltery of bitter laments, remnants of a ruined glory that the wind of death was carrying away in tatters. After almost an hour of delirium, noises in the corridor and the metal of an arrogant voice awoke him. He snorted abruptly and spoke in his faded waking voice without opening his eyes:

"What the hell's going on?"

What was going on was that General Lorenzo Cárcamo, a veteran of the wars of emancipation with a thorny disposition and an almost demented personal courage, was trying to force his way into the bedroom before the hour scheduled for interviews. He had pushed Colonel Wilson aside after hitting a lieutenant of the grenadiers with his saber, and he had bowed only to the other-worldly power of the priest, who led him, unprotesting, to an adjacent office. The General, informed by Wilson, shouted in indignation:

"Tell Cárcamo I died! That's all, just tell him I died!"

Colonel Wilson went to the office to confront the obstreperous soldier, who was dressed for the occasion in his parade uniform and a constellation of combat medals. But by then his arrogance had collapsed and his eyes were flooded with tears.

"No, Wilson, don't give me the message," he said. "I've already heard it."

When the General opened his eyes he realized the

clock still read seven minutes past one. José Palacios wound it, set it from memory, and then confirmed the time on his two watches. A little later Fernanda Barriga came in and tried to have the General eat some vegetable stew. He resisted, although he had not eaten anything since the previous day, but he ordered the food brought to the office so that he could eat during the interviews. In the meantime he succumbed to temptation and picked up one of the many guavas in the gourd. He was intoxicated by its aroma for a moment, gave it a greedy bite, chewed the flesh with childish delight, tasted the fruit on all sides, and swallowed it little by little with a long sigh of memory. Then he sat on the hammock with the gourd of guavas between his legs, and he ate them all, one after the other, almost not taking the time to breathe. José Palacios took him by surprise when there was only one left.

"We'll kill ourselves!"

The General mimicked him with good humor:

"No deader than we are already."

At three-thirty sharp, the prearranged hour, he gave orders for the visitors to begin to come into the office in twos, for in this way he could finish with one in the shortest time by letting him see his haste to attend to the other. Dr. Nicasio del Valle, who was among the first, found him sitting with his back to a glass-paned window through which one could see the entire farm and beyond that the steaming swamps. In his hand he held the plate of vegetable stew that Fernanda Barriga had brought him and that he did not even taste because he was already beginning to feel the effects of his overindulgence in the guavas. Dr. del Valle later summarized his impression of the interview in unadorned language: "That man's goose was cooked." Everyone who came for an interview agreed, each in his own way. Nevertheless, even those most touched by his weakness lacked compassion, for they urged him to travel to neighboring villages to be god-father to children, or to inaugurate public works, or to see for himself the poverty in which people lived because of the government's negligence.

After an hour the nausea and stomach cramps caused by the guavas became alarming, and he had to call a halt to the interviews despite his desire to accommodate every-one who had been waiting since the morning. There was no room in the patio for more calves, goats, chickens, or the different kinds of wild game that had been brought as gifts. The grenadiers had to intervene to prevent a disturbance, but by dusk the situation had returned to normal thanks to a second providential downpour, which cleared the air and enhanced the silence.

Despite the General's explicit refusal, a dinner in his honor had been prepared for four o'clock at a nearby house. But it was held without him, for the carminative power of the guavas kept him in a state of emergency until after eleven o'clock that night. He stayed in the hammock, prostrate with torturous shooting pains and fragrant farts, feeling his soul slip away in abrasive waters. The priest brought a medicine prepared by the pharma-cist at the Academy. The General refused it. "If I lost power with one emetic, Old Nick will carry me away with a second," he said. He abandoned himself to his fate, shivering with the icy sweat in his bones, his only con-solation the occasional snatches of beautiful string music wafting in from the banquet held without him. Little by little the flood from his belly subsided, the pain passed, the music ended, and he remained floating in nothingness.

His previous visit to Mompox had almost been the last. He was returning from Caracas after effecting, through the magic of his person, an emergency reconciliation with General José Antonio Páez, who was, nevertheless, very far from renouncing his separatist dream. At that time his enmity with Santander was public knowledge and had gone to the extreme of the General's refusing to receive any more of his letters because he no longer trusted either his heart or his morality. "Save yourself the trouble of calling yourself my friend," he wrote to him. The immediate pretext for Santanderist animosity was a hurried proclamation the General had made to the people of the city in which he said, without thinking too much about it, that all his actions had been guided by the liberty and glory of Caracas. On his return to New Granada he had tried to smooth things over with an appropriate phrase for Cartagena and Mompox: "If Caracas gave me life, you gave me glory." But it looked too much like rhetorical fence-mending to placate the demagoguery of the Santanderists.

In an attempt to hold off the final disaster, the General was returning to Santa Fe de Bogotá with a column of troops, hoping to gather others along the way, in order to begin once again the struggle for national integrity. He had said then that this was his decisive moment, which is just what he had said when he marched off to prevent the separation of Venezuela. A little more reflection would have permitted him to realize that for almost twenty years no moment of his life had not been decisive. "The entire Church, the entire army, the immense majority of the nation, were on my side," he would write later, remembering those days. But despite all these advantages, he said, it had been proved over and over again that when he abandoned the south to march north, and vice versa, the country he left behind was lost, devastated by new civil wars. It was his destiny.

The Santanderist press missed no opportunity to attribute military defeats to his nocturnal excesses. Among the many other lies intended to diminish his glory, at that time they published the story in Santa Fe de Bogotá that not he but General Santander had been in command at the battle of Boyacá, where independence had been assured at seven o'clock in the morning of August 7, 1819, while he was pleasuring himself in Tunja with a lady of dubious reputation in viceregal society.

In any case, it was not just the Santanderist press that evoked his libertine nights in order to discredit him. Even before the final victory it was said that at least three battles in the wars for independence had been lost only because he was not where he was supposed to be but in some woman's bed instead. During another of his visits to Mompox, a caravan of women of diverse ages and colors came down the second of the three streets and left the air heavy with cheap perfume. They rode sidesaddle, carried parasols of printed satin, and wore dresses of exquisite silk the likes of which had never been seen in the city. No one denied the speculation that they were the General's concubines, traveling ahead of him. A false speculation, like so many others, for his wartime harems were one of the many salon fabrications that pursued him beyond the grave.

There was nothing new in these methods of slanted reporting. The General himself had used them during the war against Spain, when he ordered Santander to print false news items in order to deceive the Spanish commanders. And therefore when the Republic was already established and he criticized this same Santander for his misuse of the press, he responded with exquisite sarcasm:

"We had a good teacher, Excellency."

"A bad teacher," the General replied, "for you must remember that the news we invented was turned against us."

He was so sensitive to everything said about him, true or false, that he never recovered from any falsehood, and until the moment of his death he struggled to disprove them. Nevertheless, he did little to protect himself from lies. As he had on other occasions, the last time he was in Mompox he gambled his glory for the sake of a woman.

She was Josefa Sagrario, a highborn Mompoxina who, disguised in a Franciscan habit, made her way past seven guard stations using the password given to her by José Palacios: "God's country." She was so white that her dazzling body made her visible in the darkness. That night, moreover, she had succeeded in surpassing the miracle of her beauty with that of her ornamentation, for over the front and the back of her dress she had hung a cuirass of magnificent local goldwork. And when he tried to carry her to the hammock he could scarcely lift her because of the weight of the gold. At dawn, after a night of abandon, she felt the terror of transience and begged him to stay another night.

It was an enormous risk, since according to the General's secret agents Santander had organized a conspiracy to strip him of his power and dismember Colombia. But he stayed, and not just one night. He stayed ten, and they were so happy they both came to believe that in fact they loved each other more than anyone in this world ever had before.

She gave him her gold. "For your wars," she said. He did not use it because of his scruples regarding treasure earned in bed and therefore ill-gotten, and he left it in the keeping of a friend. He forgot it. After the attack caused by the guavas on his final visit to Mompox, the General had the chest opened to verify its contents, and only then did he find the gold, along with her name and date, in his memory.

It was a miraculous vision: Josefa Sagrario's gold cuirass made of different kinds of exquisite metalwork, with a total weight of thirty pounds. And there was a case with twenty-three forks, twenty-four knives, twenty-four teaspoons, and a small sugar tongs, all of gold, as well as other household items of great value, also left behind on different occasions for safekeeping, and also forgotten. In the fabulous disorder of the General's treasuries, these discoveries in the most unthought-of places no longer surprised anyone. He gave instructions that the flatware should be added to his baggage and that the trunk full of gold should be returned to its owner. But the priest who was rector of San Pedro Apóstol astounded him with the news that Josefa Sagrario and her family were living in exile in Italy for conspiring against the security of the state.

"More of Santander's shit, of course," said the General.

"No, General," said the priest. "You exiled them yourself without realizing it after the troubles in '28."

He left the chest of gold where it was while he clarified

the matter, and then he did not concern himself anymore about her exile. For as he told José Palacios, he was certain that Josefa Sagrario would return along with the horde of his proscribed enemies as soon as he lost sight of the Cartagena coastline.

"Cassandro must be packing his trunks by now," he said.

And in fact, many exiles began their own repatriation as soon as they learned he was on his way to Europe. But General Santander, a man of sober reflections and unfathomable decisions, was one of the last. The news of the renunciation put him on the alert, but he gave no signs of returning, and he did not hasten to conclude the avid study trips through the countries of Europe that he had undertaken as soon as he disembarked in Hamburg in October of the previous year. On March 2, 1831, when he was in Florence, he read in the *Journal du Commerce* that the General had died. Nevertheless, he did not begin his slow return until six months later, when a new government restored his military ranks and honors and the Congress elected him President of the Republic in absentia.

Before weighing anchor in Mompox, the General made an apologetic visit to Lorenzo Cárcamo, his old comrade in arms. Only then did he learn that he was gravely ill and got up from his bed the previous afternoon only to greet him. Despite the ravages of illness, Cárcamo had to make an effort to control the power of his body, and his voice thundered while he used pillows to dry the flood of tears that poured from his eyes without any connection at all to his state of mind.

Together they lamented their misfortunes, mourned

the frivolity of nations and the ingratitude of victory, and ranted against Santander, who was always an obligatory topic for them. The General had not often been so explicit. During the campaign of 1813 Lorenzo Cárcamo had been witness to a violent altercation between the General and Santander when the latter refused to obey his order to cross the frontier in order to liberate Venezuela a second time. General Cárcamo still thought this had been the origin of a deep-seated bitterness that the passage of time did no more than exacerbate.

The General, on the other hand, believed this was not the end but rather the beginning of a great friendship. Nor was it true that the origin of their antagonism lay in the privileges granted to General Páez, or the ill-fated Constitution of Bolivia, or the imperial investiture the General accepted in Perú, or the lifelong presidency and Senate membership he dreamed of in Colombia, or the absolute powers he assumed after the Ocaña Convention. No: these reasons and many others like them had not caused the terrible animosity that grew more bitter with the years until it culminated in the assassination attempt of September 25. "The real reason was that Santander could never assimilate the idea that this continent should be a single nation," said the General. "The unity of America was too much for him." He looked at Lorenzo Cárcamo, lying on his bed as if it were the last battlefield of a war that had been doomed from the start, and he ended the visit.

"Of course none of this means anything now that the patient has died," he said.

Lorenzo Cárcamo watched him stand up, sad and stripped of everything, and he realized that for both the

General and himself, memories were more of a burden than the years. When he grasped the General's hand between both of his he also realized that each had a fever, and he wondered which of their deaths would keep them from seeing each other again.

"We lost a world, Simón my old friend," said Lorenzo Cárcamo.

"They lost it for us," said the General. "And the only thing to do now is start again from the beginning."

"And we will," said Lorenzo Cárcamo.

"Not me," said the General. "All that's left for me is for them to throw me out with the garbage."

As a memento Lorenzo Cárcamo gave him a pair of pistols in a beautiful crimson satin case. He knew the General did not like firearms, and that in his few personal quarrels he had trusted to the sword. But these pistols possessed the moral virtue of having once been used with success in a duel for love, and the General accepted them with emotion. A few days later, in Turbaco, the news would reach him that General Cárcamo had died.

The signs were auspicious when the voyage was resumed at dusk on May 23. Propelled more by favorable currents than by the oarsmen, the barges left behind the slate precipices and the mirages on the wide beaches. The rafts made of tree trunks, which they were seeing now in greater numbers, seemed swifter. Unlike the ones they had observed earlier, these had dreamy little houses with flowerpots, and clothes hung to dry in the windows, and they carried wire chicken coops, milk cows, and shabby children who continued to wave at the barges long after they had passed by. They traveled all night through a flock of stars. At dawn they sighted the town of Zambrano, brilliant in the early light.

Don Cástulo Campillo, nicknamed The Kid, was waiting for them under the huge ceiba tree in port, having prepared a coastal *sancocho* stew at his house in honor of the General. The invitation was inspired by the legend that on his first visit to Zambrano he had eaten lunch in a poor inn on the rocky hill overlooking the port and had said that he had to come back once a year if only for the succulent coastal *sancocho*. The landlady was so impressed by the importance of her guest that she borrowed dishes and flatware from the distinguished house of the Campillo family. The General did not remember many details of that occasion, and neither he nor José Palacios was certain if coastal *sancocho* was the same as Venezuelan *hervido*. Nevertheless, General Carreño thought it was the same dish, and that they had in fact eaten it on the hill in the port, not during the river campaign, however, but when they were there three years earlier on the steamboat. The General, more and more disquieted by the leaks in his memory, accepted Carreño's version with humility.

The luncheon for the grenadiers was set under the large almond trees in the patio of the Campillo family's seignorial home and served on wooden planks covered with plantain leaves instead of tablecloths. On the interior terrace overlooking the patio a splendid table was laid with rigorous formality in the English manner for the General, his officers, and a few guests. The lady of the house explained that the news from Mompox had taken them by surprise at four o'clock in the morning, and they had just had time to slaughter the fattest animal in their herds. There it was, cut into succulent pieces and cooked at a merry boil in great pots, along with all the fruits of the garden.

The announcement that they had prepared a banquet for him without first notifying him soured the General's humor, and José Palacios had to call on his best arts as conciliator so that he would agree to disembark, but the hospitable atmosphere at the fiesta improved his mood. He had well-deserved praise for the good taste of the house and for the sweetness of the young girls in the family, who were modest and diligent and served the table of honor with old-fashioned grace. Above all he praised the fineness of the china and the quality of the silver, emblazoned with the heraldic emblems of some house brought down by the fatality of modern times, but he ate with his own.

The only unpleasantness was caused by a Frenchman who was living under the protection of the Campillo family and who attended the luncheon with an insatiable need to demonstrate before such notable guests his universal knowledge regarding the enigmas of this life and the next. He had lost everything in a shipwreck, and with his entourage of assistants and servants he had occupied half the house for almost a year while he waited for uncertain assistance that was supposed to come to him from New Orleans. José Palacios learned that his name was Diocles Atlantique, but he could not determine either his field of knowledge or the nature of his mission to New Granada. Naked and with a trident in his hand, he would have been identical to King Neptune, and he had a well-established reputation in the town as a swinish boor.

But luncheon with the General moved him to come to the table bathed and with clean fingernails and dressed for the stifling heat of May as if it were the wintry salons of Paris, wearing a blue jacket with gold buttons and striped trousers in the outdated style of the Directorate.

No sooner were the first greetings concluded than he embarked on an encyclopedic lecture in meticulous Spanish. He stated that a classmate of his from the primary school in Grenoble had just deciphered the Egyptian hieroglyphics after fourteen sleepless years. That corn did not originate in Mexico but in a region of Mesopotamia where fossils had been discovered that antedated the arrival of Columbus in the Antilles. That the Assyrians had obtained experimental proof of the influence of celestial bodies on disease. That contrary to the claims of a recent encyclopedia, the Greeks had possessed no knowledge of cats until 400 B.C. While he pontificated without mercy on these and many other matters, he made emergency pauses only to lament the cultural deficiencies of American cuisine.

The General sat opposite him and paid him no more than the scant attention civility demanded, pretending to eat more than he really ate and not raising his eyes from the plate. From the start the Frenchman attempted to speak to him in his own language, and the General responded in kind for the sake of courtesy but then returned without delay to Spanish. His patience that day surprised José Laurencio Silva, who knew how the absolutism of Europeans exasperated him.

The Frenchman addressed the various guests in a loud voice, even those sitting farthest from him, but it was evident he was interested only in the attention of the

General. Then, leaping from the rooster to the burro, as he called it, he asked the General a direct question: What would be the one correct system of government suitable to the new republics? Without raising his eyes from the plate, the General asked in turn:

"And what is your opinion?"

"My opinion is that the example of Bonaparte is a good one not only for us but for the entire world," said the Frenchman.

"I don't doubt that you think so," said the General without hiding the irony. "Europeans believe that only what Europe invents is good for the entire universe, and anything else is detestable."

"It had been my understanding that Your Excellency advocated the monarchist solution," said the Frenchman.

The General raised his eyes for the first time. "Well, don't let it be your understanding anymore," he said. "My brow will never be sullied by a crown." He pointed at the group of his aides-de-camp, and concluded:

"I have Iturbide there to remind me."

"Speaking of which," said the Frenchman, "the statement you made when they shot his father the Emperor gave great encouragement to European monarchists."

"I would not change a letter of what I said then," said the General. "It amazes me that a man as ordinary as Iturbide could do such extraordinary things, but may God save me from his fate as He has saved me from his actions, although I know He will never save me from the same ingratitude."

Then he tried to temper his harshness and explained that the initiative for establishing a monarchical regime in the new republics had come from General José Antonio Páez. The idea proliferated, driven by all manner of equivocal interests, and even he had come to think of it, hidden under the cloak of a presidency for life, as a desperate formula for achieving and maintaining the integrity of America at any cost. But he soon realized how senseless it was.

"With federalism the opposite occurs," he concluded. "It seems too perfect for our countries because it demands virtues and talents far superior to our own."

"In any case," said the Frenchman, "it is not systems but their excesses that dehumanize history."

"We know that speech by heart," said the General. "At bottom it's the stupidity of Benjamin Constant, the greatest pastry chef in Europe, who was against the Revolution and then for the Revolution, who fought against Napoleon and then was one of his courtiers, who often goes to bed republican and wakes up monarchist, or vice versa, and who has now established himself as the absolute repository of our truth by the act and grace of European arrogance."

"Constant's arguments against tyranny are very lucid," said the Frenchman.

"Señor Constant, like a good Frenchman, is a fanatic for absolute interests," said the General. "On the other hand, Abbot Pradt made the only lucid statement in that polemic when he pointed out that policy depends on where and when it is formulated. During the War to the Death I myself gave the order to execute eight hundred Spanish prisoners in a single day, including the patients in the hospital at La Guayra. Today, under the same circumstances, my voice would not tremble if I gave the order again, and Europeans would not have the moral authority to reproach me, for if any history is drowned in blood, indignity, and injustice, it is the history of Europe."

The deeper he delved into his analysis in the great silence that seemed to take possession of the entire town, the more he fed the fire of his own rage. The Frenchman was thunderstruck and attempted to interrupt, but he cut him off with a wave of his hand. The General evoked the hideous slaughters of European history. On Saint Bartholomew's Night the number of slain reached more than two thousand in ten hours. During the splendor of the Renaissance twelve thousand mercenaries in the pay of the imperial armies sacked and devastated Rome and cut the throats of eight thousand of its inhabitants. And the apotheosis: Ivan IV, Czar of all the Russias, who deserved the name The Terrible, exterminated the entire population of the cities between Moscow and Novgorod, and in Novgorod, in a single assault, massacred all twenty thousand inhabitants on the simple suspicion of a conspiracy against him.

"So stop doing us the favor of telling us what we should do," he concluded. "Don't attempt to teach us how we should be, don't attempt to make us just like you, don't try to have us do well in twenty years what you have done so badly in two thousand."

He crossed his cutlery on his plate, and for the first time he fixed his flaming eyes on the Frenchman:

"Damn it, please let us have our Middle Ages in peace!"

He was breathless, overcome by another attack of coughing. But when at last he could control it, there was not a vestige of rage left in him. He turned toward Kid Campillo and favored him with his best smile.

"Pardon me, my dear friend," he said. "Such ravings were not worthy of so memorable a luncheon."

Colonel Wilson related this incident to a chronicler of the time, who did not take the trouble to record it. "The poor General's case is closed," he said. That was the fundamental belief of all who saw him on his final journey, and perhaps that was why no one left a written record. Indeed, in the opinion of some of his companions, the General would have no place in history.

The jungle was less dense after Zambrano, the towns became gayer and more colorful, and in some there was music in the streets for no reason at all. The General stretched out in the hammock, trying to digest the Frenchman's impertinence with a peaceful siesta, but it was not easy to do. He could not stop thinking about him, and with José Palacios he lamented not having found the well-aimed sentences and invincible arguments that occurred to him only now, in the solitude of the hammock and with his adversary out of reach. Nevertheless, by nightfall he felt better, and he gave General Carreño instructions that the government should try to improve the lot of the unfortunate Frenchman.

Most of the officers, enlivened by their proximity to the sea, which was becoming more and more evident in the heaving excitement of nature, loosened the reins on their natural high spirits by helping the oarsmen, hunting for alligators with bayonet harpoons, complicating the easiest tasks in order to find release for their excess energy in the toil of galley slaves. José Laurencio Silva, on the other hand, slept by day and worked by night whenever possible because of his long-standing terror of developing cataracts and going blind, as did several members of his mother's family. He got up in darkness to learn how to be a useful blind man. During bouts of insomnia in the encampments, the General had often heard him at his artisan's work, sawing boards from trees he had trimmed himself, assembling the pieces, muffling the hammer in order not to disturb others as they slept. In the full light of the following day it was difficult to believe that such artful cabinetry had been accomplished in the dark. On the night in Puerto Real, José Laurencio Silva just had time to give the password to a sentry who was about to shoot him, thinking that someone was trying to slip through the darkness to the General's hammock.

Navigation was more rapid and serene, and the only mishap occurred when one of Commodore Elbers' ships steamed past them, moving in the opposite direction, and its wake endangered the barges and capsized the one loaded with provisions. High on the hull one could read its name in large letters: *The Liberator*. The General looked at it, pensive, until the danger was past and the vessel disappeared from view. "The Liberator," he murmured. Then, like someone turning the page, he said to himself:

"To think I'm that man!"

At night he lay awake in the hammock, while the oarsmen wagered on who could identify the voices of the jungle: the capuchin monkeys, the cockatoos, the anaconda. Then, out of the blue, one of them said that the Campillos had buried the English china, the Bohemian crystal, and the Holland linen tablecloths in the patio because they were terrified of being infected by consumption.

It was the first time that the General heard this popular diagnosis, although it was already current up and down the river and would soon be repeated along the entire coast. José Palacios realized it had made an impression on him, for he stopped swaying in the hammock. After long reflection he said:

"I ate with my own place setting."

The next day they moored in the village of Tenerife to replace the provisions lost in the accident. The General remained incognito on the barge, but he sent Wilson to inquire after a French merchant whose last name was Lenoit, or Lenoir, and whose daughter Anita would be about thirty years old. Since the inquiries in Tenerife were unsuccessful, the General wanted them repeated in the neighboring towns of Guáitaro, Salamina, and El Piñón, until he was convinced the legend had no basis at all in reality.

His interest was understandable, because for years he had been pursued from Caracas to Lima by insidious gossip regarding a reckless, illicit passion that had sprung up between him and Anita Lenoit while he was in Tenerife during the river campaign. It troubled him, although he could do nothing to disprove it. First, because his father, Colonel Juan Vicente Bolívar, had also been obliged to undergo various proceedings and hearings before the Bishop of San Mateo for alleged violations of women, some of whom were minors, and for the notoriety of his liaisons with many others in avid exercise of his *droit du seigneur*. Second, because during the river campaign he had been in Tenerife for only two days, insufficient time for so tempestuous a love affair. Nevertheless, the legend prospered so well that in the Tenerife cemetery Señorita Anne Lenoit's tombstone was a place of pilgrimage for lovers until the end of the century.

In the General's entourage the discomfort José María Carreño experienced in the stump of his arm was reason for cordial teasing. He felt the movements of his hand, the sense of touch in his fingers, the pain bad weather caused in bones he did not have. He had retained enough of a sense of humor to laugh at himself. On the other hand, he was disturbed by his habit of answering questions when he was asleep. He engaged in conversations on any subject with none of his waking inhibitions, he revealed goals and frustrations he doubtless would have kept to himself had he been awake, and on one occasion he was accused, without any basis in fact, of betraying a military secret in his sleep. On the last night of the voyage, while José Palacios watched beside the General's hammock, he heard Carreño speaking in the bow of the barge:

"Seven thousand eight hundred eighty-two."

"What are we talking about?" José Palacios asked him.

"The stars," said Carreño.

The General opened his eyes, convinced that Carreño was talking in his sleep, and sat up in the hammock to look through the window at the night. It was immense and radiant, and the bright stars filled the sky.

"There must be ten times that number," said the General.

"It's the number I said," replied Carreño, "plus two shooting stars that went by while I was counting."

Then the General left the hammock and saw Carreño lying on his back in the prow, more awake than ever, his naked torso crisscrossed by a tangle of scars, counting stars with the stump of his arm. That was how they found him after the battle of Cerritos Blancos in Venezuela, covered with blood and cut to ribbons, and left for dead in the mud. He had suffered fourteen saber cuts, several of which caused him to lose his arm. Later he received more wounds in other battles. But his morale remained intact, and he learned to be so dexterous with his left hand that he was famous not only for his ferocious swordsmanship but for his exquisite handwriting as well.

"Not even stars escape the ruin of life," said Carreño. "There are fewer now than there were eighteen years ago."

"You're crazy," said the General.

"No," said Carreño. "I'm old, but I refuse to believe it."

"I'm eight long years older than you," said the General.

"I count two extra years for each wound," said Carreño. "And so I'm older than everybody."

"In that case José Laurencio must be the oldest," said the General, "wounded six times by bullet, seven by lance, and twice by arrow."

Carreño took offense and replied with disguised venom: "And you must be the youngest: not a scratch."

It was not the first time the General heard that truth spoken as a reproach, but he did not seem to resent it in the mouth of Carreño, whose friendship had already been proved in the sorest trials. He sat beside him to help him contemplate the stars on the river. When Carreño spoke again after a long pause, he was deep in the abyss of sleep.

"I refuse to accept that with this journey our life is ended," he said.

"Lives don't end only with death," said the General. "There are other ways, some even more honorable."

Carreño resisted.

"There must be something we can do," he said. "Even if it's taking a good bath in purple verbena. And not just us: the whole liberating army."

On his second trip to Paris the General had not yet heard of baths in purple verbena, the lantana blossom popular in his own country for conjuring away bad luck. It was Dr. Aimé Bonpland, Humboldt's collaborator, who spoke to him with dangerous scientific seriousness about the virtues of those flowers. During the same period he met a venerable magistrate in the French Court of Justice who had been a young man in Caracas and who often appeared in the literary salons of Paris with his beautiful flowing hair and apostle's beard stained purple by the purifying baths.

The General laughed at everything that smelled of superstition or supernatural artifice, at any cult contrary to the rationalism of his tutor, Simón Rodríguez. At that time he had just turned twenty, he was a recent and wealthy widower bedazzled by the coronation of Napoleon Bonaparte, he had become a Mason, he would recite from memory his favorite pages in Rousseau's *Émile* and *La nouvelle Héloïse*, which had been his bedside reading for some time, and he had traveled by foot, led by his tutor and carrying a knapsack on his back, through almost all of Europe. On one of the hills, with Rome at their feet, Don Simón Rodríguez pronounced another of his high-sounding prophecies regarding the destiny of the Americas. His own vision was clearer.

"What has to be done with those immigrant Spanish

pricks is to kick them out of Venezuela," he said. "And I swear I'll do it."

When at last he reached his majority and had control of his inheritance, he undertook the kind of life that the frenzied times and his high-spirited character demanded of him, and in three months he spent one hundred fifty thousand francs. He had the most expensive rooms in the most expensive hotel in Paris, two liveried servants, a carriage drawn by white horses, a Turkish driver, and a different lover for every occasion, whether it was his favorite table at the Café de Procope, the dances in Montmartre, or his private box at the Opéra, and he told anyone who would believe him that on a single unlucky night he had lost three thousand pesos at roulette.

When he returned to Caracas he was still closer to Rousseau than to his own heart, and with shameless passion he continued to reread the edition of *La nouvelle Héloïse* that was beginning to fall apart in his hands. Nevertheless, a short while before the assassination attempt of September 25, when he had more than honored his Roman vow, he interrupted Manuela Sáenz during her tenth reading of *Émile* because the book seemed abominable to him. "Nowhere have I been so bored as in Paris in the year 1804," he said to her then. On the other hand, while he was there he had thought himself not only happy but the happiest man in the world, and he had not colored his destiny with the auspicious waters of purple verbena.

Twenty-six years later, absorbed in the magic of the river, dying, in defeat, perhaps he wondered if he might not have the courage to say to hell with the oregano and sage leaves and bitter oranges of José Palacios' distracting baths, to follow Carreño's advice and sink down into a redemptive ocean of purple verbena along with his armies of beggars, his useless glories, his memorable errors, the entire country.

It was a night of vast silences, like those on the colossal estuaries of Los Llanos, whose resonance allowed you to hear intimate conversations several leagues away. Christopher Columbus had lived a moment like this one and had written in his diary: "All night I heard the birds flying." For land was near after sixty-nine days at sea. The General heard them too. They began to fly past at about eight o'clock, while Carreño was sleeping, and an hour later there were so many overhead that the wind stirred by their wings was stronger than the wind. A short while later some immense fish, lost among the stars on the river bottom, began to swim under the barges, and they could detect the first gusts of the northeast's putrefaction. There was no need to see it in order to recognize the inexorable power this strange sensation of freedom inspired in their hearts. "Merciful God!" sighed the General. "We've arrived." And it was true. For there was the sea, and on the other side of the sea was the world.

AND SO HE WAS in Turbaco once again. In the same house with its shadowy rooms, its great lunar arches and floor-to-ceiling windows facing the graveled square, and the monastic patio where he had seen the ghost of Don Antonio Caballero y Góngora, Archbishop and Viceroy of New Granada, who on moonlit nights would seek relief from his many sins and insoluble trespasses by walking among the orange trees. In contrast to the prevalent hot and humid climate of the coast, the weather was cool and healthful in Turbaco since it was situated above sea level, and along the banks of its streams there were immense laurel trees with tentacular roots where the soldiers would lie down to rest in the shade.

Two nights earlier they had reached Barranca Nueva, the longed-for end of the river journey, where they had to spend a sleepless night in a foul-smelling storage shed of cane and mud, surrounded by sacks of rice and heaps of untanned hides, because they had reserved no lodgings and the mules they had ordered in advance were not ready for them. As a consequence the General arrived in

Turbaco drenched and aching, desperate for sleep but not sleepy.

They had not finished unloading, and the news of his arrival had already reached Cartagena de Indias, only six leagues away, where General Mariano Montilla, quartermaster general and military commander of the province, had prepared a public reception for the following day. But the General was in no mood for inopportune fiestas. He greeted those who waited in the rain for him along the King's Highway with the warmth reserved for old friends, but he requested with the same openness that they leave him alone.

In reality, regardless of how he struggled to disguise it, his condition was worse than his bad humor suggested, and day after day even his entourage could see the insatiable decline. He could not master his soul. The color of his skin had gone from pale green to mortal yellow. He was feverish, and the pain in his head had become eternal. The local priest offered to send for a doctor, but he refused: "If I'd listened to my doctors I'd have been buried years ago." He had arrived in Turbaco ready to continue on to Cartagena the next day, but in the course of the morning he was informed that no ship bound for Europe was in port and no passport had come for him in the last mail. Therefore he decided to stay and rest for three days. His officers rejoiced, not only for the sake of his body but also because the first secret reports that arrived regarding the situation in Venezuela were not the most salutary for his soul.

Nevertheless, he could not prevent his friends from shooting off rockets until they ran out of powder, or stationing a corps of bagpipers near the house, who would play until late that night. They also arranged for a troupe of black men and women from the neighboring marshes of Marialabaja, dressed as sixteenth-century European aristocrats, to perform with African artfulness their burlesques of Spanish court dances, because on his previous visit he had liked them so much that he had called them back several times. Now he did not even glance at them.

"Get that noisy mob out of here," he said.

Viceroy Caballero y Góngora had built the house and lived in it for some three years, and the phantasmagorical echoes in its rooms were attributed to the spell of his soul in torment. The General refused to return to the bedroom he had used on his last visit, which he remembered as the room of nightmares because each night he slept there he dreamed over and over again until daybreak about a woman with illuminated hair who tied a red ribbon around his neck until she woke him. He had the hammock hung instead from the metal rings in the drawing room, and he slept for a while without dreaming. The rain came down in torrents, and a group of children stood peering through the street windows to watch him sleep. One of them woke him with a whispered "Bolívar, Bolívar." He searched for him through the mists of fever, and the boy asked:

"Do you love me?"

The General assented with a tremulous smile, but then he ordered the chickens wandering through the house to be chased out, the children made to leave, and the windows closed, and he fell asleep again. When he awoke the second time it was still raining and José Palacios was preparing the mosquito netting for the hammock.

"I dreamed a boy on the street was asking me strange

questions through the window," the General told him.

He agreed to drink an infusion, the first in twenty-four hours, but he could not finish it. He lay down again in the hammock, victim of a dizzy spell, and for a long while he remained submerged in a twilight meditation, contemplating the line of bats hanging from the ceiling beams. At last he sighed:

"We're ready for a pauper's grave."

He had been so prodigal with the former officers and ordinary soldiers of the liberating army who told him their misfortunes all along the river that in Turbaco he had no more than a quarter of his travel funds left. It remained to be seen if the provincial government had enough money in its battered treasury to cover the draft, or could at least negotiate it with a speculator. For his immediate accommodation in Europe he counted on the gratitude of England, for which he had done so many favors. "The English love me," he would say. For him, his servants, and his minimal entourage to live with the dignified decorum of his nostalgia, he counted on the dream of selling the Aroa Mines. Nevertheless, if he really wanted to leave, passage and travel expenses for him and his entourage were of immediate urgency, and the amount of cash he had on hand made it unthinkable. But he could not renounce his infinite capacity for illusion at the very moment he needed it most. On the contrary. Although he saw fireflies where there were none because of fever and the pain in his head, he overcame the somnolence that dulled his senses and dictated three letters to Fernando.

The first was a heartfelt response to Field Marshal Sucre's farewell, in which he said nothing about his illness although he often did so in situations where he was pressed for compassion, as he was that afternoon. The second letter was to Don Juan de Dios Amador, the Prefect of Cartagena, urging payment of the eight-thousand-peso draft from the provincial treasury. "I am in dire need of that money for my departure," he told him. His plea bore fruit, and before four days had passed he received a favorable reply and Fernando went to Cartagena for the money. The third was to the poet José Fernández Madrid, the Colombian Minister to London, requesting that he pay a letter of credit on his behalf to Sir Robert Wilson and another to the Englishman Professor Joseph Lancaster, who was owed twenty thousand duros for establishing his innovative system of reciprocal education in Caracas. "My honor is involved in this matter," he told him. For he trusted that his long-standing case would be resolved very soon and that the mines would be sold. A useless effort: by the time the letter reached London, Minister Fernández Madrid had died.

José Palacios signaled for quiet to the officers shouting their disputes as they played cards in the interior gallery, but they continued to argue in whispers until the bells in the nearby church tower sounded eleven o'clock. A short while later the bagpipes and drums at the public fiesta stopped playing, the breeze from the distant sea blew away the dark clouds that had gathered again after the downpour in the afternoon, and the full moon caught fire in the patio filled with orange trees.

José Palacios did not leave the General for a moment, for he had been in the hammock, delirious with fever, since nightfall. He prepared one of the usual potions and gave him a senna enema, hoping that someone with more authority would dare to suggest a doctor, but no one did. The General barely dozed for an hour at dawn.

That day General Mariano Montilla came to visit him with a select group of his friends from Cartagena, among them the men known as the three Juans of the Bolivarist party: Juan García del Río, Juan de Francisco Martín, and Juan de Dios Amador. The three were horrified at the sight of the body in torment that tried to sit up in the hammock and lacked the breath to embrace them all. They had seen him at the Admirable Congress, in which they had participated, and they could not believe he had deteriorated so much in so short a time. His bones were visible under his skin, and he could not focus his eyes. He must have been aware of the hot stench of his breath, for he was careful to speak from a distance and almost in profile. But what struck them most was the evidence that he had lost height, to the point where it seemed to General Montilla, when they embraced that he reached no higher than his waist.

He weighed eighty-eight pounds and would weigh ten pounds less just before he died. His official height was one meter sixty-five centimeters, although his medical and military records did not always agree, and on the autopsy table he would measure four centimeters less than that figure. His feet were as small as his hands in relation to his body, and they too seemed smaller. José Palacios had noted that he wore his trousers almost around his chest and had to turn back his shirt cuffs. The General observed his visitors' curiosity and admitted that the boots he always wore, a French size thirty-five, had been too big for him since January. General Montilla, famous for his flashes of wit even in the least opportune situations, put an end to the poignancy.

"The important thing," he said, "is that Your Excellency doesn't shrink on the inside."

As always, he underscored his own humor with uproarious laughter. The General gave him in return the smile of an old comrade and changed the subject. The weather had improved and was fine for a conversation outdoors, but he preferred to receive his visitors sitting in the hammock in the same room where he had slept.

Their main topic was the state of the nation. The Cartagena Bolivarists refused to recognize the new constitution and the chosen leaders on the pretext that Santanderist students had exerted unacceptable pressure on Congress. On the other hand, the loyal military had remained on the sidelines, by order of the General, and the rural clergy that supported him had not had the opportunity to mobilize. General Francisco Carmona, commander of a garrison in Cartagena and a man loyal to his cause, had been about to instigate an insurrection and still threatened to do so. The General asked Montilla to send Carmona to see him, so he could attempt to pacify him. Then, addressing them all but not looking at anyone, he gave them a brutal synthesis of the new government:

"Mosquera is an asshole and Caycedo is a pastry chef, and both of them are scared shitless by the boys from San Bartolomé."

What he was saying in Caribbean was that the President was a weakling and the Vice-President an opportunist capable of changing party depending on how the wind blew. He also pointed out with the sourness typical of his worst times that it was not at all strange that each of them was a cleric's brother. Yet the new constitution seemed better than anyone could have expected at a historical moment when the danger was not electoral defeat but the civil war that Santander was fomenting with his letters from Paris. In Popayán the President-elect had made repeated calls for order and unity but still had not said if he would accept the presidency.

"He's waiting for Caycedo to do the dirty work," said the General.

"Mosquera must be in Santa Fe de Bogotá by now," said Montilla. "He left Popayán on Monday."

The General had not known, but he was not surprised. "You'll see: he'll collapse like a rotten squash when the time comes for action," he said. "That man couldn't do the porter's work in a government." He fell into deep thought and was overcome by sadness.

"Too bad," he said. "Sucre was the man."

"The worthiest of the generals," said de Francisco Martín, smiling.

By now the phrase was famous throughout the country despite the General's efforts to prevent its circulation.

"Urdaneta's brilliant phrase," joked Montilla.

The General ignored the interruption and made ready to hear the secrets of local politics, more in jest than in a serious way, but then without warning Montilla reestablished the solemnity he himself had just broken. "You'll forgive me, Excellency," he said, "you know better than anyone my devotion to the Field Marshal, but he is not the man." And he concluded with theatrical emphasis:

"You are."

The General cut him off on the spot:

"I don't exist."

Then, taking up the thread, he recounted the manner in which Field Marshal Sucre resisted his pleas to accept the presidency of Colombia. "He has everything to save us from anarchy," he said, "but he allowed himself to be charmed by the sirens' song." García del Río thought the real reason was that Sucre had an absolute lack of vocation for power. The General did not think this was an insurmountable obstacle. "In the long history of humanity it has often been shown that vocation is the legitimate child of necessity," he said. In any case, these longings came too late, because he knew as no one else did that the worthiest general in the Republic now belonged to forces less ephemeral than his own.

"The greatest power lies in the force of love," he said, and he concluded his gibe: "Sucre himself said so."

While the General was reminiscing about him in Turbaco, Field Marshal Sucre was leaving Santa Fe de Bogotá for Quito, disenchanted and alone, but in the prime of his age and health and at the height of his glory. His last piece of business the night before he left was a secret visit to a well-known fortune-teller in the Egyptian district who had guided him in several of his wartime enterprises, and she had seen in the cards that even during the stormy season the most favorable routes for him were still by sea. The Field Marshal of Ayacucho thought they were too slow for his urgent love, and he risked the hazards of land against the good judgment of the cards.

"So there's nothing to be done," concluded the General. "We're so screwed up, our best government is the worst."

He knew his local supporters. They had been illustrious heroes who had performed great deeds in the struggle for liberation, but in political affairs they were petty traffickers in jobs and man-eating schemers who had even gone as far as forming alliances with Montilla against him. As he did with so many others, he gave them no peace until he had succeeded in charming them. And then he asked them to support the government, even at the expense of their personal interests. His reasoning, as usual, had a prophetic air: Tomorrow, when he was no longer there, the same government he was asking them to support would call back Santander, who would return, crowned with glory, to eradicate the wreckage of his dreams, and the immense, unified nation he had forged during so many years of wars and sacrifices would break apart, factions would divide it among themselves, and in the memory of the centuries his name would be vilified and his work distorted. But none of that mattered to him now if he could at least prevent more bloodshed. "Insurrections, like the waves of the sea, come one after the other," he said. "That's why I've never liked them." And to the amazement of his visitors, he concluded:

"Believe it or not, these days I even deplore the one we made against the Spanish."

General Montilla and his friends felt he had come to his end. Before they said goodbye he gave them each a gold medal engraved with his likeness, and they could not avoid the impression that it was a posthumous gift. As they walked to the door García del Río said in a low voice:

"He has the face of a dead man."

The words, amplified and repeated by the echoes in the house, pursued the General all night. Nevertheless, the next day General Francisco Carmona was surprised at how well he looked. He found him in the patio perfumed by orange blossoms, in a hammock with his name embroidered on it in silk thread, which had been made for him in the neighboring town of San Jacinto and which José Palacios had hung between two orange trees. He had just bathed, his hair was pulled back, and he wore a blue tunic without a shirt, which lent him an air of innocence. As he swayed very slowly, he dictated an indignant letter for President Caycedo to his nephew Fernando. He did not seem as moribund to General Carmona as they had said, perhaps because he was intoxicated by one of his legendary rages.

Carmona was too visible to pass unnoticed anywhere, yet the General looked at him but did not see him as he dictated a sentence attacking the perfidy of his detractors. Only when he had completed it did he turn toward the giant who stood looking at him without blinking, his whole body facing the hammock, and ask with no preliminary greeting:

"And do you think I'm an instigator of insurrections too?"

General Carmona, anticipating a hostile reception, asked with a touch of arrogance:

"Where does the General get that idea?"

"From the same place they do," he said.

He handed him the news clippings he had just received in the mail from Santa Fe de Bogotá, which accused him once again of having instigated in secret the rebellion of the grenadiers in order to return to power despite the decision of Congress. "What vile trash," he said. "While I waste my time preaching union, these half-baked imbeciles accuse me of conspiracy." General Carmona suffered a certain disillusionment when he read the clippings.

"Well, I not only believed it," he said, "I was delighted to think it was true."

"I can imagine," said the General.

He showed no signs of irritation but asked him to wait while he finished dictating the letter, in which he again requested official permission to leave the country. When he finished he had recovered his composure with the same sudden ease he had shown in losing it when he read the newspapers. He stood up without help and took General Carmona by the arm for a stroll around the cistern.

After three days of rain, the light was a gold powder that filtered through the leaves of the trees and moved the birds to sing among the orange blossoms. The General listened for a moment, heard them in his soul, and almost sighed: "At least they still sing." He gave General Carmona an erudite explanation of why birds in the Antilles sing better in April than in June, and then, with no transition, he returned to the business at hand. He needed no more than ten minutes to convince him to respect without conditions the authority of the new government. Afterwards he accompanied Carmona to the door, and then he went to the bedroom to write in his own hand to Manuela Sáenz, who continued to complain about the obstacles the government was placing in the way of her letters.

He did no more than taste the cornmeal mush that Fernanda Barriga brought to the bedroom while he was writing. At siesta he asked Fernando to continue reading aloud the book on Chinese botanicals they had begun the night before. A short while later José Palacios came into the room with oregano water for the warm bath and found Fernando asleep on the chair with the open book on his lap. The General was awake in the hammock, and he placed his index finger over his lips to signal quiet. For the first time in two weeks he had no fever.

In this way, marking time between one mail and the next, he spent twenty-nine days in Turbaco. He had been there twice before but appreciated its medicinal virtues only on the second visit, three years earlier, when he was returning from Caracas to Santa Fe de Bogotá in order to thwart Santander's separatist plans. On that occasion the climate had agreed with him so well that he stayed ten days instead of the two nights he had planned. They were days filled with patriotic fiestas. At the end there was a gala bullfight, despite his adversion to such spectacles, and he himself faced a heifer that tore the cape from his hands and brought a shout of fear from the crowd. Now, on the third visit, his painful destiny was fulfilled, and the passage of the days confirmed this to a maddening degree. The rains became more frequent and more desolate, and life was reduced to waiting for news of further reversals. One night, in the lucidity of advanced insomnia, he was heard by José Palacios as he sighed in the hammock:

"God knows where Sucre can be!"

General Montilla had returned twice and found him much better than he had been on the first day. Furthermore, it seemed to him that little by little the General was recovering his old drive, above all because of the insistence with which he complained that his supporters in Cartagena had not yet voted for the new constitution or recognized the new government, as had been agreed on the previous visit. General Montilla invented the excuse that they were waiting to find out if Joaquín Mosquera would accept the presidency.

"They'll be in a better position if they do it beforehand," said the General.

On the next visit he complained with even greater energy, for he had known Montilla since they were boys and realized that the resistance he attributed to others was in fact his own. Not only were they bound by a friendship based on class and profession, but they had spent their lives in common as well. At one time their relations cooled to the point where they stopped speaking to each other because Montilla left the General without reinforcements in Mompox, at one of the most dangerous moments in the war, and the General accused him of both moral degeneracy and responsibility for all his calamities. Montilla's reaction was so impassioned that he challenged the General to a duel, but he continued to serve the cause of independence despite personal animosities.

He had studied mathematics and philosophy at the Military Academy in Madrid and had been a personal bodyguard to King Fernando VII until the day the first news of Venezuelan emancipation reached him. He was a good conspirator in Mexico, a good arms smuggler in Curaçao, and a good fighter everywhere from the time he was first wounded, at the age of seventeen. In 1821 he rid the coast of Spaniards from Riohacha to Panamá and took Cartagena from a larger and better-equipped army. Then he offered reconciliation to the General with a gallant gesture: he sent him the gold keys of the city, which the General returned along with his promotion to the rank of brigadier general and orders to take over the government of the coast. He was not a well-loved governor, although he tended to mitigate his excesses with a sense of humor. His house was the best in the city, his hacienda, Aguas Vivas, was one of the most desirable in the province, and in broadsides on the walls the people asked where he got the money to buy them. But after eight years of a difficult and solitary exercise of power he was still governor, having become an astute politician, difficult to oppose.

Montilla replied to each insistent complaint with a different argument. Nevertheless, at one point he told the unadorned truth: The Bolivarists in Cartagena were resolved not to swear to a compromise constitution or recognize a weak government whose origins lay not in harmony but in widespread discord. This was typical of local politicians, whose disagreements had been the cause of great historical tragedies. "And they are not mistaken if Your Excellency, the most liberal of us all, leaves us at the mercy of men who have appropriated the name liberal in order to destroy your work," said Montilla. And therefore the only way to settle matters was for the General to remain in the country and prevent its disintegration.

"Fine. If that's the case, tell Carmona to come back and we'll persuade him to revolt," replied the General with characteristic sarcasm. "It won't be as bloody as the civil war the Cartagenans are going to provoke with their insolence."

But before he said goodbye to Montilla he had regained his composure, and he asked him to bring the leaders of his party to Turbaco to air their objections. He was still waiting for them when General Carreño arrived with the news that Joaquín Mosquera had assumed the presidency.

He slapped his forehead. "Fuck it!" he exclaimed. "I won't believe it until I see it with my own eyes."

That same afternoon General Montilla went to confirm the report in person, in a downpour with crosswinds that uprooted trees, devastated half the town, destroyed the house's farmyard, and swept away the drowned animals. But it also softened the blow of the bad news. The official escort, in an agony of tedium in the empty days, prevented the disaster from becoming worse. Montilla threw on a battlefield rain cape and directed rescue operations. The General sat on a rocking chair in front of the window, wrapped in the sleeping blanket, his look thoughtful and his respiration calm, contemplating the torrent of mud that carried along the wreckage left by the disaster. Those Caribbean disturbances had been familiar to him since he was a boy. Nevertheless, while the troops hurried to reestablish order in the house, he told José Palacios that he could not remember seeing anything like it. When at last calm was restored, Montilla came into the room, dripping water and muddied up to his knees. The General was still intent on his idea.

"Well, Montilla," he said. "Mosquera is President now, and Cartagena still hasn't recognized him."

Montilla would not allow storms to distract him either.

"If Your Excellency were in Cartagena it would be much easier," he said.

"There's the danger it would be interpreted as interference by me, and I don't want to be the protagonist of anything," he said. "Furthermore, I'm not moving from here until this matter is resolved."

That night he wrote a letter of support to General Mosquera. "I have just learned, with no surprise, that you accepted the presidency, which makes me happy for the country and for myself," he told him. "But I regret it, and will always regret it, for your sake." And he ended the letter with a sly postscript: "I have not left because my passport has not arrived, but I am leaving without fail when it does."

On Sunday General Daniel Florencio O'Leary arrived in Turbaco and joined the entourage. He was a prominent member of the British Legion, who for some time had been an aide-de-camp and a bilingual secretary to the General. Montilla, in a better humor than ever, had accompanied him from Cartagena, and they and the General spent a pleasant afternoon as old friends under the orange trees. At the end of a long conversation with O'Leary concerning his military career, the General asked his favorite question:

"And what are people saying?"

"That it isn't true you're leaving," said O'Leary.

"Aha," said the General. "Why not this time?"

"Because Manuelita is staying behind."

The General responded with disarming sincerity:

"But she's always stayed behind!"

O'Leary, a close friend of Manuela Sáenz, knew the General was right. It was true she always stayed behind, not because she wanted to but because the General would leave her on any pretext in a foolhardy effort to escape the servitude of formalized love. "I'll never fall in love again," he once confessed to José Palacios, the only human being with whom he ever permitted himself that sort of confidence. "It's like having two souls at the same time." Manuela asserted herself with a determination that could not be contained and with none of the hindrances of dignity, but the more she attempted to conquer him, the more eager the General seemed to free himself from her chains. It was a love of perpetual flight. In Quito, after their first two weeks of passionate love, he had to travel to Guayaquil for a meeting with General José de San Martín, the liberator of Río de la Plata, and she stayed behind, asking herself what kind of lover left the table in the middle of the meal. He had promised to write every day, everywhere he went, so that he could swear with all his heart that he loved her more than he had ever loved anyone else in this world. He did write to her, in fact, and sometimes in his own hand, but he did not send the letters. In the meantime he consoled himself in a multiple idyll with the five indistinguishable women of the Garaycoa matriarchy, never knowing for certain if he had chosen the grandmother of fifty-six, the daughter of thirty-eight, or the three granddaughters in the flower of their youth. When his mission in Guayaquil was over, he escaped from them all with promises of eternal love and a prompt return, and he went back to Quito to sink into the quicksands of Manuela Sáenz.

Early the following year he left her again, to complete the liberation of Perú, which was the final enterprise of his dream. Manuela waited four months, but she set sail for Lima as soon as letters began to arrive that not only were written by Juan José Santana, the General's private secretary, which was not unusual, but were thought and felt by him as well. She found him in the pleasure palace of La Magdalena, invested with dictatorial powers by the Congress and besieged by the beautiful bold women of the new republican court. The Presidential Palace was so disorderly that a colonel of the lancers had moved out one midnight because the agonies of love in the bedrooms did not let him sleep. But Manuela was now in territory that she knew all too well. She had been born in Quito, the illegitimate daughter of a wealthy American landowner and a married man, and at the age of eighteen she had jumped out the window of the convent where she was a student and run off with an officer in the king's army. Nevertheless, two years later she was married in Lima, and with a virgin's orange blossoms, to Dr. James Thorne, a complaisant physician who was twice her age. And therefore, when she returned to Perú in pursuit of the love of her life, she did not need lessons from anyone on how to hold her own in the midst of scandal.

O'Leary was her best aide-de-camp in these battles of the heart. At first Manuela did not live at La Magdalena, but she came and went as she pleased, through the main door and with military honors. Astute and indomitable, she had irresistible grace, a sense of power, and unbounded tenacity. She spoke good English because of her husband, as well as an elementary but comprehensible French, and she played the clavichord in the sanctimonious style of novices. Her handwriting was difficult to read, her syntax impassable, and she would convulse with laughter at what she called her orthographical horrors. The General named her curator of his archives in order to keep her near him, and this made it easy for them to make love anytime, anywhere, surrounded by the clamor of the wild Amazonian animals that Manuela tamed with her charms.

Nevertheless, when the General began the conquest of the difficult territories of Perú, which were still in the hands of the Spanish, Manuela could not persuade him to take her along as a member of his general staff. She followed him without his permission, with her trunks worthy of a first lady, the chests filled with archives, and her court of slavewomen, in a rear guard of Colombian troops who adored her for her barracks language. She traveled three hundred leagues on the back of a mule along the dizzying precipices of the Andes, and in four months she managed to spend only two nights with the General, one of them because she succeeded in frightening him with a suicide threat. Some time went by before she learned that while she could not be with him, he consoled himself with other, transitory loves that he found along the way. Among them was Manuelita Madroño, an untamed eighteen-year-old mulatta who sanctified his bouts of insomnia.

After her return from Quito, Manuela decided to leave her husband, whom she described as an insipid Englishman who loved without pleasure, conversed without wit, walked without haste, greeted people with bows, sat down and stood up with caution, and did not laugh even at his own jokes. But the General convinced her to preserve at all costs the privileges of her legal status, and she acceded to his wishes.

A month after the victory at Ayacucho, when he was master of half the world, the General left for Alto Perú, which would later become the Republic of Bolivia. He not only left without Manuela, but before leaving suggested as a matter of state the advantage of a definitive separation. "I see that nothing can unite us under the auspices of innocence and honor," he wrote to her. "In the future you will be alone, although at your husband's side, and I will be alone in the midst of the world. The glory of having conquered ourselves will be our only consolation." Before three months had passed he received a letter in which Manuela announced her departure for London with her husband. The news found him in the alien bed of Francisca Zubiaga de Gamarra, a spirited woman of action married to a field marshal who would later be President of the Republic. The General did not wait for the second lovemaking of the night to write an immediate reply to Manuela that seemed more like an order in battle: "Tell the truth and don't go anywhere." And with his own hand he underlined the last sentence: "*My love for you is steadfast.*" She obeyed, delighted.

The General's dream began to fall apart on the very day it was realized. No sooner had he founded Bolivia and concluded the institutional reorganization of Perú than he had to hurry back to Santa Fe de Bogotá, spurred by General Páez' first separatist attempts in Venezuela and Santander's political intrigues in New Granada. On this occasion Manuela had a longer wait until he allowed her to follow him, but when at last he did she traveled in a caravan worthy of Gypsies, with her trunks on the backs of a dozen mules, her immortal slavewomen, and eleven cats, six dogs, three monkeys educated in the art of palace obscenities, a bear trained to thread needles, and nine cages of parrots and macaws that railed against Santander in three languages.

She arrived in Santa Fe de Bogotá just in time to save the little life remaining to the General on the evil night of September 25. Six years had gone by since they had met, but he was as aged and full of doubt as if it had been fifty, and Manuela had the impression that he was wandering without direction through the mists of solitude. He would return to the south a short while later to curb the colonial ambitions of Perú in Quito and Guayaquil, but by that time all his efforts were in vain. On this occasion Manuela stayed behind in Santa Fe de Bogotá without the least desire to follow him, for she knew that her eternal fugitive no longer had a place to escape to.

In his memoirs O'Leary observed that the General had never been so willing to recall his furtive loves as on that Sunday afternoon in Turbaco. Montilla thought at the time, and wrote years later in a private letter, that this was an unmistakable symptom of old age. Encouraged by the General's good humor and confidences, Montilla could not resist the temptation of a cordial provocation.

"Was Manuela the only one who stayed behind?" he asked.

"They all stayed behind," said the General with complete seriousness. "But Manuela more than any of them."

Montilla winked at O'Leary and said:

"Confess, General: how many were there?"

The General eluded him.

"Many fewer than you think," he said.

That night, while he was in the warm bath, José Palacios tried to clarify matters for him. "According to my calculations there were thirty-five," he said. "Not counting the one-night birds, of course." The figure matched the General's own calculations, but he had not wanted to say so during the visit.

"O'Leary is a great man, a great soldier, and a faithful friend, but he takes notes on everything," he explained. "And there's nothing more dangerous than a written memoir."

The next day, after a long private interview held to inform him of conditions on the border, he asked O'Leary to go to Cartagena for the formal purpose of bringing him up-to-date on the movement of ships bound for Europe, although the real mission was to keep him advised regarding the hidden details of local politics. No sooner had O'Leary arrived than, on Saturday, June 12, the Cartagena Congress swore loyalty to the new constitution and recognized the chosen officials. Montilla sent the General an inevitable message along with the news:

"We're waiting for you."

He was still waiting when a rumor that the General had died made him leap out of bed. He rode to Turbaco at full gallop, not taking time to confirm the report, and there he found the General better than ever, lunching with a Frenchman, the Count de Raigecourt, who had come with an invitation that they travel together to Europe on an English packet boat arriving in Cartagena the following week. It was the culmination of a salubrious day for the General, who had decided to confront his poor health with moral fortitude, and no one could say he had not been successful. He had awakened early, walked through the farmyards at milking time, visited the grenadiers in their barracks, listened to them as they spoke about their living conditions, and given categorical orders to improve them. On his way back he stopped at an inn in the market, drank some coffee, and took the cup with him to avoid the humiliation of their destroying it. He was walking toward his house when he turned a corner and the children leaving school ambushed him, singing and clapping in rhythm: "*Long live The Liberator! Long live The Liberator!*" He was bewildered and would not have known what to do if the children themselves had not made way for him.

At his house he found the Count de Raigecourt, who had arrived unannounced in the company of the most beautiful, elegant, and haughty woman he had ever seen. She wore riding clothes, although in reality they had come in a chaise drawn by a burro. All she revealed of her identity was that her name was Camille and that she was a native of Martinique. The Count gave no additional information, although in the course of the day it would become far too evident that he was mad with love for her.

The mere presence of Camille revived the General's high spirits of other days, and he lost no time in ordering a gala luncheon. Although the Count spoke correct Spanish, conversation was carried on in French, which was Camille's language. When she said she had been born in Trois-Îlets, he gestured with enthusiasm and his faded eyes flashed.

"Ah," he said. "Where Josephine was born."

She laughed.

"Please, Excellency, I was hoping for a more intelligent observation than the one everybody else makes."

He indicated that he was wounded and defended himself with a lyrical evocation of La Pagerie Plantation, the birthplace of Marie-Josèphe, Empress of France, which was visible at a distance of several leagues across the vast canebrakes and through the clamor of the birds and the hot smell from the distilleries. She was surprised that the General knew it so well.

"The truth is I've never been there or anywhere else on Martinique," he said.

"*Et alors?*" she said.

"I prepared and spent years learning about it," said the General, "because I knew I would need it one day in order to please the most beautiful woman from those islands."

He was dressed in embossed cotton trousers, a satin tunic, and red slippers, and he spoke without pause, his voice broken but eloquent. She noticed the breath of cologne floating through the dining room. He confessed it was a weakness of his, to the point where his enemies accused him of having spent eight thousand pesos of public funds on cologne. He was as weak as he had been the day before, but only his meager body betrayed the severity of his illness.

In the company of men the General was capable of swearing like the most shameless horse thief, but the mere presence of a woman was enough to refine his manners and language to the point of affectation. He himself uncorked, decanted, and served a *grande classe* Burgundy that the Count described without hesitation as a velvet caress. They were serving the coffee when Captain Iturbide whispered something in his ear. He listened with utmost gravity, but then he leaned back in his chair and laughed out loud.

"Listen to this, please," he said. "A delegation from Cartagena has arrived for my funeral."

He had them come in. Montilla and his companions had no other recourse than to go along with his joke. The aides-de-camp called in the bagpipers from San Jacinto who had been in the vicinity since the previous night, and a group of old men and women danced the *cumbia* in honor of the guests. Camille was amazed at the elegance of that folk dance of African origin, and she wanted to learn it. The General had a reputation as a fine dancer, and some of his dining companions remembered that on his last visit he had danced the *cumbia* like a master, but when Camille asked him to join her, he declined the honor. "Three years is a long time," he said, smiling. She danced alone after she was shown two or three steps. Then, when the music stopped for a moment, they heard sudden cheering, a series of fearful explosions, and the sound of gunfire. Camille was frightened.

The Count said in all seriousness:

"Damn it, it's a revolution!"

"You can't imagine how much we need one." The General laughed. "Sad to say, it's only a cockfight."

Almost without thinking about it, he finished his coffee and with a circular gesture of his hand invited all of them to the cockpit.

"Come with me, Montilla, so you can see how dead I am," he said.

And so at two o'clock in the afternoon he visited the cockpit, accompanied by a large group with the Count de Raigecourt in the lead. But in that kind of gathering, composed only of men, everyone noticed Camille, not the General. No one could believe that so dazzling a woman was not one of his many lovers, and in a place forbidden to women, above all when they were told she had come with the Count, for it was well known that the General had other men accompany his clandestine lovers in order to cloud the truth.

The second fight was horrifying. A red cock scratched out his opponent's eyes with a pair of well-aimed spurs. But the blinded one did not surrender. He attacked the other cock in ferocious rage until he tore off his head and ate it with great pecks of his bill.

"I never imagined a fiesta could be so bloody," said Camille. "But I love it."

The General explained that it was even bloodier when the audience provoked the roosters with obscene shouts and fired their weapons in the air, but that afternoon they were inhibited by the presence of a woman, above all one so beautiful. He gave her a flirtatious look and said: "And so the fault is yours." She laughed in amusement:

"It's yours, Excellency, for having governed this country for so many years and not making a law that would require men to behave the same whether there are women present or not."

He began to lose his patience.

"I beg you not to call me Excellency," he said. "I'm satisfied with being reasonable."

That night, as he was floating in the futile water of the bath, José Palacios said: "She's the best-looking woman we've seen." The General did not open his eyes.

"She's abominable," he said.

His appearance in the cockpit, according to widespread opinion, was a premeditated action taken to counteract the differing versions of his illness, which had become so serious in recent days that no one doubted the rumor of his death. It had its effect, for the mail leaving Cartagena carried the news of his good health along various routes, and his followers celebrated with public fiestas that were more defiant than jubilant.

The General had succeeded in deceiving even his own body, for his animation continued in the days that followed, and he permitted himself to sit again at the gaming table with his aides-de-camp, who whiled away the tedium with endless games of cards. Andrés Ibarra, who was the youngest and most joyful and still preserved a romantic sense of war, had written during this time to a lover in Quito: "I prefer death in your arms to this peace without you." They played for days and nights on end, sometimes absorbed in the enigma of the cards, sometimes shouting their disagreements, and always pursued by the mosquitoes that during the rainy season assaulted them even in broad daylight, despite the dung fires the orderlies kept burning. He had not played since the evil night in Guaduas, for the harsh incident with Wilson had left a bitterness that he wanted to erase from his heart, but in the hammock he listened to their shouts, their confidences, their memories of war during the idleness of an elusive peace. One night he walked around the house a few times and could not resist the temptation to stop in the corridor. He signaled those facing him to keep quiet, and came up behind Andrés Ibarra. As if they were falcon's claws, he placed a hand on each of his shoulders and asked:

"Tell me something, Cousin: do you think I look like a dead man too?"

Ibarra, accustomed to his ways, did not turn around to look at him.

"Not me, General," he said.

"Well, either you're blind or you're lying," he said.

"Or my back is turned," said Ibarra.

The General became interested in the game, sat down, and after a while began to play. For everyone it was like a return to normalcy, not only that night but on the following nights as well. "While we're waiting for the passport," as the General said. Nevertheless, José Palacios told him again that despite the ritual of the cards, despite his personal attention, despite himself, the officers of his entourage were sick to death of all their coming and going to nowhere.

No one was more concerned than he for the fate of his officers, for the daily minutiae as well as the broad horizon of their destiny, but when problems had no solution he resolved them by deceiving himself. Ever since the incident with Wilson, and then all along the river, he had interrupted his own suffering to think about them. Wilson's conduct was unspeakable, and only very deep frustration could have inspired such harshness. "He's as good a soldier as his father," the General had said when he saw him fighting at Junín. "And more modest," he had added when Wilson refused the promotion to colonel granted him by Field Marshal Sucre after the battle of Tarqui, which he had obliged him to accept.

The regimen he imposed on all of them, in peace as well as war, required not only heroic discipline but a loyalty that almost demanded clairvoyance. They were fighting men but not barracks soldiers, for they had fought so much they had almost not had time to make camp. There were all kinds of men among them, but the nucleus of those who won independence, the ones closest to the General, were the flower of American aristocracy, who had been educated in the schools of princes. They had spent their lives fighting, far from their homes, their wives, their children, far from everything, and necessity had turned them into politicians and officeholders. They were all Venezuelans except Iturbide and the European aides-de-camp, and almost all of them were related to the General by blood or by marriage: Fernando, José Laurencio, the Ibarras, Briceño Méndez. The links of class or blood identified and unified them.

One was different from the rest: José Laurencio Silva was the son of a midwife from the town of El Tinaco, on Los Llanos, and a fisherman on the river. Through his father and his mother he was a dark-skinned member of the lower class of *pardo* half-breeds, but the General had married him to Felicia, another of his nieces. During his career he had risen from a sixteen-year-old volunteer in the liberating army to a field general at the age of fifty-eight, and he had suffered more than fifteen serious wounds and numerous minor ones, inflicted by a variety of weapons, in fifty-two battles in almost all the campaigns for independence. The only difficulty he encountered as a *pardo* was his rejection by a lady of the local aristocracy during a gala ball. The General then requested that they repeat the waltz, and he danced it with Silva himself.

At the opposite extreme was General O'Leary, who was tall and blond and had an elegant appearance, enhanced by his Florentine uniforms. He had come to Venezuela at the age of eighteen as a second lieutenant in the Red Hussars and spent his entire career fighting in almost all the battles of the wars for independence. He too, like the others, had suffered his moment of disgrace: when the General sent him to find a formula for reconciliation, he had agreed with Santander in the latter's dispute with José Antonio Páez. The General refused to speak to him, leaving him to his fate for fourteen months, until his anger cooled.

The personal merits of each of them were undeniable. The difficulty was that the General was never conscious of the barricade of power that he himself maintained with them, which became even more insurmountable the more he thought he was being accessible and kind. But on the night when José Palacios made him see their state of mind, he played cards as an absolute equal, losing with good grace until the officers allowed themselves to express their feelings.

It was clear they were not burdened by old frustrations. They did not care about the sense of defeat that took hold of them even after winning a war. They did not care about the slowness he imposed on their promotions to avoid the appearance of privilege, and they did not care about their uprooted, wandering life or the misfortunes of occasional love. Military salaries had been reduced by two thirds because of the nation's financial straits, and still their pay was three months late, and then it was issued in government bonds of uncertain value, which they sold at a loss to speculators. Nevertheless, they did not care, as they did not care about the General's leaving, slamming the door with a noise that would echo around the world, or about his abandoning them to the mercy of their enemies. Not at all: glory was for others. What they could not endure was the uncertainty he had inspired in them ever since his decision to renounce power, which became more and more unbearable the more he continued to slog his way through this endless journey to nowhere.

That night the General felt so gratified as he was taking his bath that he told José Palacios there was not the slightest shadow between himself and his officers. Yet the impression he left with the officers was that they had inspired neither gratitude nor guilt in the General but rather a germ of mistrust.

Above all José María Carreño, who since the night of their conversation on the barge had continued to show his rancor and without realizing it had fed the rumor that he was in touch with the Venezuelan separatists. Or, as they said at the time, that he was a turncoat. Four years earlier the General had expelled him from his heart, as he had expelled O'Leary, Montilla, Briceño Méndez, Santana, and so many others, on the mere suspicion that he desired popularity at the expense of the army. As he had done four years before, the General had him followed now, smelled out his tracks, listened to all the gossip brewing against him, in an effort to glimpse some light in the darkness of his own doubts.

One night when he did not know if Carreño was asleep or awake, he heard him say in the adjoining room that for the sake of the nation's health even treason was legitimate. Then the General took him by the arm, walked him to the patio, and subjected him to the irresistible magic of his charm with a calculated intimacy that he called on only in times of emergency. Carreño confessed the truth. In fact, it made him bitter that the General would leave his work adrift, with no concern for how orphaned they all felt. But his plans to defect were loyal. Weary of searching for a ray of hope on this blind men's journey, incapable of living bereft of a soul, he had decided to flee to Venezuela and lead an armed movement in favor of integration.

"I can think of nothing more meritorious," he concluded.

"And do you really think you'll be better treated in Venezuela?" the General asked him.

Carreño did not dare to say yes.

"Well, but at least there I'm in my own country," he said.

"Don't be an ass," said the General. "For us America is our own country, and it's all the same: hopeless."

He did not allow him to say anything more. He spoke to him at length, revealing in every word what seemed to be his heart, although neither Carreño nor anyone else would ever know if it really was. At last he patted him on the shoulder and left him in the darkness.

"Stop hallucinating, Carreño," he said. "It's all gone to hell."

ON WEDNESDAY, June 16, he received the news that the government had confirmed the pension for life granted him by the Congress. He wrote his acknowledgment to President Mosquera in a formal letter that was not free of irony, and when he finished dictating he said to Fernando, imitating José Palacios' majestic plural and ceremonial emphasis: "We are rich." On Tuesday, June 22, he received the passport to leave the country, and he waved it in the air, saying: "We are free." Two days later, when he awoke from an hour of restless sleep, he opened his eyes in the hammock and said: "We are sad." Then he decided to leave for Cartagena without delay, taking advantage of the cool, cloudy day. His only specific order was that the officers in his entourage should travel in civilian clothes and carry no weapons. He gave no explanation, no sign that would permit conjecture regarding his motives, and he allowed no time for saying goodbye to anyone. They started out as soon as his personal guards were ready, leaving behind the baggage that would follow with the rest of the traveling party.

The General in His Labyrinth

On his journeys the General was in the habit of making casual stops to inquire about the problems of the people he met along the way. He asked about everything: the age of their children, the nature of their illnesses, the condition of their business, what they thought about everything. On this occasion he did not say a word, he did not change his pace, he did not cough, he did not give signs of fatigue, and he had nothing but a glass of port all day. At about four o'clock in the afternoon the old convent on La Popa Hill was outlined on the horizon. It was the season for public prayers, and from the King's Highway they saw the lines of pilgrims like *arriera* ants ascending along the rugged precipice. A short while later they spied in the distance the eternal stain of turkey buzzards circling the public market and the waters of the slaughterhouse. In sight of the walls the General motioned to José María Carreño, who approached and offered his robust falconer's stump for him to lean on. "I have a confidential mission for you," the General told him in a very low voice. "As soon as we arrive, find out where Sucre's gotten to." He gave him his customary farewell pat on the shoulder and concluded:

"Just between us, of course."

A large party led by Montilla was waiting for them on the King's Highway, and the General found himself obliged to finish the journey in the Spanish governor's old carriage pulled by a team of lighthearted mules. Although the sun was low, the great mangrove branches seemed to boil in the heat of the dead swamps surrounding the city, whose pestilential stink was less bearable than that of the bay, corrupted for over a century by the blood and offal from the slaughterhouse. When they passed through the

Media Luna Gate a gale of startled turkey buzzards rose from the open-air market. There were still traces of the panic caused that morning by a rabid dog that had bitten several people of various ages, among them a white woman from Castile, who had been snooping where she had no business being, and some children from the slave quarter, who had managed to stone the dog to death themselves. The body was hanging from a tree at the school door. General Montilla had it burned, not only for reasons of hygiene but also to prevent people from trying to exorcise the dog's evil spell with African magic.

The population of the walled district, called by an urgent summons, had taken to the streets. The afternoons were turning translucent and slow in the June solstice, and on the balconies there were garlands of flowers and women dressed in the exaggerated popular style of Madrid, and the bells in the cathedral, the music of the regimental bands, and the artillery salutes thundered all the way to the sea, but nothing could mitigate the misery they wanted to hide. As he waved his hat in greeting from the rickety carriage, the General could not help seeing himself in a pitiful light when he compared this impoverished reception to his triumphal entry into Caracas in August of 1813, when he was crowned with laurels in a carriage drawn by the six most beautiful maidens in the city and surrounded by a weeping multitude that eternalized him that day with the name of his glory: The Liberator. Caracas was still a remote town in the colonial provinces, and it was ugly, sad, and commonplace, but the afternoons in Ávila tore at his nostalgia.

The two memories did not seem to belong to the same life, for the very noble and heroic city of Cartagena de

Indias, which had been capital of the viceregency several times and had been celebrated a thousand times as one of the most beautiful cities in the world, was not even a shadow of what it once had been. It had suffered nine military sieges by land and by sea and had been sacked on various occasions by pirates and generals. Nevertheless, nothing had devastated it as much as the battles for independence followed by the factional wars. The wealthy families from its golden age had fled. The former slaves had been set adrift in a useless freedom, and from the marquises' palaces taken over by the poverty-stricken, rats as big as cats poured onto the rubbish heaps of the streets. The cordon of invincible bastions that the King of Spain had wanted to view with his telescopes from the watchtowers of his palace could not even be imagined among the brambles. The commerce that had been the most flourishing in the seventeenth century because of the slave traffic was reduced to a handful of ruined shops. It was impossible to reconcile glory with the stench from the open sewers. The General sighed into Montilla's ear:

"What a price we've had to pay for an independence that's not worth shit!"

That night Montilla gathered the cream of the city in his seignorial house on Calle La Factoría, where the Marquis de Valdehoyos had lived a villainous life and his Marquise had prospered from smuggling flour and trafficking in blacks. Easter lights had been lit in the principal houses, but the General had no illusions because he knew that in the Caribbean anything, even an illustrious death, could be the excuse for public revels. And in fact it was a false fiesta. Vile broadsides had been in circulation for several days, and the opposition party had incited its gangs to throw stones through windows and battle the police with cudgels. "It's just as well there are no more windows left to break," said Montilla with his customary humor, well aware that popular anger was directed at him more than at the General. He reinforced the grenadiers of the guard with local troops, cordoned off the area, and ordered that his guest not be told of the war in the streets.

That night the Count de Raigecourt came to tell the General that the English packet boat was in sight of the castles on Boca Chica but that he was not leaving. The public reason was his not wanting to share the immensity of the ocean with a group of women, who were all crowded into the only cabin. But the truth was that despite the urbane lunch at Turbaco, despite the adventure at the cockpit, despite all the General had done to overcome the misfortunes of his health, the Count realized he was in no condition to undertake the voyage. He thought perhaps the General's spirit could endure the crossing, but not his body, and he refused to do death a favor. Nevertheless, these reasons and many others like them failed to shake the General's determination that night.

Montilla did not admit defeat. He said early goodbyes to his guests so that the sick man might rest, but he kept him a good while longer on the interior balcony while a languid adolescent girl in an almost invisible muslin tunic played seven romanzas for them on the harp. They were so beautiful, and were performed with so much tenderness, that the two soldiers did not have the heart to speak until the sea breeze had cleared the last ashes of music from the air. The General sat dozing in the rocking chair, floating on the waves of the harp, when without warning he shuddered inside and sang all the words of the last song in a very low but clear and harmonious voice. When the song was over he turned to the harpist, murmuring thanks that came from his soul, but the only thing he saw was the harp, hung with a garland of withered laurels. Then he remembered.

"There's a man in prison in Honda for justifiable homicide," he said.

Montilla's laughter preceded his own witticism:

"What color are his horns?"

The General let the remark pass and explained the case in all its details except for his earlier acquaintance with Miranda Lyndsay in Jamaica. Montilla had a simple solution.

"He should ask to be transferred here for reasons of health," he said. "Once he's here we'll arrange his pardon."

"Can you do that?" asked the General.

"No," said Montilla, "but we do it."

The General closed his eyes, oblivious to the sudden loud barking of the dogs in the night, and Montilla thought he had gone back to sleep. After deep reflection he opened his eyes again and filed the matter away.

"All right," he said. "But I don't know anything."

Only then did he notice the barking that spread in concentric waves from the walled district to the remotest swamps, where there were dogs trained in the art of not barking so they would not betray their owners. General Montilla told him they were poisoning the street dogs to prevent the spread of rabies. In the slave quarter they had succeeded in capturing only two of the children who had been bitten. The others, as always, had been hidden by their parents so they could die under their own gods, or had been taken beyond the reach of the government to the strongholds of the fugitive slaves in the swamps of Marialabaja, in an effort to save them with the witch doctors' arts.

The General had never attempted to suppress those calamitous rites, but he thought that poisoning dogs was unworthy of the human condition. He loved them as much as horses and flowers. When he sailed for Europe the first time, he carried a pair of pups with him all the way to Veracruz. He had more than ten dogs with him when he left Los Llanos in Venezuela and crossed the Andes at the head of four hundred barefoot plainsmen to liberate New Granada and found the Republic of Colombia. He always took them into battle. Nevado, the most famous, who had been with him from his earliest campaigns and had defeated without help a brigade of twenty bloodthirsty dogs belonging to the Spanish armies, had been killed by a lance during the first battle of Carabobo. In Lima, Manuela Sáenz owned more than she could care for, in addition to the numerous animals of all kinds that she kept on the estate at La Magdalena. Someone had told the General that when a dog died it had to be replaced without delay by another just like it, and with the same name, so you could go on believing it was the same animal. He did not agree. He always wanted them to be distinctive so he could remember them all with their own identities, their yearning eyes and eager spirits, and could mourn their deaths. Among the victims of the attack on the evil night of September 25 were the two bloodhounds whose heads had been cut off by the conspirators. Now, on his final journey, he had with him the two that survived, as well as the ferocious, ill-favored stray they had picked up on the river. Montilla's announcement that on the first day alone they had poisoned over fifty dogs ruined the state of mind created in him by the harp of love.

Montilla was truly sorry and promised there would be no more dogs killed in the streets. The promise calmed him, not because he believed it would be kept, but because the good intentions of his generals were a consolation to him. The splendor of the night was responsible for the rest. The scent of jasmine rose from the illuminated patio, the air seemed like diamonds, and there were more stars than ever in the sky. "Like Andalusia in April," he had once said, remembering Columbus. A crosswind swept away the noises and the smells, and all that remained was the thunder of the waves against the walls.

"General," pleaded Montilla. "Don't go."

"The ship is in port," he said.

"There'll be others," said Montilla.

"It doesn't matter," he replied. "They're all the last one."

He would not budge. After much pleading, to no avail, Montilla had no other recourse than to reveal the secret he had sworn to keep until just before it was to take place: General Rafael Urdaneta, at the head of the Bolivarist officers, was preparing a coup in Santa Fe de Bogotá for early in September. Contrary to Montilla's expectations, the General did not seem surprised.

"I didn't know," he said, "but it was easy to imagine."

Then Montilla disclosed the details of the military conspiracy brewing in all the loyal garrisons in the country, with the compliance of officers in Venezuela. The General gave it deep thought. "It makes no sense," he said. "If Urdaneta really wants to save the world, let him make peace with Páez and repeat the history of the last fifteen years all the way from Caracas to Lima. Then it will just be a patriotic excursion down to Patagonia." Nevertheless, before he retired he left a small opening.

"Does Sucre know?" he asked.

"He's against it," said Montilla.

"Because of his quarrel with Urdaneta, of course," said the General.

"No," said Montilla. "Because he's against everything that keeps him from Quito."

"In any event, he's the one you have to talk to," said the General. "You're wasting your time with me."

It seemed his final word. Very early the next day he even gave José Palacios orders to load the baggage while the packet was in the bay, and he sent him to ask the ship's captain to anchor her opposite the fortress of Santo Domingo during the afternoon so that he could watch from the balcony of his house. The arrangements were so precise that his officers thought he would not take any of them because he had not said who was traveling with him. Wilson proceeded in accordance with the plan made in January and loaded his luggage without consulting anyone.

Even those least convinced of his departure went to say goodbye when they saw the six loaded wagons rolling through the streets toward the wharf on the bay. The Count de Raigecourt, accompanied on this occasion by Camille, was the guest of honor at luncheon. Her hair was pulled back into a chignon, she wore a green tunic and slippers, and she looked younger, her eyes less cruel. The General concealed with a compliment his displeasure at seeing her.

"The lady must be very certain of her beauty for green to look so well on her," he said in Spanish.

The Count translated on the spot, and Camille burst into the laughter of a free woman, saturating the entire house with her licorice breath. "Let's not start again, Don Simón," she said. Something had changed in them both, for neither dared to take up the rhetorical jousting of their first meeting for fear of wounding the other. Camille forgot him as she flitted at her pleasure through a crowd educated to speak French on just such occasions as this. The General went to converse with Friar Sebastián de Sigüenza, a saintly man who enjoyed well-deserved prestige for having cured Humboldt of the smallpox he contracted on his visit to the city in the year 1800. The friar was the only person who attributed no importance to what he had done. "The Lord has willed that some die of smallpox and others not, and the Baron was one of the latter," he would say. The General had asked to meet him on his previous trip, when he learned that he cured three hundred different diseases using medicines with an aloe base.

Montilla had already given orders to prepare the farewell military parade, when José Palacios returned from the port with the official message that the packet would be in front of the house after lunch. As protection against the afternoon sun in mid-June, Montilla ordered awnings placed on the tenders that would carry the General from

the fortress of Santo Domingo to the ship. At eleven
o'clock, when the house was crowded with invited guests
and casual visitors suffocating in the heat, all manner of
curiosities of the local cuisine were served on the long
table. Camille could not explain the reason for the com-
motion that shook the room until she heard the faint voice
very close to her ear: "*Après vous, madame.*" The General helped her to a little of everything, explaining the
name, recipe, and origin of each dish, and then to the
astonishment of his cook he served himself an even larger
portion, for an hour before he had refused delicacies more
exquisite than those displayed on the table. Then, making
his way through the groups searching for a place to sit,
he led her to the oasis of large tropical flowers on the
interior balcony, and he made his proposition without
preambles.

"It would be very pleasant to see each other in Kingston," he said.

"Nothing would please me more," she said, without a
trace of surprise. "I adore the Blue Mountains."

"Alone?"

"No matter whom I'm with I'll always be alone," she
said. And she added with a roguish touch: "Excellency."

He smiled.

"I'll find you through Hyslop," he said.

That was all. He led her back through the room to the
spot where he had found her, took his leave with a bow
worthy of a contredanse, left his plate untouched on a
windowsill, and returned to his place. Nobody knew
when he made the decision to stay, or why he made it.
He was besieged by politicians discussing local dissensions,

when he turned suddenly to de Raigecourt and made a remark that had no bearing on the subject and was intended for everyone's ears:

"You're right, Count. What will I do with so many women, in the lamentable state in which I find myself?"

"Just so, General," said the Count with a sigh. And he hastened to add: "On the other hand, the *Shannon* arrives next week, an English frigate with a good stateroom and an excellent physician as well."

"That's worse than a hundred women," said the General.

In any case, the explanation was only a pretext, because one of the officers was prepared to give him his cabin until they reached Jamaica. José Palacios was the only man who offered a precise reason, with his infallible: "Only my master knows what my master is thinking." And he could not have sailed in any event, because the packet ran aground on its way to pick him up across from Santo Domingo and suffered serious damage.

And so he stayed, and the only condition was that he would not remain in Montilla's house. The General thought it the most beautiful in the city, but because of its proximity to the sea it was too humid for his bones, above all in winter, when he awoke with the sheets soaked through. His health demanded winds less heraldic than those of the walled district. Montilla interpreted this as a sign that he would be staying for some time, and he hastened to accommodate him.

On the spur of La Popa Hill was a holiday suburb burned in 1815 by the Cartagenans so that the royalist troops who had come back to reconquer the city would have no place to make camp. The sacrifice was futile, because the Spanish captured the fortified area after one hundred sixteen days, during which time those under siege ate even the soles of their shoes, and six thousand died of hunger. Fifteen years later the calcined plain was still exposed to the furious two o'clock sun. One of the few rebuilt houses belonged to the English merchant Judah Kingseller, who was away on a journey. It had attracted the General's attention when he arrived from Turbaco, for its palm roof was well cared for and its walls were painted in festive colors, and it was almost hidden in a grove of fruit trees. General Montilla thought it was too modest a house for so splendid a tenant, but the General reminded him that he was as accustomed to sleeping on the floor of a pigsty, wrapped in his cape, as in a duchess' bed. And so he rented the house for an indefinite period, with an extra charge for the bed, the water jug, the six leather taborets in the drawing room, and the handmade still in which Señor Kingseller brewed his own liquor. General Montilla also brought a velvet armchair from Government House and had a cane-and-mud barracks built for the grenadiers of the guard. The house was cool during the hours when the sun shone hottest, less humid at any hour than the Marquis de Valdehoyos' mansion, and it had four airy bedrooms where iguanas strolled. His insomnia was less arid at dawn as he listened to the sudden explosions of ripe soursop fruit falling from the trees. In the afternoons, above all when the rains were heavy, the processions of the poor could be seen bearing their drowned to the convent for a vigil.

After he moved to the foot of La Popa, the General returned to the walled district no more than three times, and then only to pose for Antonio Meucci, an Italian painter who was visiting Cartagena. He felt so weak that he had to sit down on the interior terrace of the Marquis's mansion, surrounded by wildflowers and boisterous birds, and in any event he could not sit still for longer than an hour. He liked the portrait, although it was evident that the artist had viewed him with too much compassion.

The New Granadan artist José María Espinosa had painted his portrait in Government House in Santa Fe de Bogotá not long before the September assassination attempt, and it seemed so unlike the image he had of himself that he could not resist the impulse to discuss it with General Santana, his secretary at the time.

"Do you know who this portrait looks like?" he said. "Olaya, that old man from La Mesa."

When Manuela Sáenz found out, she did not hide her indignation, for she knew the old man too.

"It seems to me you don't have a very good opinion of yourself," she said. "Olaya was almost eighty years old the last time we saw him, and he couldn't even stand up."

The oldest of his portraits was an anonymous miniature painted in Madrid when he was sixteen. When he was thirty-two another was painted in Haiti, and both were faithful to his age and Caribbean character. He had a strain of African blood through a paternal great-great-grandfather, who had fathered a son by a slavewoman, and it was so evident in his features that the aristocrats in Lima called him Sambo. But as his glory increased, the painters began to idealize him, washing his blood, mythologizing him, until they established him in official memory with the Roman profile of his statues. But Espinosa's portrait resembled no one but him, wasted at the age of forty-five by the disease he did everything to hide, even from himself, until the eve of his death.

One rainy night when he awoke from a restless sleep in the house at the foot of La Popa, the General saw a young girl sitting in a corner of the bedroom and wearing the rough burlap tunic of a lay evangelical congregation, her hair adorned with a crown of shining fire beetles. During the colonial period European travelers were amazed to see Indians lighting their way with a flask full of the fire beetles that later became a republican fashion, when women used them as shining garlands on their hair, as diadems of light on their foreheads, as phosphorescent brooches on their bosoms. The girl who came into the bedroom that night had them sewn in a band that illuminated her face with phantasmal light. She was languid and mysterious, her hair was graying at the age of twenty, and he soon detected the marks of the virtue he valued most in a woman: untamed intelligence. She had come to the grenadiers' camp to offer herself for any purpose, and she seemed so extraordinary to the officer on duty that he sent her with José Palacios in case he might be interested in her for the General, who invited her to lie down beside him, for he did not have the strength to carry her to the hammock. She removed the headband, placed the fire beetles inside a stalk of sugarcane she carried with her, and lay down at his side. After a desultory conversation the General dared to ask her what they thought of him in Cartagena.

"They say Your Excellency is well but pretends to be sick so people will feel sorry for you," she said.

He took off his nightshirt and asked the girl to examine him by the light of the candle. Then she gained thorough knowledge of the most ravaged body one could imagine: the meager belly, the ribs pushing through the skin, the legs and arms reduced to mere bone, all of it enclosed in a hairless hide as pale as death except for the face, which was so weathered by exposure to the elements that it seemed to belong to another man.

"The only thing lacking is for me to die," he said.

The girl persisted.

"People say you've always been like this but now it suits you to let them know about it."

He did not concede to her testimony. He continued to offer conclusive proofs of his illness, while she drifted in and out of an easy slumber and answered him as she slept without losing the thread of the dialogue. He did not even touch her all night: it was enough for him to feel the warm sun of her adolescence. Then, just outside the window, Captain Iturbide began to sing: "*If the tempest continues and the hurricane blows, put your arms round my neck, let the sea swallow us.*" It was a song from another time, when his stomach could still endure the awful evocative power of ripe guavas and the rigors of a woman in the dark. The General and the girl listened to it together, almost with devotion, but she fell asleep in the middle of the next song, and a short while later he fell into an unquiet stupor. The silence was so pure after the music that the dogs began to bark when she stood and tiptoed away in order not to awaken the General. He heard her feeling for the latch in the dark.

"You're leaving a virgin," he said.

She answered with a festive laugh:

"No one is a virgin after a night with Your Excellency."

She left, as they all did. For of all the women who passed through his life, many of them for a few brief hours, there was none to whom he had even suggested the idea of staying. In his urgencies of love he was capable of changing the world in order to go to them. Once satisfied, he was content with the illusion that he would keep them in his memory, give himself to them from a distance in passionate letters, send them extravagant gifts to protect himself from oblivion, but, with an emotion that resembled vanity more than love, he would not commit the least part of his life to them.

As soon as he was alone that night he got up to join Iturbide, who was still talking with other officers around the fire in the patio. He had him sing until dawn, accompanied on the guitar by Colonel José de la Cruz Paredes, and because of the songs he requested, all of them realized he was in a bad humor.

He had returned from his second trip to Europe with an enthusiasm for the fashionable tunes of the day, which he sang at the top of his voice and danced with insuperable grace at the weddings of well-born mestizos in Caracas. The war changed his taste. The romantic popular songs that had led him by the hand through the countless doubts of his first love affairs were replaced by sumptuous waltzes and triumphal marches. That night in Cartagena he again requested the songs of his youth, some so old he had to teach them to Iturbide, who was too young to remember them. The audience slipped away as the General bled inside, and he was left alone with Iturbide beside the embers.

It was a strange night, without a star in the sky, and a sea wind was blowing, heavy with the weeping of orphans and the fragrance of decay. Iturbide was a man of great silences, as inspired in his unblinking contemplation of frozen ashes as in his ability to sing all night without stopping. The General, as he poked the fire with a stick, broke the spell:

"What are they saying in Mexico?"

"I don't have anyone there," said Iturbide. "I'm an exile."

"All of us here are exiles," said the General. "I've lived in Venezuela only six years since this began, and the rest of the time has been spent heading off calamities in half the world. You can't imagine what I'd give right now to be eating an *hervido* in San Mateo."

His mind must have truly flown away to the sugar mills of his childhood, for his silence was deep as he watched the dying fire. When he spoke again he was back on solid ground. "The damn problem is that we stopped being Spaniards and then we went here and there and everywhere in countries that change their names and governments so much from one day to the next we don't know where the hell we come from," he said. He contemplated the ashes again for a long time and asked in a different tone of voice:

"And since there are so many countries in this world, how did it occur to you to come here?"

Iturbide's answer had a long preamble. "At military school they taught us to make war on paper," he said. "We fought with little lead soldiers on plaster maps. On Sundays they would take us to the nearby meadows, along with the cows and the ladies coming back from

Mass, and the Colonel would shoot the cannon so we could grow accustomed to the shock of the explosion and the smell of gunpowder. Imagine, the most famous teacher was a disabled Englishman who taught us how to fall off our horses when we were killed."

The General interrupted him.

"And you wanted real war."

"Your war, General," said Iturbide. "But it'll be two years since the army accepted me, and I still don't know what a flesh-and-blood battle is like."

The General still had not looked him in the face. "Well, you chose the wrong destiny," he said. "The only wars here will be civil wars, and those are like killing your own mother." From the shadows José Palacios reminded him that it was almost dawn. Then he scattered the ashes with the stick, and as he stood up, clutching Iturbide's arm, he said:

"If I were you I'd get out of here as fast as I could before dishonor caught up with me."

Until the day he died José Palacios insisted that the house at the foot of La Popa was possessed by evil spirits. They were still settling in when the ship's officer, José Tomás Machado, arrived from Venezuela with the news that several military cantonments had disavowed the separatist government and that a new party in favor of the General was gaining strength. He received Machado alone and listened to him with attention, but he was not very enthusiastic. "The news is good, but it comes too late," he said. "And as for me, what can a poor invalid do against the whole world?" He gave instructions to lodge the emissary with all honors, but he did not promise him a reply.

"I do not expect health for our native land," he said.

Nevertheless, as soon as he said goodbye to Captain Machado, the General turned to Carreño and asked him: "Did you locate Sucre?" Yes, he had left Santa Fe de Bogotá in the middle of May, in a rush to spend his saint's day with his wife and daughter.

"He left in plenty of time," concluded Carreño, "because President Mosquera passed him on the Popayán road."

"I can't believe it!" said the General, surprised. "He traveled by land?"

"That's right, General."

"Merciful God!" he said.

It was a presentiment. That same night he received the news that on June 4 Field Marshal Sucre had been ambushed and assassinated by a bullet in the back as he was traveling the dark stretch of road at Berruecos. Montilla arrived with the bad news when the General had finished his evening bath, and he did not listen to the entire report. He slapped his forehead and tore at the tablecloth where the supper dishes still lay, maddened by one of his biblical rages.

"Fuck it!" he shouted.

The echoes of his outburst were still resonating through the house when he regained control of himself. He fell into the chair, bellowing, "It was Obando." And he repeated it many times: "It was Obando, the Spaniards' paid assassin." He referred to General José María Obando, the commander of Pasto, on the southern frontier of New Granada, who had thus deprived the General of his only possible successor and assured for himself the presidency of the Republic that had been cut to pieces in order to hand it over to Santander. In his memoirs one of the conspirators recounted that as he was leaving the house on the main square of Santa Fe de Bogotá where the crime had been planned, he had suffered a disturbance in his soul when he saw Field Marshal Sucre in the icy fog of nightfall, wearing his black wool greatcoat and his poor man's hat as he walked alone, his hands in his pockets, through the atrium of the cathedral.

On the night he learned of Sucre's death the General vomited blood. José Palacios hid the fact, as he had in Honda when he surprised the General on all fours washing the bathroom floor with a sponge. He kept the two secrets without being asked to, thinking it was not appropriate to add more bad news when there was already so much of it.

On a night like this, in Guayaquil, the General had become aware of his premature aging. He still wore his hair down to his shoulders and for convenience tied it at the back of his neck with a ribbon for his battles in war and in love, but on that occasion he realized his hair was almost white and his face was withered and sad. "If you saw me you wouldn't recognize me," he had written to a friend. "I'm forty-one years old, but I look like an old man of sixty." That night he cut his hair. A short while later, in Potosí, trying to hold back the gale winds of fugitive youth escaping between his fingers, he shaved off his mustache and sideburns.

After the assassination of Sucre he had no further dressing table artifices to hide his age. The house at the foot of La Popa sank into mourning. The officers stopped playing cards and spent the nights talking until all hours in the patio, around the perpetual fire intended to drive away the mosquitoes, or lying in hammocks hung at different levels in the common bedroom.

The General gave himself over to distilling his bitterness drop by drop. He chose two or three of his officers at random, and he kept them awake, showing them the worst of what he kept hidden in his festering heart. He made them listen once again to the old tale about the time his armies were at the verge of dissolution because of the niggardliness with which Santander, as appointed President of Colombia, resisted sending him troops and money to complete the liberation of Perú.

"He's a miser and a skinflint by nature," he said, "but his reasoning was even more perverse: he didn't have the brains to see beyond the colonial borders."

He repeated for the thousandth time the old story that the fatal blow to integration was inviting the United States to the Congress of Panamá, as Santander had done on his own account, when it was a question of nothing less than proclaiming the unity of America.

"It was like inviting the cat to the mice's fiesta," he said. "And all because the United States threatened to accuse us of turning the continent into a league of popular states opposed to the Holy Alliance. What an honor!"

He repeated one more time his horror at the inconceivable sangfroid with which Santander accomplished his purposes. "He's as cold as a dead fish," he said. He repeated for the thousandth time his diatribe against the loans Santander received from London, and the complacency with which he sponsored the corruption of his friends. Each time he recalled him, in private or in public, he added poison to a political atmosphere that did not seem able to contain another drop. But he could not restrain himself.

"That was how the world began to fall apart," he said.

He had been so rigorous in his handling of public funds that he could not return to this subject without losing his temper. As President he had decreed the death penalty for any official employee who misappropriated or stole more than ten pesos. Yet he was so openhanded with his personal wealth that in a few years he spent a large portion of the fortune he inherited from his parents on the wars for independence. His earnings were divided among the war widows and the men disabled in battle. He gave his nieces and nephews the sugar plantations he had inherited, he gave his sisters the house in Caracas, and most of his lands he divided among the numerous slaves he freed before the abolition of slavery. He refused the million pesos offered him by the Congress of Lima in the euphoria of liberation. A few days before his renunciation he presented to a friend in financial difficulties the Monserrate estate awarded him by the government so he would have a worthy place to live. In Apure he got up from the hammock where he was sleeping and presented it to a scout so he could sweat out his fever, while he slept on the ground wrapped in a battle cloak. The twenty thousand duros in hard cash that he wanted to pay out of his own funds to the Quaker educator Joseph Lancaster was not his personal debt but the state's. He left the horses he loved so well with friends—even Palomo Blanco, the best-known and most glorious, who stayed behind in Bolivia to preside over the stables of Field Marshal de Santa Cruz. And therefore the topic of embezzled loans drove him unrestrained to the extremes of perfidy.

"Cassandro came out clean, of course, just as he did on September 25, because he's a wizard at observing good form," he would say to anyone who would listen. "But his friends took back to England the same money the English had lent the nation at savage interest, and they increased it and made a profit through usury."

He revealed to everyone, all night long, the muddiest depths of his soul. At dawn of the fourth day, when the crisis seemed to have become eternal, he appeared at the patio door in the same clothes he was wearing when he received news of the crime, called General Briceño Méndez aside, and spoke with him alone until the first roosters crowed, the General in his hammock with the mosquito netting and Briceño Méndez in another that José Palacios hung beside it. Perhaps neither of them was aware of how much they had abandoned the sedentary habits of peace and returned in a few days to the uncertain nights of military camp. That conversation made it clear to the General that the disquiet and desires expressed by José María Carreño in Turbaco were not his alone but were shared by most of the Venezuelan officers. After the actions of the New Granadans against them, they felt more Venezuelan than ever but were prepared to die for integration. If the General had ordered them to fight in Venezuela, they would have hurried there in droves. And Briceño Méndez would have been the first.

Those were the worst days. The only visitor the General agreed to receive was the Pole, Colonel Miecieslaw Napierski, hero of the battle of Friedland and survivor of the disaster at Leipzig, who had come with a recommendation from General Poniatowski to join the Army of Colombia.

"You've come too late," the General had told him. "There's nothing left here."

After the death of Sucre there was less than nothing. This is what he said to Napierski, and this is what Napierski said in his travel journal, which a great New Granadan poet would recover for history one hundred eighty years later. Napierski had arrived aboard the *Shannon*. The ship's captain accompanied him to the General's house, and the General spoke to them of his desire to travel to Europe, but neither one could detect in him a real disposition to sail. As the frigate would make a stop in La Guayra and return to Cartagena before sailing for Kingston, the General gave the captain a letter for his Venezuelan agent in the negotiations concerning the Aroa Mines, hoping he would send him money on the return trip. But the frigate came back without a reply, which disheartened him so much that nobody thought to ask him if he was leaving.

There was not a single piece of consolatory news. José Palacios, for his part, was careful not to make the reports they received worse and tried to hold back as much as possible. Something that concerned the officers of the entourage, which they hid from the General in order not to complete his mortification, was that the hussars and grenadiers of the guard were sowing the fiery seed of an immortal gonorrhea. It had begun with two women who passed through the entire garrison during the nights in Honda, and the soldiers had continued to disseminate it wherever they went with their dissolute lovemaking. At that moment none of the troops had escaped, although there was no academic medicine or witch doctor's artifice they had not tried.

The measures that José Palacios took to protect his master from unnecessary bitterness were not infallible. One night a note without a salutation was passed from hand to hand, and no one knew how it reached the General's hammock. He read it without his spectacles, holding it at arm's length, and then he put it in the candle flame and held it there between his fingers until it was consumed.

It was from Josefa Sagrario. She had arrived on Monday with her husband and children on the way to Mompox, encouraged by the news that the General had been deposed and was leaving the country. He never revealed what the message said, but he showed signs of great restlessness all night, and at dawn he sent Josefa Sagrario a proposal of reconciliation. She resisted his pleas and continued her journey as planned without a moment's vacillation. Her only motive, as she told José Palacios, was that it seemed senseless to make peace with a man she already considered dead.

That week it was learned that Manuela Sáenz' personal war for the return of the General had broken out in Santa Fe de Bogotá. In an attempt to make her life impossible, the Ministry of the Interior had asked her to turn over the archives she had in her care. She refused and set in motion a campaign of provocations that drove the government mad. In the company of two of her warrior slavewomen she fomented scandals, distributed pamphlets glorifying the General, and erased the charcoal slogans scrawled on public walls. It was common knowledge that she entered barracks wearing the uniform of a colonel and was as apt to take part in the soldiers' fiestas as in the officers' conspiracies. The most serious rumor was that right under Urdaneta's nose, she was promoting an armed rebellion to reestablish the absolute power of the General.

It was difficult to believe he had the strength for such an enterprise. The fevers at nightfall were becoming more and more punctual, and his cough was heartrending. One dawn José Palacios heard him shout: "Cunt of a country!" He burst into the bedroom, alarmed by an exclamation that the General reproached his officers for using, and found him with his cheek bathed in blood. He had cut himself shaving, and he was not as indignant at the mishap itself as at his own clumsiness. The apothecary who treated him, brought in on an emergency call by Colonel Wilson, found him in such despair that he tried to calm him with some drops of belladonna. The General stopped him short.

"Let me be," he said. "Despair is the health of the damned."

His sister María Antonia wrote to him from Caracas. "Everyone complains about your refusing to come and settle this disorder," she said. The village priests had decided in his favor, desertions from the army were uncontrollable, and the mountains were full of armed men who said they wanted no one but him. "This is a fandango for lunatics who can't get along even after they've made their revolution," his sister said. For while some people clamored for him, every morning the walls in half the country were painted with insulting slogans. His family, said the broadsides, should be exterminated to the fifth generation.

The coup de grace came from the Congress of Venezuela, meeting in Valencia, who crowned their deliberations with a resolution for definitive separation and a solemn declaration that there would be no agreement with New Granada and Ecuador as long as the General remained in Colombian territory. As much as the action itself, it grieved him that the official communiqué from Santa Fe de Bogotá was sent through a September 25 conspirator and his mortal enemy, whom President Mosquera had brought back from exile in order to name him Minister of the Interior. "I must say that this is the event that has affected me most in my life," said the General. He spent the night dictating different versions of his reply to a variety of secretaries, but his rage was so great that he fell asleep. At dawn, after a disturbed sleep, he said to José Palacios:

"The day I die the bells in Caracas will ring in jubilation."

That was not all that happened. When he heard the news of the General's death the Governor of Maracaibo would write: "I hasten to share the news of this great event, which, beyond all doubt, will produce untold benefits for the cause of liberty and the well-being of the country. The genius of evil, the firebrand of anarchy, the oppressor of the nation, has ceased to exist." The announcement, intended at first to inform the government in Caracas, ended as a national proclamation.

In the midst of the horror of those ill-fated days, José Palacios sang out to the General the date of his birth at five o'clock in the morning: "The twenty-fourth of July, feast day of Saint Christina, Virgin and Martyr." He opened his eyes and once again must have been aware of himself as one chosen by adversity.

It was his custom to celebrate not his birthday but his saint's day. There were eleven Simons in the Catholic calendar of saints, and he would have preferred to be named for the one who helped Christ carry his cross, but destiny gave him another Simon, the apostle and preacher in Egypt and Ethiopia, whose day is October 28. Once, on that date, in Santa Fe de Bogotá, he was crowned with a laurel wreath during the fiesta. He removed it with good humor and placed it, along with all his malice, on the head of General Santander, who accepted it without changing expression. But he reckoned his life not by his name but by his age. Forty-seven had a special significance for him, because on July 24 of the previous year, in the midst of bad news from all sides and the delirium of his pernicious fevers, he had been shaken by a presentiment—he, who never admitted the reality of presentiments. The message was clear: If he could stay alive until his next birthday, then there would be no death that could kill him. The mystery of that secret oracle was the force that had sustained him until now, against all reason.

"Forty-seven years old, damn it," he murmured. "And I'm still alive!"

He sat up in the hammock, his strength restored and his heart elated by the marvelous certainty that he was safe from all harm. He called Briceño Méndez, the ringleader of those who wanted to go to Venezuela to fight for the integrity of Colombia, and through him he granted his officers' wish because it was his birthday.

"Starting with the rank of lieutenant," he said, "let everyone who wants to fight in Venezuela pack up his gear."

General Briceño Méndez was the first. Another two generals, four colonels, and eight captains from the Cartagena garrison joined the expedition. But when Carreño reminded the General of his earlier promise, he told him:

"You're reserved for a higher destiny."

Two hours before their departure he decided that José Laurencio Silva should go as well, for he had the impression that the rust of routine was worsening his obsession with his eyes. Silva declined the honor.

"This idleness is also a war, and one of the most difficult," he said. "And therefore I'll stay here, if my General does not order otherwise."

On the other hand, Iturbide, Fernando, and Andrés Ibarra were denied permission to join the others. "If you leave, it will be to another destination," the General told Iturbide. He informed Andrés, with strange reasoning, that General Diego Ibarra was already in the struggle, and two brothers were too many for the same war. Fernando did not even volunteer, because he was sure he would receive the same answer he always did: "A man must be whole to go to war, but he cannot allow his two eyes and right hand to go without him." He resigned himself with the consolation that this answer was, in a certain sense, a kind of military distinction.

Montilla brought the travel funds on the same night they were approved, and he took part in the simple ceremony in which the General said goodbye to each of them with an embrace and a few words. They left one by one, taking different routes, some headed for Jamaica, others for Curaçao, others for Guajira, and all wearing civilian clothes, without weapons or anything else that could betray their identity, just as they had learned to do in their clandestine actions against the Spanish. At dawn the house at the foot of La Popa was a dismantled barracks, but the General was sustained by the hope that a new war would make the laurels of long ago green again.

GENERAL RAFAEL URDANETA took power on September 5. The Constituent Congress had come to the end of its mandate, and there was no other valid authority to legitimatize the coup, but the insurgents appealed to the City Council of Santa Fe de Bogotá, which recognized Urdaneta as the man entrusted with power until it was assumed by the General. This was the culmination of an insurrection by Venezuelan troops and officers garrisoned in New Granada, who defeated the government forces with the support of the small landowners on the savanna and the rural clergy. It was the first coup d'état in the Republic of Colombia, and the first of the forty-nine civil wars we would suffer in what remained of the century. President Joaquín Mosquera and Vice-President Caycedo, isolated in the midst of nothing, renounced their offices. Urdaneta picked up the power left lying on the ground, and his first governmental act was to send a personal delegation to Cartagena to offer the General the presidency of the Republic.

It had been a long while since José Palacios could remember his master's health as stable as it was during this time, for the headaches and twilight fevers surrendered their weapons as soon as news of the military coup was received. But neither had he seen him more restless. This worried Montilla, who sought the cooperation of Friar Sebastián de Sigüenza in providing the General with covert relief. The friar was a willing and able accomplice, allowing himself to be beaten at chess during the arid afternoons when they were waiting for Urdaneta's messengers.

The General had learned how to move the pieces on his second trip to Europe, and he came close to mastery playing with General O'Leary on dull nights during the long campaign in Perú. But he did not feel capable of going any further. "Chess isn't a game, it's a passion," he would say. "And I prefer bolder ones." Nevertheless, in his programs for public education he had included it among the useful and honest games that should be taught in school. The truth was he had not continued because his nerves were not made for so circumspect a game, and he needed the concentration it demanded for more serious matters.

Friar Sebastián found him swaying with violent lurches in the hammock he had ordered hung in front of the street door so he could keep watch over the parched dust of the road where Urdaneta's messengers were to appear. "Ah, Father," the General said when he saw him approach. "You're a glutton for punishment." He remained seated only long enough to move the pieces, for after every play he would stand up while the friar was thinking.

"Don't distract me, Excellency," the friar would say. "I'm going to skin you alive."

The General laughed:

"Pride goeth before a fall."

O'Leary would stop by the table to study the board and make suggestions to the General, who would reject them with indignation. But each time he won he would go out to the patio where his officers were playing cards to announce his victory. In the middle of one game Friar Sebastián asked if he planned to write his memoirs.

"Never," he said. "They're nothing but dead men making trouble."

The mail, which was one of his dominant obsessions, became his martyrdom. It was even worse during those weeks of confusion when the mail carriers in Santa Fe de Bogotá would delay their departure in expectation of the latest news and the connecting riders would grow weary of waiting for them. On the other hand, the clandestine mails became faster and more frequent. As a consequence the General had news of the news before it arrived, and there was more than enough time for his decisions to ripen.

On September 17, when he learned that the emissaries were near, he sent Carreño and O'Leary to meet them on the Turbaco road. The first surprise for Colonels Vicente Piñeres and Julián Santa María was the good spirits in which they found the hopeless invalid who was the subject of so much talk in Santa Fe de Bogotá. A solemn ceremony was improvised in the house, with civilian and military dignitaries, secondhand speeches, and toasts to the health of the nation. But when it was over he took the emissaries aside and truths were told in private. Colonel Santa María, who found solace in melodrama, struck the culminating note: If the General did not accept command, the most awful anarchy would break out in the country. The General was evasive.

"Existence comes before modifications," he said. "We won't know if there's a nation or not until the political horizon clears."

Colonel Santa María did not understand.

"I mean that the most urgent matter is to reunify the country by force of arms," said the General. "But the road begins in Venezuela, not here."

From then on, that would be his fixed idea: to begin again from the beginning, knowing that the enemy was not external but inside the house. The oligarchies in each country, represented in New Granada by the Santanderists and by Santander himself, had declared war to the death against the idea of integrity because it was unfavorable to the local privileges of the great families.

"This is the real cause, the only cause, of the war of dispersion that is killing us," said the General. "And the saddest part is that they think they're changing the world when they're really perpetuating the most reactionary thought in Spain."

He drew breath and continued: "I know I'm ridiculed because in the same letter, on the same day, and to the same person I say first one thing and then the opposite, because I approved the plan for monarchy, or I didn't approve it, or somewhere I agreed with both positions at the same time." He was accused of being capricious in the way he judged men and manipulated history, he was accused of fighting Fernando VII and embracing Morillo, of waging war to the death against Spain and promoting her spirit, of depending on Haiti in order to win the war and then considering Haiti a foreign country in order to exclude her from the Congress of Panamá, of having been a Mason and reading Voltaire at Mass but of being the paladin of the Church, of courting the English while wooing a French princess, of being frivolous, hypocritical, and even disloyal because he flattered his friends in their presence and denigrated them behind their backs. "Well, all of that is true, but circumstantial," he said, "because everything I've done has been for the sole purpose of making this continent into a single, independent country, and as far as that's concerned I've never contradicted myself or had a single doubt." And he concluded in pure Caribbean:

"All the rest is bullshit!"

In a letter he sent two days later to General Briceño Méndez he wrote: "I have not wanted to accept the command conferred on me by events because I do not want to appear to be the leader of rebels or be named by dint of the victors' military might." Nevertheless, in two letters he dictated that same night to Fernando and sent to General Rafael Urdaneta, he was careful not to be so radical.

The first was a formal reply, and his solemnity was far too evident, beginning with the salutation: "Most Excellent Sir." He justified the coup because of the anarchy and lawlessness that prevailed in the Republic following the dissolution of the previous government. "In such cases the people are not deceived," he wrote. But there was no possibility of his accepting the presidency. All he could offer was his willingness to return to Santa Fe de Bogotá to serve the new government as a simple soldier.

The other was a private letter, and he indicated this at the outset: "My dear General." It was extensive and explicit, and it did not leave the slightest doubt regarding the reasons for his hesitancy. Since Don Joaquín Mosquera had not renounced his title, he could claim recognition as the legal President tomorrow, making the General a usurper. And so he reiterated what he had said in the official letter: As long as there was no clear mandate from a legitimate source, there was no possibility of his assuming power.

The two letters were sent by the same mail, along with the original copy of a proclamation in which he asked the country to forget its passions and support the new government. But he distanced himself from any commitment. "Although I may seem to offer a good deal, I offer nothing," he would say later. And he recognized that he had written some words with the sole object of flattering those who wanted him in office. What was most significant in the second letter was his tone of command, surprising in someone who had been stripped of all power. He requested the promotion of Colonel Florencio Jiménez so he could go west with enough troops and equipment to resist the pointless war being waged against the central government by Generals José María Obando and José Hilario López: "The men who assassinated Sucre," he insisted. He also recommended other officers for various high positions. "Take care of this," he told Urdaneta, "and I'll see to the rest from the Magdalena to Venezuela, including Boyacá." He was prepared to leave for Santa Fe de Bogotá at the head of two thousand men and in that way contribute to the reestablishment of public order and the consolidation of the new government.

He did not receive direct news again from Urdaneta for forty-two days. But in any case he continued to write to him during the long month when he did nothing but impart military orders to the four winds. The ships came and went, but there was no more talk of the voyage to Europe, although he brought it up from time to time as a way of exerting political pressure. The house at the foot of La Popa was turned into headquarters for the entire country, and few military decisions during those months were not inspired or made by him from his hammock. Step by step, almost without intending to, he also became involved in decisions that went beyond military affairs. He even concerned himself with trivial matters, such as finding a position in the mail offices for his good friend Señor Tatis, or returning General José Ucrós to active service because he could no longer endure peace at home.

During this time he repeated one of his old phrases with renewed emphasis: "I'm old, sick, tired, disillusioned, harassed, slandered, and unappreciated." Nevertheless, no one who saw him would have believed it. For while he seemed to twist and turn like a scalded cat only to strengthen the government, in reality he was planning, with the authority and power of the commander in chief, each piece of the detailed military strategy with which he proposed to regain Venezuela and from there begin to restore the largest alliance of nations in the world.

A more propitious moment could not have been imagined. New Granada, with the liberal party in defeat and Santander anchored in Paris, was safe in Urdaneta's hands. Ecuador was assured by Flores, the same ambitious, contentious Venezuelan leader who had separated Quito and Guayaquil from Colombia in order to create the new republic but whom the General was certain of bringing back to the cause after he defeated Sucre's assassins. Bolivia was secure with his friend Field Marshal de Santa Cruz, who had just offered him the post of Ambassador to the Holy See. And therefore his immediate objective was to wrest the control of Venezuela from General Páez once and for all.

The General's military plan seemed aimed at launching a major offensive from Cúcuta while Páez was engaged in the defense of Maracaibo. But on September 1 the Province of Riohacha deposed its military commander, refused to recognize the authority of Cartagena, and declared itself Venezuelan. Maracaibo not only offered immediate support but also sent in its defense the leader of the September 25 attempt, General Pedro Carujo, who had fled punishment to the protection of the Venezuelan government.

Montilla brought the news as soon as he received it, but the General had already heard it and was exultant because the Riohacha insurrection justified his mobilizing new and better forces on another front to move against Maracaibo.

"And furthermore," he said, "Carujo is in our hands."

That same night he closeted himself with his officers and outlined the strategy with great precision, describing the irregularities of the terrain, moving entire armies like chessmen, anticipating the enemy's most unexpected purposes. He did not have an academic education even comparable to that of any of his officers, most of whom had been educated at the best military schools in Spain, but he had the ability to conceptualize an entire situation down to the smallest details. His visual memory was so remarkable that he could describe an obstacle seen in passing many years before, and although he was far from a master of the arts of war, no one surpassed him in inspiration.

At dawn the plan was finished. It was thorough and ferocious and so visionary that the attack on Maracaibo was planned for the end of November or, if worst came to worst, the beginning of December. When the final revision was completed at eight o'clock on a rainy Tuesday morning, Montilla pointed out the noteworthy absence of a New Granadan general in the plan.

"There isn't one from New Granada who's worth anything," the General said. "Those who aren't incompetent are scoundrels."

Montilla hastened to sweeten the conversation:

"And you, General, where will you be going?"

"Right now I don't care if it's Cúcuta or Riohacha," he said.

He turned to leave, and General Carreño's hard frown reminded him of the promise he had not kept several times over. The truth was he wanted to have him at his side at any cost but could no longer bear his restlessness. He gave him his usual pat on the shoulder and said:

"Word of honor, Carreño, you're going too."

The expeditionary force of two thousand men set sail from Cartagena on September 25, a date that seemed chosen for its symbolism. It was under the command of Generals Mariano Montilla, José Félix Blanco, and José María Carreño, each of whom had a separate commission to find a country house in Santa Marta where the General could follow the war at close range while he recovered his health. He wrote to a friend: "In two days I leave for Santa Marta to take some exercise, to escape the ennui in which I find myself, and to improve my disposition."

No sooner said than done: On October 1 he set out on the journey. On October 2, while he was en route, he was more straightforward in a letter to General Justo Briceño: "I am on my way to Santa Marta with the intention of contributing my influence to the expedition against Maracaibo." The same day he wrote again to Urdaneta: "I am on my way to Santa Marta with the intention of visiting that region, which I have never seen, and to learn if I can disillusion some enemies who have too great an influence on opinion." Only then did he disclose the real purpose of his journey: "I will observe at first hand the operations against Riohacha, and I will approach Maracaibo and the troops to discover if I can influence some important operation." Viewed in the proper light, he was no longer a defeated pensioner fleeing into exile but a general on campaign.

The departure from Cartagena had been preceded by the pressing demands of combat. There was no time for official farewells, and he informed very few friends in advance. On his instructions, Fernando and José Palacios left half the baggage in the care of friends and commercial establishments to avoid carrying unnecessary encumbrances to an uncertain war. They left ten trunks of private papers with the local merchant Don Juan Pavajeau, along with instructions to send them to an address in Paris that would be given to him later. On the receipt it was stipulated that Señor Pavajeau would burn the papers in the event the owner could not reclaim them because of circumstances beyond his control.

In the banking establishment of Busch and Company, Fernando deposited two hundred ounces of gold that he discovered at the eleventh hour, with no clue as to their

origin, among his uncle's writing implements. He also
deposited with Juan de Francisco Martín a chest containing thirty-five gold medals, as well as a velvet pouch with
two hundred ninety-four large silver medals, sixty-seven
small ones, and ninety-six medium-size ones, and an identical pouch with forty commemorative medals of silver
and gold, some with the General's profile. He also left
with him the gold table settings they had brought from
Mompox in an old wine crate, some well-worn bed linen,
two trunks of books, a sword studded with diamonds,
and a useless rifle. Among many other, smaller items, the
vestiges of times gone by, there were several pairs of old
spectacles, which increased in strength from the time the
General first discovered his incipient farsightedness, when
he had difficulty shaving at the age of thirty-nine, until
the moment his arm was not long enough for him to
read.

José Palacios, for his part, left in the care of Don Juan
de Dios Amador a chest that had traveled everywhere
with them for several years but whose contents were not
known. It was typical of the General: at one moment he
could not resist a voracious desire for the most unexpected objects or for men with no outstanding merits,
and then, after a time, he had to drag them along with him,
not knowing how to get rid of them. He had carried that
chest from Lima to Santa Fe de Bogotá in 1826, and he
still had it with him after the September 25 attempt,
when he returned to the south for his last war. "We can't
leave it behind when we don't even know if it's ours,"
he would say. When he returned to Santa Fe de Bogotá
for the last time, ready to present his definitive renunciation to the Constituent Congress, the chest was part of the

little that remained of his former imperial baggage. At last they decided to open it in Cartagena during a general inventory of his goods, and inside they discovered a jumble of personal items that had long since been given up for lost. There were four hundred fifteen ounces of gold coined in Colombia, a portrait of General George Washington and a lock of his hair, a gold snuffbox given to him by the King of England, a gold case with diamond keys containing a reliquary, and the great star of Bolivia encrusted with diamonds. José Palacios left all of it, described and annotated, in the house of Juan de Francisco Martín and requested the usual receipt. Their baggage was then reduced to a more rational size, although they still had three of the four trunks with his everyday clothing, another containing ten worn cotton and linen tablecloths, and a chest with gold and silver place settings of unmatched styles, which the General did not want to leave behind or sell, in the event that they needed to set the table for meritorious guests sometime in the future. He had often been advised to auction these articles in order to increase his scant resources, but he always refused, with the argument that they belonged to the state.

With lightened baggage and a reduced entourage, they traveled as far as Turbaco on the first day. They continued the next day in good weather, but before noon they had to take refuge under a roadside shelter, where they spent the night exposed to rain and the malignant winds out of the swamps. The General complained of pains in the spleen and the liver, and José Palacios prepared a potion from the French manual, but the pains became more severe and his fever increased. At dawn he was so prostrate that they carried him, unconscious, to the town of Soledad, where an old friend, Don Pedro Juan Visbal, took him into his house. There he remained for over a month, suffering all manner of pains made worse by the oppressive October rains.

Soledad was well named; its solitude consisted of four burning, desolate streets lined with the houses of the poor, located some two leagues from the place once called Barranca de San Nicolás, which in a few years would become the most prosperous and hospitable city in the country and would later be named Barranquilla. The General could not have found a more peaceful spot or a house more favorable to his health: six Andalusian balconies flooded it with light, and the patio was well suited to meditation under the centenarian ceiba tree. The bedroom window overlooked the deserted little square with its ruined church and the houses painted in holiday colors, with roofs of bitter palm.

But domestic peace did not help him either. The first night he suffered a slight attack of vertigo, but he refused to admit that it was new evidence of his prostration. In accordance with the French manual, he described his illness as an attack of black bile aggravated by a general chill, and a recurrence of rheumatism brought on by exposure. This multiple diagnosis increased his querulous diatribes against simultaneous medicines for different illnesses, for he said that the ones that were good for some ailments were bad for the others. But he also recognized that no medication helps the man who refuses to take it, and he complained every day about not having a good doctor, although he refused to be examined by the many who were sent to him.

In a letter he wrote to his father during this time,

Colonel Wilson said that the General could die at any moment but that his rejection of doctors was the result of lucidity, not contempt. In reality, said Wilson, disease was the only enemy the General feared, and he refused to confront it so that he would not be distracted from the greatest enterprise of his life. "Attending to an illness is like working on a ship," the General had told him. Four years earlier, in Lima, O'Leary had suggested that he accept thorough medical treatment while he was preparing the Constitution of Bolivia, and his reply was decisive:

"You can't win two races at the same time."

He seemed convinced that continual movement and self-reliance were a charm against disease. Fernanda Barriga had been in the habit of tying a bib around his neck and feeding him with a spoon, as if he were a child, and he would accept the food and chew it in silence and even open his mouth again when he had finished. But now he took the plate and spoon from her and ate with his own hand, without a bib, so that everyone would know he did not need anyone. It broke José Palacios' heart when he found the General attempting to do for himself the domestic chores that his servants or orderlies or aides-de-camp had always done for him, and José Palacios was not consoled to see him spill a flask of ink over himself while trying to fill an inkwell. This was something extraordinary, because everyone marveled that the General's hands did not tremble no matter how sick he was, and that his wrist was so steady he still cut and buffed his nails once a week and shaved himself every day.

In his paradise in Lima he had spent a joyous night with a young girl who was covered with fine, straight down over every millimeter of her Bedouin skin. At dawn, while he was shaving, he looked at her lying naked in the bed, adrift in the peaceful sleep of a satisfied woman, and he could not resist the temptation of possessing her forever with a sacramental act. He covered her from head to foot with shaving lather, and with a pleasure like that of love he shaved her clean with his razor, sometimes using his right hand and sometimes his left as he shaved every part of her body, even the eyebrows that grew together, and left her doubly naked inside her magnificent newborn's body. She asked, her soul in shreds, if he really loved her, and he answered with the same ritual phrase he had strewn without pity in so many hearts throughout his life:

"More than anyone else in this world."

In the town of Soledad, again while he was shaving, he submitted to the same sacrificial rite. He began by cutting off one of the few limp white locks of hair he had left, obeying what seemed to be a childish impulse. And then he cut off another in a more conscious way, and after that all of them at random, as if he were cutting grass, while through the cracks in his voice he declaimed his favorite stanzas from *La Araucana*. José Palacios came into the bedroom to see whom he was talking to and found him shaving his lathered skull. Not a hair was left on his head.

The exorcism did not redeem him. He wore the silk cap during the day, and at night he put on the red hood, but he could not moderate the icy gusts of despondency. He got up to pace through the darkness in the enormous moonlit house, only now he could not walk naked on hot nights but wrapped himself in a blanket so he would not shiver with cold. During the day the blanket was not enough, and he resolved to wear the red hood over the silk cap.

The military's quibbling intrigues and the abuses of the politicians exasperated him so much that one afternoon he decided with a blow to the table that he could not endure any of them any longer. "Tell them I'm consumptive so they won't come back," he shouted. His determination was so drastic that he forbade military uniforms and rituals in the house. But he could not survive without them, so that the consolatory interviews and sterile secret meetings continued as always, against his own orders. And then he felt so ill that he agreed to a doctor's visit on the condition that he not examine him or ask him questions about his pains or attempt to give him anything to drink.

"Just to talk," he said.

The physician selected could not have been more to his liking. Hércules Gastelbondo was an immense, placid old man, anointed with contentment, whose skull was radiant with total baldness and who possessed the patience of a drowned man, which in itself alleviated the suffering of others. His incredulity and scientific daring were famous all along the coast. He prescribed chocolate cream with melted cheese for disturbances of the bile, he advised lovemaking during the languors of digestion as a fine palliative promoting long life, and he smoked endless wagon drivers' cigars, which he rolled with rag paper and prescribed to his patients for all sorts of equivocations of the body. The patients themselves said he never effected a complete cure but entertained them instead with his florid eloquence. He would break into plebeian laughter.

"Other doctors lose as many patients as I do," he would say. "But with me they die happier."

He arrived in the carriage of Señor Bartolomé Molinares, which came and went several times a day carrying all kinds of spontaneous visitors until the General prohibited their coming without an invitation. He arrived dressed in wrinkled white linen, making his way through the rain, his pockets overflowing with things to eat, and carrying an umbrella so full of holes that it invited more water than it held back. The first thing he did after the formal greetings was to beg pardon for the stench of his half-smoked cigar. The General, who could not abide tobacco smoke, not then or ever, had already forgiven him.

"I'm used to it," he said. "Manuela smokes cigars more disgusting than yours, even in bed, and of course she's closer to me than you are when she blows the smoke."

Dr. Gastelbondo seized an opportunity that burned his soul.

"Of course," he said. "How is she?"

"Who?"

"Doña Manuela."

The General's reply was abrupt.

"All right."

And he changed the subject in so obvious a manner that the doctor laughed out loud to conceal his impertinence. There was no doubt the General knew that none of his gallant escapades was safe from the gossip of his entourage. He never boasted about his conquests, but there had been so many, and they had been so flagrant, that the secrets of his bedroom were public knowledge.

An ordinary letter took three months to travel from Lima to Caracas, but the gossip about his adventures seemed to fly with the speed of thought. Scandal followed him like a second shadow, and his lovers were marked forever with a cross of ashes, but he complied with the useless duty of protecting his secrets of love under a sacred code. No one ever heard an indiscretion from him regarding a woman he had made love to except José Palacios, who was his accomplice in everything—not even to satisfy a curiosity as innocent as Dr. Gastelbondo's, not even concerning Manuela Sáenz, whose intimacy with him was so public that there was little left to hide.

Except for that momentary unpleasantness, Dr. Gastelbondo was a providential presence. He revived him with his learned lunacies, he shared with him the honey-dipped candies, the almond-paste confections, the chocolate and cassava drops he carried in his pockets, which the General accepted out of courtesy and ate out of distraction. One day he complained that these salon sweets were good only for staving off hunger but not for gaining back weight, which is what he desired. "Don't worry, Excellency," the doctor replied. "Everything that enters the mouth adds weight, and everything that leaves it is debased." The argument seemed so amusing to the General that he agreed to drink a large glass of wine and a cup of arrowroot with the doctor.

Nevertheless, the humor improved by the doctor with so much painstaking care was disturbed by bad news. Someone told the General that, fearing contagion, the owner of the house where he had lived in Cartagena had burned the cot he slept in, the mattress and the sheets, and everything that had passed through his hands during his stay. He ordered Don Juan de Dios Amador to use the money he had left with him to reimburse the owner for the destroyed items as if they were new and to pay for the rental of the house. But not even this could appease his bitterness.

He felt worse a few days later when he learned that Don Joaquín Mosquera had passed through the area on his way to the United States and had not deigned to visit him. By questioning various people without concealing his disquiet, he learned that in fact Mosquera had been on the coast for more than a week while he waited for the ship, seen many mutual friends as well as some enemies, and expressed to all of them his resentment of what he termed the General's ingratitude. At the moment they weighed anchor, when he was already in the launch that would carry him to the ship, he had summarized his fixed idea for everyone who came to see him off.

"Never forget," he told them. "That man doesn't love anybody."

José Palacios knew how sensitive the General was to such reproaches. Nothing pained or bewildered him more than people casting doubt on his affections, and he was capable of parting oceans and moving mountains with the terrible power of his charm until he convinced them of their error. During the plenitude of his glory, Delfina Guardiola, the belle of Angostura, became enraged by his inconstancy and slammed the doors of her house in his face. "You're a great man, General, greater than anyone," she told him. "But love is still too big for you." He climbed through the kitchen window and spent three days with her, and he almost lost a battle as well as his life while he was persuading Delfina to trust in his heart.

Mosquera was beyond his reach, but he spoke about his rancor to everyone he could find. He never wearied of asking how a man had the right to talk of love who had permitted the General to be notified by official communiqué that Venezuela had resolved to repudiate and exile him. "He should be thankful I didn't respond and saved him from the condemnation of history," he shouted. He recalled everything he had done for Mosquera, how much he had helped him become who he was, how he had been obliged to tolerate the stupidities of his rural narcissism. At last he wrote a long, desperate letter to a mutual friend to make certain the sound of his indignation would reach Mosquera anywhere in the world.

On the other hand, the news he did not receive shrouded him like an invisible fog. Urdaneta still had not answered his letters. Briceño Méndez, his man in Venezuela, had sent him a letter along with some of the Jamaican fruits he was so fond of, but the messenger had drowned. The inaction of Justo Briceño, his man on the eastern frontier, drove him to despair. Urdaneta's silence had cast a shadow over the country. The death of Fernández Madrid, his correspondent in London, had cast a shadow over the world.

What the General did not know was that while Urdaneta sent him no news, he maintained an active correspondence with the officers of his entourage, encouraging them to extract from him an unequivocal response. He wrote to O'Leary: "I need to know once and for all if the General does or does not accept the presidency, or if we will spend the rest of our lives chasing after an unreachable phantom." O'Leary as well as others around him tried to hold casual conversations that would provide some answer for Urdaneta, but the General's evasions were insurmountable.

When at last definitive news was received from Riohacha, it was more serious than any evil premonition. General Manuel Valdés, according to plan, had taken the city without resistance on October 20, but the following week Carujo wiped out two of his reconnaissance companies. Valdés presented what was intended as an honorable resignation to Montilla, but the General thought it ignoble. "That swine, he's dying of fright," he said. In only two weeks they were to attempt the capture of Maracaibo, according to the original plan, but simple control of Riohacha was by now an impossible dream.

"God damn it!" shouted the General. "The cream of my generals haven't been able to put down a barracks revolt."

Nevertheless, the news that affected him most was that the people fled at the approach of government troops because they identified them with the General, whom they considered the murderer of Admiral Padilla, an idol in his native Riohacha. This calamity, moreover, seemed to coincide with others throughout the country. Anarchy and chaos raged everywhere, and Urdaneta's government was incapable of controlling them.

On the day he found the General hurling biblical curses at a special emissary who had just brought the latest news from Santa Fe de Bogotá, Dr. Gastelbondo was amazed once again at the revivifying power of rage. "The government's not worth shit! Instead of engaging the people and the men who matter, it paralyzes them," the General shouted. "It will fall again, and it will not rise up a third time, because the men who form it and the masses who sustain it will be exterminated."

The physician's attempts to calm him were futile, for when he finished lashing out against the government he began, at the top of his lungs, to go down the black list of his staff. He said that Colonel Joaquín Barriga, hero of three major battles, was capable of anything: "Even murder." He said that General Pedro Margueytío, whom he suspected of taking part in the conspiracy to kill Sucre, was not competent to command troops. He slashed General González, his most devoted follower in Cauca, with a brutal: "His diseases are feebleness and farting." He collapsed, gasping, into the rocking chair to give his heart the rest it had needed for twenty years. Then he saw Dr. Gastelbondo standing paralyzed with astonishment in the doorway, and he raised his voice.

"After all," he said, "what can you expect of a man who gambled away two houses at dice?"

Dr. Gastelbondo was perplexed.

"Whom are we talking about?" he asked.

"Urdaneta," said the General. "He lost them in Maracaibo to a navy commander, but he made it appear on the documents as if he had sold them."

He took in the air he needed. "Of course they're all saints compared to the slippery bastard Santander," he continued. "His friends stole money from the English loans, they bought state bonds for a tenth of their real value, and the state bought them back at one hundred percent." He explained that in any event he had not opposed the loans for fear of corruption but because he knew they threatened the independence that had cost so much blood.

"I despise debt more than I do the Spanish," he said. "That's why I warned Santander that whatever good we had done for the nation would be worthless if we took on debt because we would go on paying interest till the end of time. Now it's clear: debt will destroy us in the end."

In the early days of the current government he not only had agreed with Urdaneta's decision to respect the lives of the defeated but had celebrated it as a new war ethic: "Our present enemies should not do to us what we did to the Spanish." That is, wage war to the death. But during his dark nights in Soledad he reminded Urdaneta in a terrible letter that every civil war had been won by the side that was most savage.

"Believe me, my dear Doctor," he told the physician. "Our authority and our lives cannot be saved except at the cost of our enemies' blood."

Then, with as little warning as when it began, his rage passed without a trace, and the General undertook the historical absolution of the officers he had just insulted. "In any case, I am the one who is wrong," he said. "They only wanted to win independence, something immediate and concrete, and damned if they haven't done that very well!" He stretched out a hand that was just skin and bone so the doctor could help him to stand, and he concluded with a sigh:

"But I've become lost in a dream, searching for something that doesn't exist."

It was during this time that he decided Iturbide's fate. Toward the end of October Iturbide received a letter from his mother, who still lived in Georgetown, telling him that the progress made by the liberal forces in Mexico had moved the family further and further away from any hope of repatriation. This uncertainty, added to the doubts he had carried with him since childhood, became unbearable. One afternoon, when the General was walking along the corridor leaning on Iturbide's arm, he happened to evoke an unexpected memory.

"I have only one bad recollection of Mexico," he said. "In Veracruz the harbor captain's mastiffs tore apart two pups I was taking with me to Spain."

In any event, he said, that was his first experience of the world, and it had marked him forever. Veracruz was supposed to be a brief stopover on his first trip to Europe, in February 1799, but his stay lasted almost two months because of an English blockade of Havana, which was the next port of call. The delay gave him time to travel by coach to Mexico City, climbing almost three thousand meters between snowcapped volcanoes and hallucinatory deserts, which were nothing like the pastoral dawns of the Aragua Valley, where he had lived until then. "I thought it was how the moon must look," he said. In Mexico City he was amazed at the purity of the air, dazzled by the profusion and cleanliness of the public markets, where red maguey worms, armadillos, river worms, mosquito eggs, grasshoppers, the larvae of black ants, wildcats, water beetles in honey, corn wasps, cultivated iguanas, rattlesnakes, all kinds of birds, midget dogs, and a strain of beans that jumped without stopping, as if they had a life of their own, were all sold as food. "They eat everything that moves," he said. He was astounded by the clear waters of the numerous canals crossing the city, the boats painted in Sunday colors, the splendor and abundance of the flowers. But he was depressed by the short February days, the taciturn Indians, the eternal drizzle, everything that would later oppress his heart in Santa Fe de Bogotá, in Lima, in La Paz, up and down the entire length and height of the Andes, which he suffered then for the first time. The Bishop, to whom he brought letters of introduction, took him by the hand to an audience with the Viceroy, who seemed more episcopal than the Bishop and paid almost no attention to the thin, dark boy who dressed like a dandy and declared his admiration for the French Revolution. "It could have cost me my life," the General said in amusement. "But perhaps I thought one had to say something about politics to a viceroy, and at the age of sixteen that was all I knew." Before continuing his journey he wrote to his uncle, Don Pedro Palacio y Sojo, the first of his letters that would be preserved. "My handwriting was so bad even I couldn't read it," he said, weak with laughter. "But I explained to my uncle that the fatigue of travel made it look the way it did." In a page and a half he made forty spelling mistakes, two of them in the same word: "sunn" for "son."

Iturbide could not comment, for his memory had nothing to remember. All he retained of Mexico was a recollection of misfortunes that had worsened his congenital melancholy, and the General had reason to understand this.

"Don't stay with Urdaneta," he told him. "And don't go with your family to the United States. It's omnipotent and terrible, and its tale of liberty will end in a plague of miseries for us all."

The effect of his words was to throw yet another doubt into a swamp of uncertainty. Iturbide exclaimed:

"Don't frighten me, General!"

"Don't be frightened," said the General in a calm voice. "Go to Mexico, even if they kill you or even if you die. And go now while you're still young, because one day it will be too late, and then you won't feel at home here or there. You'll feel like a stranger everywhere, and that's worse than being dead." He looked him straight in the eye, placed his open hand on his own chest, and concluded:

"Just look at me."

And so Iturbide left at the beginning of December with two letters for Urdaneta. In one of them the General said that Iturbide, Wilson, and Fernando were the most trustworthy people in his house. He stayed in Santa Fe de Bogotá with no fixed destination until April of the following year, when Urdaneta was deposed by a Santanderist conspiracy. With her exemplary persistence, his mother arranged for him to be named secretary of the Mexican legation in Washington. He spent the rest of his life in the oblivion of public service, and nothing was heard of the family until thirty-two years later, when Maximilian of Hapsburg, installed as Emperor of Mexico by French arms, adopted two Iturbide boys of the third generation and named them as successors to his chimerical throne.

In the General's second letter to Urdaneta he asked that all his past and future letters be destroyed so that no trace would remain of his dark hours. Urdaneta did not oblige the General, who had made a similar request to General

Santander five years before: "Don't have my letters published, whether I'm alive or dead, because they are written with a good deal of freedom and disorder." He was not obliged by Santander either, whose letters, unlike those of the General, were perfect in form and content, and it was evident at first glance that he wrote them with the awareness that their ultimate destination was history.

Starting with the letter from Veracruz and ending with the last one he dictated, six days before his death, the General wrote at least ten thousand letters, some in his own hand, others dictated to his secretaries, still others composed by them according to his instructions. A little over three thousand letters and some eight thousand documents with his signature have been preserved. Sometimes he drove his secretaries mad. Or vice versa. Once he thought a letter he had just dictated was not written in a fair hand, and instead of ordering another copy he himself added a line about the secretary: "As you must realize, Martell is more imbecilic than ever today." In 1817, on the eve of his departure from Angostura to complete the liberation of the continent, he brought his governmental affairs up-to-date with fourteen documents dictated in a single sitting. Perhaps this was the origin of the legend, which has never been disproved, that he would dictate several letters to several different secretaries at the same time.

October was reduced to the sound of rain. He did not leave his room again, and Dr. Gastelbondo had to call on his most learned resources so that he would permit the doctor to visit and feed him. During the General's pensive siestas, when he lay in the hammock without moving and contemplated the rain in the deserted square, José Palacios had the impression that he was calling to mind even the smallest details of his past life.

"Merciful God," he sighed one afternoon. "What has happened to Manuela!"

"All we know is that she's well, because we haven't heard anything about her," said José Palacios.

For a silence had surrounded her ever since Urdaneta assumed power. The General had not written to her again, but he instructed Fernando to keep her up-to-date on their journey. Her last letter had arrived late in August, and it contained so much confidential news concerning preparations for the military coup that between her illegible writing and the deliberate obfuscation of facts in order to throw the enemy off the track, it was not easy to unravel its mysteries.

Forgetting the General's good advice, and with thorough and perhaps excessive jubilation, Manuela had assumed her role as the nation's leading Bolivarist and unleashed her own paper war against the government. President Mosquera did not dare take action against her, but he did not prevent his ministers from doing so. Manuela responded to the aggressions of the official press with printed diatribes that she distributed on horseback, escorted by her slavewomen, along the Calle Real. Her lance at the ready, she pursued those who distributed broadsides against the General down the cobbled alleys of the outlying districts, and with even more insulting slogans she covered over the painted insults that appeared every day on the walls.

In the end, the official war was waged against her in her own name. But she did not flinch. Her confidants inside the government informed her, on a day of patriotic fiestas, that fireworks were being mounted on the main square with a caricature of the General dressed as the king of fools. Manuela and her slavewomen rode roughshod over the guards and knocked down the structure in a cavalry charge. Then the Mayor himself, at the head of a squad of soldiers, tried to arrest her in her bed, but she was waiting for them with a pair of cocked pistols, and mediation by friends of both parties was all that prevented an even greater misfortune.

The only thing that placated her was General Urdaneta's assumption of power. She had a true friend in him, and Urdaneta had in her his most enthusiastic accomplice. When she was alone in Santa Fe de Bogotá, while the General was fighting in the south against the Peruvian invaders, Urdaneta was the trusted friend who saw to her safety and attended to her needs. When the General made his unfortunate statement in the Admirable Congress, it was Manuela who convinced him to write to Urdaneta: "I offer you all my old friendship and an absolute and heartfelt reconciliation." Urdaneta accepted the gallant offer, and after the military coup Manuela returned the favor. She disappeared from public life in so absolute a fashion that by the beginning of October the rumor was circulating that she had gone to the United States, and no one disputed it. And therefore José Palacios was right: Manuela was fine, because they had heard nothing about her.

During one of those meticulous examinations of the past, when he was lost in the rain, sick of waiting and not knowing for what or for whom, or why, the General touched bottom: he cried in his sleep. When José Palacios heard the quiet sobs he thought they came from the stray dog picked up on the river. But they came from his master. He was disconcerted because during their long years of intimacy he had seen him cry only once, and that had been with rage, not with sorrow. He called Captain Ibarra, who was standing watch in the corridor, and he too listened to the sound of tears.

"That will help him," said Ibarra.

"It will help all of us," said José Palacios.

The General slept later than usual. He was not awakened by either the birds in the nearby orchard or the church bells, and José Palacios bent over the hammock several times to see if he was breathing. When he opened his eyes it was past eight o'clock, and the heat had begun.

"Saturday, October 16," said José Palacios. "The Day of Purity."

The General got up from the hammock and looked through the window at the solitary, dusty square, the church with the peeling walls, the turkey buzzards fighting over the remains of a dead dog. The harshness of the early sun announced a day of suffocating heat.

"Let's get out of here," said the General. "I don't want to hear the shots of the firing squad."

José Palacios shuddered. He had lived that moment in another place and another time, and the General, just as he had been then, was barefoot on the rough bricks of the floor, wearing long underpants and the sleeping cap on his shaved head. It was an old dream repeated in reality.

"We won't hear them," said José Palacios, and he added with deliberate precision: "General Piar was shot in Angostura, and not today at five in the afternoon but on a day like today thirteen years ago."

General Manuel Piar, a hard mulatto from Curaçao who at the age of thirty-five had earned as much glory as anyone in the national militias, had put the General's authority to the test at a time when the liberating army required its forces united as never before in order to stop Morillo's advances. Piar called on blacks, mulattoes, zambos, and all the destitute of the country to resist the white aristocracy of Caracas, personified by the General. Piar's popularity and messianic aura were comparable only to those of José Antonio Páez, or the royalist Boves, and he even made a favorable impression on some white officers in the liberating army. The General had exhausted all his arts of persuasion, and on his orders Piar was arrested and brought to Angostura, the provisional capital, where the General was entrenched with the officers close to him, several of whom would accompany him on his final journey along the Magdalena River. A court-martial named by him, which included friends of Piar, passed summary judgment. José María Carreño acted as prosecutor. Piar's official advocate did not have to lie when he praised him as one of the outstanding heroes in the struggle against the power of Spain. He was declared guilty of desertion, insurrection, and treason, and was condemned to death and the loss of his military titles. Knowing his merits, no one believed that the sentence would be confirmed by the General, least of all at a time when Morillo had recaptured several provinces and morale was so low among the patriots that there was fear of a rout. The General was subjected to every kind of pressure, he listened with cordiality to the opinions of his closest friends, Briceño Méndez among them, but his determination was unshakable. He revoked the sentence of demotion and confirmed the sentence of death by firing squad, which he made even worse by ordering a public execution. It was an endless night when anything evil could happen. On October 16, at five o'clock in the afternoon, the sentence was carried out under the brutal sun in the main square of Angostura, the city that Piar himself had wrested from the Spanish six months before. The commander of the firing squad had ordered the removal of the remains of a dead dog that the turkey buzzards were devouring, and he had the gates closed to keep stray animals from disrupting the dignity of the execution. He denied Piar the final honor of giving the order to fire and blindfolded him against his will, but he could not prevent him from bidding farewell to the world with a kiss to the crucifix and a salute to the flag.

The General had refused to witness the execution. The only man with him in his house was José Palacios, who saw him struggling to hold back the tears when he heard the volley. In his proclamation to the troops he said: "Yesterday was a day of sorrow for me." For the rest of his life he would repeat that it was a political necessity that saved the country, persuaded the rebels, and avoided civil war. In any case, it was the most savage use of power in his life, but the most opportune as well, for with it he consolidated his authority, unified his command, and cleared the road to his glory.

Thirteen years later, in the town of Soledad, he did not even seem to realize that he had been the victim of one of time's caprices. He continued to look out at the square until an old woman in rags crossed the plaza, leading a burro loaded down with coconuts to be sold for their milk, and the turkey buzzards were frightened away by their shadows. Then he returned to the hammock with a sigh of relief, and without anyone's asking he gave the answer that José Palacios had wanted to hear ever since the tragic night in Angostura.

"I would do it again," he said.

THE GREATEST DANGER was walking, not because of the risk of a fall but because the effort it cost him was too evident. On the other hand, it was reasonable for someone to help him up and down the stairs in the house even if he was capable of doing it alone. Nevertheless, when he in fact needed an arm to lean on he did not allow anyone to offer him one.

"Thank you," he would say, "but I can still do it myself."

One day he could not. He was about to descend a flight of stairs alone when the world disappeared. "I lost my footing, I don't know how, I was half dead," he told a friend. It was worse than that: it was a miracle he did not kill himself, because the fainting spell threw him against the side of the stairs, and he did not roll all the way down only because his body was so light.

Dr. Gastelbondo rushed him to Barranca de San Nicolás in the carriage of Don Bartolomé Molinares, who had housed the General on an earlier visit and had ready for him the same large, airy bedroom facing Calle Ancha.

On the way a thick substance that gave him no peace began to ooze from his left tear duct. He was detached from everything as he traveled, and at times he seemed to be praying when in reality he was murmuring entire stanzas from his favorite poems. The doctor wiped his eye with his handkerchief, surprised that the General did not do it himself since he was so punctilious about his personal cleanliness. He barely roused himself at the entrance to the city when a herd of runaway cows almost trampled the carriage and did, in fact, overturn the berlin belonging to the parish priest, who somersaulted into the air and then leaped to his feet, white with sand from head to toe, and with his forehead and hands bloodied. When he recovered from the shock, the grenadiers had to open a path through the idle onlookers and naked children who wanted only to enjoy the accident and had no idea of the identity of the passenger who looked like a seated corpse in the darkness of the carriage.

The doctor introduced the priest as one of the few who had supported the General in the days when the bishops thundered against him from their pulpits and he was excommunicated for being a lecherous Mason. The General did not seem to understand what had happened and only became aware of the world when he saw blood on the cassock of the priest, who asked him to intervene with his authority to keep cows from wandering loose in a city where it was no longer possible to walk in safety because of all the carriages on public thoroughfares.

"Don't let it bother you, Your Reverence," he said without looking at him. "It's the same all over the country."

The eleven o'clock sun hung motionless over the sandpits of the wide, desolate streets, and the entire city reverberated with heat. The General was glad he did not have to spend more time there than necessary to recuperate from the fall, and he wanted to go out sailing on a day when the seas were rough, because the French manual said that seasickness was good for ridding the body of bilious humors and cleansing the stomach. He soon recovered from the fall, but it was not so easy to arrange for a boat and bad weather.

In a fury at his body's recalcitrance, the General did not have strength for any social or political activity, and if he received visitors they were old friends who came to the city to say goodbye. The house was large and as cool as November would allow, and its owners converted it into his personal hospital. Don Bartolomé Molinares was one of the many people ruined by the wars that had left him with nothing but the position of postmaster, which he had held for the past ten years without pay. He was such a kindhearted man that the General had called him Papa ever since his previous visit to the city. His wife, a splendid-looking woman with an indomitable matriarchal vocation, spent her hours making bobbin lace, which she sold at a good price on the European ships, but from the moment the General arrived she devoted all her time to him, to the point where she came into conflict with Fernanda Barriga because she put olive oil in his lentils, convinced that it was good for diseases of the chest, and he was obliged to eat them out of gratitude.

What bothered the General most during this time was the oozing tear duct, which kept him in a somber frame of mind until he at last agreed to chamomile eyewashes. After that he joined the card games, an ephemeral consolation for the torment of the mosquitoes and the sorrows of twilight. During a half-serious conversation with the owners of the house, he surprised them by declaring, in one of his few crises of repentance, that one good agreement was worth a thousand successful lawsuits.

"In politics too?" asked Señor Molinares.

"Above all in politics," said the General. "Our not making peace with Santander has ruined us all."

"As long as you have friends there is hope," said Molinares.

"On the contrary," said the General. "It was not the perfidy of my enemies but the diligence of my friends that destroyed my glory. It was they who launched me on the calamity of the Ocaña Convention, who entangled me in the disaster of the monarchy, who obliged me first to seek reelection with the same arguments they later used to force my renunciation, and who now hold me captive in this country when I no longer have any reason to be here."

The rain became eternal, and the humidity began to open cracks in his memory. The heat was so intense that even at night the General had to change his drenched shirt several times. "I feel as if I've been cooked in a double boiler," he complained. One afternoon he spent more than three hours sitting on the balcony and watching the debris of the poor districts wash down the street—the household utensils and dead animals swept away by the torrent of a seismic downpour that endeavored to pull up houses by their roots.

Commander Juan Glen, the prefect of the city, arrived in the middle of the storm with the news that he had arrested a woman in Señor Visbal's service for selling as holy relics the hair the General had cut off in Soledad. Once again he became despondent at the sorrowful thought that everything of his would turn into goods for sale.

"They already treat me as if I had died," he said.

Señora Molinares had pulled her rocking chair up to the card table so she could hear every word.

"They treat you like what you are," she said. "A saint."

"Well," he said, "if that's the case, they should let that poor innocent go."

He did not read again. If he had to write letters he was satisfied with giving instructions to Fernando, and he did not even look at the few he had to sign. He spent the morning on the balcony, contemplating the sand desert of the streets, watching the water burro pass by, and the brazen, cheerful black woman who sold sun-dried mojarra fish, and the children leaving school at the stroke of eleven, and the parish priest in his tattered, patched cassock, who blessed him from the atrium of the church and was melting in the heat. At one o'clock, while the others were taking their siestas, he walked along the putrefying gutters, frightening away with his mere shadow the flocks of turkey buzzards from the market, greeting the few people who recognized him even though he was half dead and wore civilian clothes, walking as far as the grenadiers' barracks, a large shed of cane and mud that faced the river port. He was concerned for the morale of the troops, who were rotting with a boredom that seemed far too evident in the disorder of the barracks, where the stench had become unbearable. But a sergeant, who appeared to be in a stupor because of the suffocating afternoon heat, left him flabbergasted with the truth.

"What's fucked us up isn't morale, Excellency," he told him. "It's gonorrhea."

Only then did he learn the facts. The local doctors, having exhausted their science with distracting enemas and milk sugar palliatives, had passed the problem on to the military authorities, who could not agree on what to do. The whole city was aware of the danger that threatened it, and the glorious Army of the Republic was seen as the emissary of a plague. The General, less alarmed than had been feared, resolved the matter with one stroke by imposing an absolute quarantine.

When the lack of news, either good or bad, began to drive him to despair, a courier on horseback brought an obscure message from General Montilla in Santa Marta: "The man is ours and negotiations are going well." The General thought the message so strange, and its form so irregular, that he interpreted it as a staff matter of the greatest significance, perhaps related to the Riohacha campaign, to which he attributed a historic importance that no one wished to contemplate.

Ever since governmental neglect destroyed the systems of ciphered messages that had proved so useful during the first conspiracies against Spain, it was normal at this time to intentionally obscure messages and muddle military dispatches for reasons of security. The idea that the military were deceiving him was a long-standing concern of his that was shared by Montilla, and this further complicated the enigma of the message and intensified the General's uneasiness. And therefore he sent José Palacios to

Santa Marta on the pretext that he was buying fresh fruits and vegetables and a few bottles of dry sherry and pale beer not available in the local market. But the real purpose was to decipher the mystery. It was very simple: Montilla meant that Miranda Lyndsay's husband had been transferred from the prison in Honda to the one in Cartagena and that his pardon was a matter of days. The General felt so cheated by the simplicity of the enigma that he did not even take pleasure in the service he had rendered his Jamaican savior.

Early in November the Bishop of Santa Marta, in a letter written by his own hand, informed him that it had been he, with his apostolic mediation, who had at last soothed tempers in the nearby town of La Ciénaga, where an attempt at civil insurrection in support of Riohacha had taken place the week before. The General thanked him, also in his own hand, and he asked Montilla to do the same, but he did not like the Bishop's haste in calling in the debt.

Relations between the General and Monsignor Estévez had never been very easy. Beneath his meek good shepherd's crozier, the Bishop was a passionate but unenlightened politician, opposed deep in his heart to the Republic, opposed to the integration of the continent and to everything connected with the General's political thinking. In the Admirable Congress, where he had served as vice-president, the Bishop had understood very well that his real duty was to obstruct Sucre's power, and he had done so with more malice than efficiency, both in the election of officials and in their shared mission to find an amicable solution to the conflict with Venezuela. Señor and Señora Molinares, who knew about these disagreements, were not at all surprised when the General greeted them at four o'clock tea with one of his prophetic parables:

"What will become of our children in a country where revolutions are ended by the diligence of a bishop?"

Señora Molinares replied with an affectionate but firm reproach:

"Even if Your Excellency is right, I don't want to hear it," she said. "We're old-style Catholics."

He recovered without delay:

"Much more old-style than the Bishop, no doubt, who hasn't reestablished order in La Ciénaga for the love of God but in order to keep his parishioners united in the war against Cartagena."

"We're opposed to Cartagena's tyranny here too," said Señor Molinares.

"I know," he said. "Every Colombian is an enemy country."

In Soledad the General had asked Montilla to send a light boat to the neighboring port of Sabanilla for him to use in his plan to expel bile by means of seasickness. Montilla had delayed satisfying his request because Don Joaquín de Mier, a Spanish republican and the partner of Commodore Elbers, had promised him one of the steamboats pressed into occasional service on the Magdalena River. When this proved impossible, Montilla sent an English merchant ship that arrived unannounced in Santa Marta in mid-November. As soon as he heard the news, the General let it be known that he would take advantage of the opportunity to leave the country. "I'm determined to go anywhere rather than die here," he said. Then he was shaken by the presentiment that Camille was waiting for him, watching the horizon from a flower-filled balcony facing the sea, and he sighed:

"They love me in Jamaica."

He instructed José Palacios to begin packing, and that night he stayed up very late trying to find some papers that he wanted to take with him at all costs. He was so exhausted that he slept for three hours. At dawn, when his eyes were already open, he became conscious of where he was only when José Palacios announced the saint's day.

"I dreamed I was in Santa Marta," he said. "It was a very clean city, with white houses that were all the same, but the mountain blocked the view of the sea."

"Then it wasn't Santa Marta," said José Palacios. "It was Caracas."

For the General's dream had revealed to him that they would not go to Jamaica. Fernando had been in the port since early that morning arranging the details of the voyage, and on his return he found his uncle dictating a letter to Wilson in which he requested a new passport from Urdaneta because the one issued by the deposed government was worthless. That was the only explanation he gave for canceling the trip.

Nevertheless, everyone agreed that the real reason was the news he received that morning concerning operations in Riohacha, which did nothing but make the earlier reports even more calamitous. The nation was falling apart from one ocean to the other, the specter of civil war raged over its ruins, and nothing was as distasteful to the General as running from adversity. "There is no sacrifice we are not prepared to make to save Riohacha," he said.

Dr. Gastelbondo, more disturbed by what disturbed the invalid than by his incurable diseases, was the only man who knew how to tell him the truth without mortifying him.

"The world's coming to an end and you worry about Riohacha," he said. "We never dreamed we'd be so honored."

His reply was immediate:

"The fate of the world depends on Riohacha."

He really thought it did, and he could not disguise his uneasiness at the fact that they had planned to take Maracaibo by this time but instead were further than ever from victory. And as December approached with its topaz afternoons, he feared not only that Riohacha, and perhaps the entire coast, would be lost but that Venezuela would mount an expedition to destroy the last vestiges of his illusions.

The weather had begun to change during the previous week, and where there had been mournful rains a diaphanous sky opened, and the nights were full of stars. The General remained detached from the marvels of the world, at times preoccupied in the hammock, at times playing cards with no concern for his luck. Then, when they were playing in the drawing room, a breeze laden with sea roses blew the cards out of their hands and made the window latches jump. Señora Molinares, exalted by this premature announcement of the providential season, exclaimed: "It's December!" Wilson and José Laurencio Silva hurried to close the windows in order to prevent the breeze from carrying away the house. The General was the only one who remained preoccupied with his fixed idea.

"December already, and we're still in the same place," he said. "They're right when they say it's better to have bad sergeants than useless generals."

He continued playing, and in the middle of the game he put his cards to one side and told José Laurencio Silva to prepare everything for traveling. Colonel Wilson, who on the previous day had unloaded his luggage for the second time, was perplexed.

"The boat left," he said.

The General knew that. "It wasn't the right one," he said. "We have to go to Riohacha, to see if we can persuade our illustrious generals to decide to win at last." Before leaving the table he felt obliged to justify himself to his hosts.

"By now it's not even a necessity of war," he told them, "but a question of honor."

And so he sailed at eight o'clock in the morning of December 1 on the brigantine *Manuel*, which Señor Joaquín de Mier placed at his disposal to use however he pleased: to take a sail to expel bile, to convalesce from his many illnesses and countless sorrows on Señor Mier's sugar plantation at San Pedro Alejandrino, or to continue straight on to Riohacha to attempt once again the redemption of the Americas. General Mariano Montilla, who arrived on the brigantine with General José María Carreño, arranged for the *Manuel* to be escorted by the North American frigate *Grampus*, which, in addition to being well armed, had on board a good surgeon, Dr. Night. Nevertheless, when Montilla saw the General's pitiable condition, he did not want to be guided by Dr. Night's judgment alone, and he consulted his local physician.

"I don't believe he'll even survive the crossing," said

Dr. Gastelbondo. "But let him go: anything's better than living like this."

The channels through Ciénaga Grande, the great swamp, were slow and hot and gave off fatal vapors, and so they traveled on the open sea, taking advantage of the first trade winds from the north, which were early and benign that year. A cabin was ready for him on the well-maintained square-sailed brigantine, which was clean and comfortable and had a lighthearted way in the water.

The General boarded in good spirits and wanted to remain on deck to see the estuary of the Great Magdalena River, whose mud gave an ashen color to the water for many leagues out to sea. He was wearing old corduroy trousers, the Andean cap, and an English sailor's jacket given him by the captain of the frigate, and his appearance improved in the sunlight and the vagabond breeze. In his honor the frigate's crew caught a gigantic shark, in whose belly they found a variety of metal objects, including a pair of spurs. He enjoyed everything with a tourist's pleasure until he was overcome by fatigue and sank down into his own soul. Then he signaled José Palacios to approach and whispered in his ear:

"Papa Molinares must be burning the mattress and burying the spoons by now."

Toward midday they passed Ciénaga Grande, a vast extension of muddy waters where all the birds of the air fought over a school of golden mojarra. On the burning saltpeter plain between the swamp and the sea, where the light was clearer and the air was purer, there were fishing villages with tackle spread out to dry in the patios, and beyond them lay the mysterious town of La Ciénaga, whose diurnal phantoms had caused the disciples of Humboldt to doubt their science. On the other side of Ciénaga Grande rose the crown of eternal ice on the Sierra Nevada.

The high-spirited brigantine, almost flying over the water in the silence of the sails, was so quick and stable that it did not cause the convulsion desired by the General to expel the bile from his body. Nevertheless, when they passed a ridge of the Sierra that extended toward the sea, the water turned rough and the wind blustered. The General observed those changes with growing anticipation, for the world began to spin with the carrion birds circling overhead, an icy perspiration soaked his shirt, and his eyes filled with tears. Montilla and Wilson had to hold him, for he was so light that a sudden wave could have swept him overboard. At dusk, when they entered the calm waters of Santa Marta Bay, there was nothing left for him to expel from his ravaged body, and he lay exhausted in the captain's bunk, moribund but in the rapture of a dream come true. General Montilla was so disturbed by his condition that before proceeding with disembarkation he had Dr. Night see him again, and the physician decided that the General should be carried to land in a litter.

Aside from the Santa Martans' total lack of interest in everything that smacked of officialdom, there were other reasons why so few people were waiting on the dock. Santa Marta had been one of the most difficult cities to lure to the republican cause. Even after independence was confirmed at the battle of Boyacá, Viceroy Sámano took refuge there to await reinforcements from Spain. The General himself had attempted to liberate Santa Marta several times, and only Montilla succeeded, after the Republic was already established. Royalist rancor was added to the animosity everyone felt toward Cartagena for being the central government's favored city, a feeling the General fomented without realizing it because of his passion for the Cartagenans. The strongest reason, however, even for many of his loyal supporters, was the summary execution of Admiral José Prudencio Padilla, who, to make matters even worse, had been as much a mulatto as General Piar. The bitter feelings deepened with the takeover of power by Urdaneta, who had been president of the court-martial that issued the death sentence. And so the bells in the cathedral did not ring as planned and no one could explain why, and the cannon in El Morro Fortress fired no salute because that morning it was discovered that the powder in the arsenal was wet. The soldiers had toiled until just before the General's arrival so he would not see the "Long Live José Prudencio" scrawled in charcoal on the side of the cathedral. The official announcements of his arrival had almost no effect on the handful of men in the port. The most notable absence was that of Bishop Estévez, the first and most eminent of the dignitaries who had been informed.

Don Joaquín de Mier would remember until the end of his long life the dreadful creature carried ashore in a litter in the lethargy of early evening, wrapped in a woolen blanket, wearing one cap over another and both pulled down to his eyebrows, and with hardly a breath of life. Nevertheless, what he remembered best was his burning hand, his labored breathing, the supernatural elegance with which he left the litter and stood, holding himself upright with the help of his aides-de-camp, to greet them all, one by one, with their titles and complete names.

Then he allowed himself to be carried to the berlin and collapsed on the seat, his listless head resting on the back but his avid eyes drinking in the life that for him was passing just one time and forever on the other side of the window.

The line of carriages had only to cross the avenue to reach the old customhouse that had been reserved for him. It was about to strike eight o'clock on a Wednesday, but the first December breezes brought a Saturday air to the promenade along the bay. The streets were broad and dirty, and the masonry houses with their continuous balconies were better preserved than those in the rest of the country. Whole families had brought out furniture and sat on the sidewalks, and some even received their visitors in the middle of the street. The clouds of fireflies among the trees lit the seafront avenue with a phosphorescent brilliance more intense than the lamplight.

The recently restored old customhouse, the first in the country, had been built two hundred ninety-nine years before. The bedroom on the second floor, with a view of the bay, had been prepared for the General, but he preferred to spend most of the time in the principal drawing room, where the only rings for hanging a hammock were located. In the same room was the rough, carved mahogany table where his embalmed body would lie in state sixteen days later, wearing the blue tunic of his rank without the eight buttons of pure gold that someone would tear off in the confusion of death.

He was the only one who did not seem to believe he was so close to that fate. But Dr. Alexandre Prosper Révérend, the French physician brought by General Montilla on an emergency call at nine o'clock in the evening, did not need to take his pulse to know he had begun to die years before. Because of the weakness of his neck, the contraction of his chest, and the yellowness of his face, the doctor thought it was a case of damaged lungs, which was confirmed by his observations in the days that followed. In the initial private interview, held half in Spanish and half in French, he established that the patient possessed a masterful talent for distorting his symptoms and misinterpreting his pain, and was using the little breath he had left in an effort not to cough or spit during the consultation. The initial diagnosis was confirmed by clinical examination. But beginning with that night's medical bulletin, the first of the thirty-three he would issue during the next two weeks, the physician attributed as much importance to moral torment as to physical calamities.

Dr. Révérend, at thirty-four, was self-confident, well educated, and well dressed. He had arrived six years earlier, disenchanted with the restoration of the Bourbons to the throne of France, and he spoke and wrote correct, fluent Spanish, but the General took advantage of the first opportunity to demonstrate his good French. The doctor captivated him at once.

"Your Excellency has a Parisian accent," he told him.

"The Rue Vivienne," he said, becoming animated. "How did you know?"

"I pride myself on guessing the very street in Paris where a person grew up, just by his accent," said the physician, "although I was born and raised in a village in Normandy."

"Good cheese but bad wine," said the General.

"Perhaps it's the secret of our good health," said the doctor.

He gained the General's confidence with his painless sounding of the boyish side of his spirit. He gained it even more when, instead of prescribing new medicines, he administered by his own hand a spoonful of the syrup prepared by Dr. Gastelbondo to alleviate his cough, and a tranquilizing pill that the General took with no resistance because his desire to sleep was so great. They continued chatting about this and that until the soporific took effect and the doctor tiptoed out of the room. General Montilla, who accompanied him to his house along with other officers, was alarmed when the doctor told him he planned to sleep in his clothes in the event an emergency arose in the middle of the night.

Révérend and Night held several meetings that week but came to no agreement. Révérend was convinced the General suffered from a pulmonary lesion whose origin was an ill-treated catarrh. Because of his color and evening fevers, Dr. Night was convinced it was a case of chronic malaria. They did agree, nevertheless, on the gravity of his condition. They requested other doctors to settle their differences, but the three from Santa Marta, and others from the province, refused to cooperate, giving no explanation. And therefore Drs. Révérend and Night agreed on a compromise treatment based on pectoral balms for catarrh and doses of quinine for malaria.

The patient's condition had deteriorated even further over the weekend because of a glass of donkey's milk he drank on his own account without the doctors' knowledge. His mother would drink it warm with honey, and gave it to him when he was very young to ease his cough. But that soothing taste, associated in so intimate a way with his earliest memories, disturbed his bile and devastated his body, and his prostration was so pronounced that Dr. Night sailed earlier than planned in order to send a specialist from Jamaica. He in fact sent two, who were very qualified, and he did so with a speed that was incredible for the time, but they arrived too late.

With it all, the General's state of mind did not correspond to his prostration, for he behaved as if the diseases that were killing him were no more than trivial annoyances. He spent the nights awake in the hammock contemplating the turns of the light in El Morro Fortress, enduring pain so his moans would not betray him, always staring at the splendor of the bay that he had considered the most beautiful in the world.

"My eyes hurt from looking at it so much," he would say.

During the day he made an effort to show the diligence of other times, and he would call Ibarra, or Wilson, or Fernando, or whoever was close by, to give instructions concerning the letters he no longer had the patience to dictate. Only José Palacios had a heart lucid enough to realize that these pressing matters were the urgencies of his last days. For he was arranging the destiny of those near to him, and even of some who were not in Santa Marta. He forgot the quarrel with his former secretary, General Juan José Santana, and obtained a position for him in the foreign service so he could enjoy his new life as a married man. He paid well-deserved tribute to the good heart of General José María Carreño and set him on the path that would bring him, in time, to the designated presidency of Venezuela. He requested Urdaneta to provide service documents for Andrés Ibarra and José Laurencio Silva so they could at least enjoy a regular income in the future. Silva became General in Chief and Secretary of the Army and Navy in his own country and died at the age of eighty-two, his sight clouded by the cataracts he had feared so much, and living on a certificate of disability he obtained after arduous efforts to prove his combat service by means of his numerous scars.

The General also attempted to convince Pedro Briceño Méndez to return to New Granada to become Minister of War, but the rush of history did not give him time. He left his nephew Fernando a legacy to facilitate his career in public administration. He advised General Diego Ibarra, his first aide-de-camp and one of the few people with whom he used the intimate form of address in private and in public, to go where he would be more useful than in Venezuela. On his deathbed he would even ask General Justo Briceño, toward whom he still felt some resentment, for the last favor of his life.

His officers may never have imagined to what extent this distribution of benefits joined their destinies. For better or worse, all of them would share the rest of their lives, including the historical irony of being reunited in Venezuela five years later, fighting at the side of Commander Pedro Carujo in a military adventure intended to achieve the Bolivarist idea of integration.

These were not political maneuvers but legacies to his orphans, which was confirmed by Wilson in the surprising statement the General dictated in a letter to Urdaneta: "The Riohacha enterprise is lost." That same afternoon the General received a note from Bishop Estévez the Unpredictable, who asked him to use his good offices with the central government to have Santa Marta and Rio-hacha declared departments, thus putting an end to their historic discord with Cartagena. The General made a dispirited gesture when José Laurencio Silva finished reading him the letter. "The only ideas that occur to Colombians are for ways to divide the nation," he said. Later, as he dispatched back correspondence with Fernando, he was even more bitter.

"Don't even answer it," he told him. "Let them wait until I'm six feet under, and then they can do whatever they like."

His constant longing to change the weather kept him on the brink of dementia. If it was humid he wanted it dry, if it was cold he wanted it milder, if it was mountain weather he wanted it coastal. This heightened his perpetual restless desire to have the window opened to let in the air and to have it closed again, to have the easy chair moved into the light and to have it moved back again, and he seemed to find relief only by swaying in the hammock with the meager strength remaining to him.

The days in Santa Marta became so dismal that when the General calmed down somewhat and repeated his desire to leave for Señor de Mier's country house, Dr. Révérend was the first to encourage him, aware that these were the final symptoms of a prostration from which there was no return. The night before the journey the General wrote to a friend: "I will die in a couple of months at the latest." It was a revelation to all of them, because on very few occasions in his life, and even less in recent years, had anyone heard him mention death.

La Florida de San Pedro Alejandrino, a league from

Santa Marta in the foothills of the Sierra Nevada, was a sugar plantation with a mill for making brown sugar loaves. The General rode in Señor de Mier's berlin along the dusty road. Ten days later the shell of his body, wrapped in his old upland blanket and lying in an oxcart, would travel the same road in the opposite direction. Long before he saw the house he smelled the breeze, heavy with hot molasses, and he was ensnared by nostalgia.

"It's the smell of San Mateo," he sighed.

The San Mateo Plantation, twenty-four leagues from Caracas, was the center of his longing. There he lost his father at the age of three, his mother at the age of nine, and his wife at the age of twenty. He had been married in Spain to his kinswoman, a beautiful girl of the American aristocracy, and his only dream then was to be happy with her while he increased his immense fortune as master of life and property on the San Mateo Plantation. It was never established with any certainty if the death of his wife eight months after the wedding was caused by a malignant fever or a domestic accident. For him it meant his birth into history, for he had been a rich young gentleman from the colonies, dazzled by mundane pleasures and without the slightest interest in politics, but at that moment he became, with no transition, the man he would be for the rest of his life. He never spoke of his dead wife again, he never recalled her, he never tried to replace her. Almost every night of his life he dreamed about the house at San Mateo, and he often dreamed of his father and mother, his brother and sisters, but he never dreamed about her, for he had buried her at the bottom of a watertight oblivion as a brutal means of living without her. All that could stir her momentary memory was the smell

of molasses at San Pedro Alejandrino, the impassivity of
the slaves in the mills, who did not cast so much as a
pitying glance in his direction, the immense trees around
the house that had just been whitewashed to receive him,
the other mill in his life, where an ineluctable destiny was
taking him to die.

"Her name was María Teresa Rodríguez del Toro y
Alayza," he said without warning.

Señor de Mier was at a loss.

"Who?" he asked.

"The woman who was my wife," he said, and then his
reaction was immediate: "But forget it, please: it was a
misfortune of my youth."

That was all he said.

The bedroom that had been prepared for him gave rise
to another deviation of memory, causing him to examine
it with meticulous attention as if each object were a revelation. In addition to the canopied bed there was a mahogany bureau, a mahogany night table with a marble
top, and an armchair covered in red velvet. On the wall
next to the window was an octagonal clock with Roman
numerals, which had stopped at seven minutes past one.

"We've been here before," he said.

Later, when José Palacios wound the clock and set it
for the correct time, the General lay down in the hammock, trying to sleep for a moment. Only then did he
see the clear, blue Sierra Nevada through the window,
like a painting hung on the wall, and his memory wandered to other rooms from so many other lives.

"I've never felt so close to home," he said.

His sleep was sound the first night at San Pedro Alejandrino, and the next day he seemed to have recovered

so well from his maladies that he visited the mills, admired the breeding of the oxen, tasted the honey, and surprised everyone with his knowledge of the arts of milling sugar. General Montilla, astonished at such a change, asked Révérend to tell him the truth, and the latter explained that the General's imaginary improvement was frequent in dying men. The end was a matter of days, perhaps hours. Stunned by the bad news, Montilla smashed the bare wall with his fist and broke his hand. For the rest of his life it would never be the same again. He had often lied to the General, always in good faith and for trivial political reasons. From that day on he lied to him out of charity and instructed those who had access to the General to do the same.

That week eight high-ranking officers expelled from Venezuela for activities against the government arrived in Santa Marta. Among them were several great heroes of the epic of liberation: Nicolás Silva, Trinidad Porto-carrero, Julián Infante. Montilla asked them not only to keep bad news from the dying General but to enhance the good in search of solace for the most serious of his many misfortunes. They went even further and made so encouraging a report on the situation in their country that they were able to rekindle the old fire in his eyes. The General returned to the topic of Riohacha, banished from conversation for the past week, and he spoke again of Venezuela as an imminent possibility.

"We've never had a better opportunity to start over again on the right path," he said. And he concluded with irrefutable conviction: "The day I set foot in the Aragua Valley, the entire Venezuelan nation will rise up in my favor."

In a single afternoon he outlined a new military strategy in the presence of the visiting officers, who offered the assistance of their compassionate enthusiasm. Nevertheless, for the rest of the night they had to listen to him declaim in a prophetic tone just how they would rebuild from the beginning, and this time forever, the vast empire of his dreams. Montilla was the only one who dared to dispute the utter disbelief of those who thought they were listening to the ravings of a madman.

"Watch out," he told them. "That's what they thought at Casacoima."

For no one had forgotten July 4, 1817, when the General had been forced to spend the night in the waters of Casacoima Lagoon, together with a small group of officers, Briceño Méndez among them, hiding from the Spanish troops who had almost taken them by surprise in open country. Half naked and shivering with fever, he suddenly began to declaim at the top of his voice each step he would take in the future: the immediate capture of Angostura, the crossing of the Andes to liberate New Granada and later Venezuela and to found Colombia, and at last the conquest of the immense southern territories all the way to Perú. "Then we will climb Chimborazo and plant on its snow-covered peaks the tricolor of an America that is forever great, united, and free," he concluded. Those who heard him in Casacoima also thought he had lost his mind, and nevertheless it was a prophecy fulfilled in every detail in less than five years.

Sad to say, the prophecy at San Pedro Alejandrino was no more than a vision of dire things to come. The sufferings held at bay during the first week rushed headlong into a violent windstorm of total annihilation. By this time the General had grown so small that the cuffs of his shirt-sleeves had to be turned up again and an inch was cut off the corduroy trousers. He could not sleep more than three hours in the early evening, and the rest of the night he spent strangled by coughing, or hallucinating in his delirium, or driven to despair by the recurrent attacks of hiccuping that had begun in Santa Marta and were becoming more and more tenacious. In the afternoon, while the others napped, he endured his agony by looking through the window at the snowy peaks of the Sierra.

He had crossed the Atlantic four times and ridden through the liberated territories on horseback more than anyone would ever do again, and he had never made a will, which was unheard-of at that time. "I have nothing to leave anyone," he would say. When he was preparing for his departure in Santa Fe de Bogotá, General Pedro Alcántara Herrán had recommended he do so, with the argument that it was a normal precaution for every traveler, and the General had told him, more in seriousness than in jest, that death was not part of his immediate plans. Nevertheless, at San Pedro Alejandrino, it was he who took the initiative and dictated rough drafts of his last will and testament. No one ever knew if it was a reasoned act or the stumbling of his afflicted heart.

Because Fernando was ill, he began by dictating to José Laurencio Silva a series of somewhat disordered notes that did not express his desires so much as his disillusionment: America is ungovernable, the man who serves a revolution plows the sea, this nation will fall inevitably into the hands of the unruly mob and then will pass into the hands of almost indistinguishable petty tyrants of every color and race, and many other lugubrious thoughts that had already circulated as separate ideas in letters to various friends.

He continued dictating for several hours, as if he were in a clairvoyant trance, hardly stopping for the attacks of coughing. José Laurencio Silva could not keep up with him, and Andrés Ibarra could not make the effort of writing with his left hand for very long. When all the secretaries and aides-de-camp were exhausted, one man, a cavalry lieutenant named Nicolás Mariano de Paz, was still standing, and he copied out the dictation with meticulous care and a fair hand until there was no paper left. He asked for more, but it took so long to arrive that he continued copying on the wall until it was almost covered with writing. The General was so grateful that he presented him with the two pistols for duels of love that had belonged to General Lorenzo Cárcamo.

It was his final wish that his remains be taken to Venezuela, that the two books owned by Napoleon be entrusted to the University of Caracas, that eight thousand pesos be given to José Palacios in recognition of his constant service, that the papers he had left with Señor Pavajeau in Cartagena be burned, that the medal with which the Congress of Bolivia had honored him be returned to its place of origin, that the gold sword encrusted with precious gems given him by Field Marshal Sucre be restored to the Field Marshal's widow, and that the rest of his possessions, including the Aroa Mines, be divided among his two sisters and the children of his dead brother. There was not enough for other bequests, because these same possessions had to be used to pay outstanding debts, both large and small, including the recurrent nightmare of the twenty thousand duros owed to Professor Lancaster.

Among the prescribed clauses, he had been careful to include an exceptional one in which he thanked Sir Robert Wilson for the good behavior and fidelity of his son. It was not the distinction that was strange but his not having written one as well for General O'Leary, who would not be present at his death only because he could not arrive in time from Cartagena, where by the General's order he had remained at the disposal of President Urdaneta.

Both names would be forever linked to the General's. Wilson would later be British chargé d'affaires in Lima, and then in Caracas, and would continue his frontline participation in the political and military affairs of both countries. O'Leary would move to Kingston and later to Santa Fe de Bogotá, where he would serve as his nation's consul for many years and die at the age of fifty-one, having collected in thirty-four volumes an enormous testimony of his life with the General of the Americas. His was a quiet and fruitful twilight, which he summarized in a single sentence: "After The Liberator died and his great work was destroyed, I retired to Jamaica, where I dedicated myself to arranging his papers and writing my memoirs."

From the day the General dictated his will, the doctor made exhaustive use of all the palliatives known to his science: mustard plasters on his feet, spinal massages, anodyne poultices over his entire body. He ameliorated the General's congenital constipation with enemas of immediate but devastating effect. Fearing a cerebral congestion, he subjected him to blistering plasters in order to drain the catarrh accumulated in his head. This treatment consisted of plasters made of blister beetle, a caustic insect that, when ground and applied to the skin, produced blisters capable of absorbing medicines. Dr. Révérend applied five blistering plasters to the back of the neck and one to the calf of the dying General. A century and a half later, numerous physicians would still think that the immediate cause of death had been these irritating plasters that provoked a urinary disorder in which micturition was at first involuntary, then painful, and at last bloody, until the bladder was left dry and adhered to the pelvis, as Dr. Révérend confirmed in the autopsy.

The General's sense of smell had become so acute that he obliged the doctor and the pharmacist, Augusto Tomasín, to keep their distance because they smelled of liniment. Then he had the room sprinkled with more cologne than ever, and he continued to take the illusory baths, to shave with his own hand, to clean his teeth with fierce savagery in a superhuman effort to defend himself against the obscene filth of death.

Colonel Luis Perú de Lacroix visited Santa Marta during the second week in December. He was a young veteran of Napoleon's armies who until a short while before had been aide-de-camp to the General, and after his visit the first thing he did was to write the truth to Manuela Sáenz. As soon as she received the letter Manuela set out on the journey to Santa Marta, but in Guaduas they told her she was a whole lifetime too late. The news erased her from the world. She sank into her own shadows, her only obligations the two chests of the General's papers that she managed to hide in a safe place in Santa Fe de Bogotá until, on her instructions, Daniel O'Leary rescued them several years later. General Santander, in one of his first governmental acts, exiled her from the country. Manuela submitted to her fate with festering dignity, first in Jamaica and then in a dismal pilgrimage that would end in Paita, a sordid port on the Pacific where whaling ships from all the oceans came to anchor. There she endured oblivion with embroideries, mule drivers' cigars, and little candies, which she made and sold to sailors for as long as the arthritis in her hands allowed. Dr. Thorne, her husband, was knifed to death in an empty lot in Lima during a robbery in which the little he had with him was stolen, and in his will he left Manuela a sum equal to the dowry she had brought to the marriage, but she never received it. Three memorable visitors consoled her abandonment: the tutor Simón Rodríguez, with whom she shared the ashes of glory, the Italian patriot Giuseppe Garibaldi, who was returning from the struggle against the dictatorship of Rosas in Argentina, and the novelist Herman Melville, who was wandering the oceans of the world gathering information for *Moby-Dick*. When she was old and confined by a broken hip to her hammock, she would give card readings and advice to lovers. She died in an epidemic of the plague at the age of fifty-nine, and her cabin was burned by the health officials, along with the General's precious papers, which included his intimate letters. Her only mementos of him, according to what she told Perú de Lacroix, were a lock of his hair and a glove.

Perú de Lacroix found La Florida de San Pedro Alejandrino already disordered by death. The house was adrift. The officers slept whenever fatigue overcame them and were so irritable that the prudent José Laurencio Silva went so far as to draw his sword in response to Dr. Révérend's demands for silence. Fernanda Barriga did not have the strength or good humor to attend to so many requests for food at the least expected times. The most demoralized played cards day and night, with no concern for the fact that everything they shouted could be heard by the dying man in the next room. One afternoon, while the General was lying in a feverish stupor, someone on the terrace bellowed his rage at the abusive charge of twelve pesos and twenty-three centavos for half a dozen boards, two hundred twenty-five nails, six hundred common tacks and fifty gilded ones, ten yards of madapollam, ten yards of manila ribbon and six yards of black.

It was a shouted litany, which other voices tried to silence but which in the end filled the entire hacienda. Dr. Révérend was in the bedroom changing the bandages on General Montilla's fractured hand, and both of them realized that the sick man, in the lucidity of light sleep, was listening to the list of charges. Montilla went to the window and roared at the top of his voice:

"Shut up, damn it!"

The General intervened without opening his eyes.

"Leave them alone," he said. "After all, by now there aren't any costs I can't hear."

Only José Palacios knew that the General did not need to hear any more to realize that the shouted sums came out of the two hundred fifty-three pesos, seven reales, and three cuartillos in the public collection for his funeral gathered by the municipality from private individuals and from the slaughterhouse and prison funds, and that the lists were of materials for making his coffin and building his tomb. From that time on, José Palacios, following Montilla's orders, took responsibility for keeping everyone out of the bedroom, regardless of rank, title, or dignity, and he imposed on himself so drastic a regimen of caring for the patient that it differed very little from his own death.

"If they had given me power like this from the beginning, the man would have lived to be a hundred," he said.

Fernanda Barriga attempted to enter the bedroom.

"This poor orphan liked women so much," she said, "he can't die without one at his bedside, even if she's as old and ugly and useless as I am."

They would not permit it. And so she sat outside the window, trying to sanctify the pagan ravings of the dying man with her prayers. And there she stayed, living on public charity, submerged in eternal mourning, until the age of a hundred and one.

Just after dark on Wednesday it was she who scattered flowers along the road and led the chanting when the priest from the neighboring village of Mamatoco arrived with the viaticum. He was preceded by a double row of barefoot Indian women wearing cassocks of raw linen and crowns of crape myrtle, who lit his way with oil lamps and sang prayers for the dead in their own language. They walked the path that Fernanda, at their head, was carpeting with flower petals, and it was so hair-raising a moment that no one dared to stop them. The General sat up in bed when he heard them come in the bedroom, shielded his eyes from the light with his arm, and made them leave with a shout:

"Get those altar lights out of here: this looks like a procession of lost souls."

Trying to keep the evil mood in the house from killing the doomed man, Fernando brought a band of street musicians from Mamatoco, who played without stopping for an entire day under the tamarind trees in the patio. The General responded well to the calming effect of the music. "La Trinitaria," his favorite contredanse, was repeated several times. It had become popular because in another time he distributed copies of the score wherever he went.

The slaves stopped the mills and watched the General for a long while through the vines at the window. He was wrapped in a white sheet, more emaciated and ashen than after death, and he kept time to the music with his head, which was bristling with a new growth of hair. After each piece he applauded with the conventional propriety he had learned at the Paris Opéra.

At noon, animated by the music, he drank a cup of broth and ate a ground mixture of arrowroot and boiled chicken. Afterwards, in the hammock, he asked for a hand mirror, looked at himself, and said: "With these eyes I won't die." The almost abandoned hope that Dr. Révérend could perform a miracle was reborn in everyone. But when he seemed better, the invalid confused General Sardá with one of the thirty-eight Spanish officers whom Santander had ordered shot without trial in a single day following the battle of Boyacá. Later he suffered a sudden relapse, from which he never recovered, and he shouted with the little voice left to him to get the musicians away from the house, where they could not disturb the silence of his death agony. When he was calm again he ordered Wilson to compose a letter to General Justo Briceño, asking him as an almost post-humous homage to make peace with General Urdaneta in order to save the country from the horrors of anarchy. The only part he dictated was the heading: "I am writing this letter to you in the final moments of my life."

He talked with Fernando until very late that night, and for the first time he advised him regarding the future. The idea of their writing his memoirs together would not be realized, but his nephew had lived by his side long enough to attempt to write them as a simple act of love, so that his children would have an idea of those years of glory and disaster. "O'Leary will write something if he doesn't change his mind," the General said. "But it will be different." Fernando was then twenty-six years old, and he would live to the age of eighty-eight without writing anything more than a few disordered pages, for fate granted him the immense good fortune of losing his memory.

José Palacios had been in the bedroom while the General dictated his will. Neither he nor anyone else said a word during an act imbued with sacramental solemnity. But that night, while the General was in the emollient bath, José Palacios pleaded with him to change his bequest.

"We have always been poor and we haven't needed anything," he told him.

"The truth is just the opposite," said the General. "We have always been rich and we haven't anything left."

Both extremes were true. José Palacios had entered his service when he was very young, by order of the General's mother, who was his owner, and he had not been emancipated in a formal way. He was left floating in a civil limbo in which he was never paid a salary and his status was not defined, but his personal needs formed part of the private needs of the General, with whom he identified even in his manner of dressing and eating and in his exaggerated sobriety. The General was not willing to leave him adrift without military rank or a certificate of disability, and at an age when he was not disposed to start a new life. And so there was no alternative: the legacy of eight thousand pesos was not only irrevocable but unrenounceable.

"It's the fitting thing," concluded the General.

José Palacios' reply was abrupt:

"The fitting thing is for us to die together."

And in fact that is what happened, for he managed his money as badly as the General managed his. After his death José Palacios remained in Cartagena de Indias at the mercy of public charity, attempted to drown his memories in alcohol, and succumbed to its pleasures. He died at the age of seventy-six in a den of beggars who were veterans of the liberating army, writhing in the mud with the torments of delirium tremens.

The General was so ill when he awoke on December 10 that they called Bishop Estévez with all urgency in the event he wanted to make his confession. The Bishop rushed to the house, and such was the importance he gave to the interview that he wore full episcopal attire. But by order of the General it took place behind closed doors and without witnesses and lasted only fourteen minutes.

No one ever learned a word they said. The Bishop hurried away in a state of consternation, climbed into his carriage without saying goodbye, and would not officiate at the funeral despite many requests, or even attend the burial. The General was so weak he could not get out of the hammock unassisted, and the doctor had to lift him in his arms like an infant and prop him against the pillows on the bed so he would not be strangled by coughing. When at last he caught his breath he had everyone leave so he could talk to the doctor alone.

"I never imagined this damn business was serious enough to even think about last rites," he said. "And I don't have the good fortune to believe in the afterlife."

"It's not a question of that," said Révérend. "It has been demonstrated that settling matters of conscience inspires a state of mind in the patient that facilitates the physician's task."

The General paid no attention to the masterful reply, because he was shaken by the overwhelming revelation that the headlong race between his misfortunes and his dreams was at that moment reaching the finish line. The rest was darkness.

"Damn it," he sighed. "How will I ever get out of this labyrinth!"

He examined the room with the clairvoyance of his last days, and for the first time he saw the truth: the final borrowed bed, the pitiful dressing table whose clouded, patient mirror would not reflect his image again, the chipped porcelain washbasin with the water and towel and soap meant for other hands, the heartless speed of the octagonal clock racing toward the ineluctable appointment at seven minutes past one on his final afternoon of

December 17. Then he crossed his arms over his chest and began to listen to the radiant voices of the slaves singing the six o'clock *Salve* in the mills, and through the window he saw the diamond of Venus in the sky that was dying forever, the eternal snows, the new vine whose yellow bellflowers he would not see bloom on the following Saturday in the house closed in mourning, the final brilliance of life that would never, through all eternity, be repeated again.

My Thanks

For many years I listened to Alvaro Mutis discussing his plan to write about Simón Bolívar's final voyage along the Magdalena River. When he published "El Último Rostro" [The Last Face], a fragment of the projected book, the story seemed so ripe, and its style and tone so polished, that I expected to read it in its complete form very soon afterwards. Nevertheless, two years later I had the impression that he had relegated it to oblivion, as so many writers do even with our best-loved dreams, and only then did I dare ask for his permission to write it myself. It was a direct hit after a ten-year ambush. Therefore my first thanks go to him.

At that time the Magdalena River interested me more than the glories of the central character. I began to know it as a child, traveling from the Caribbean coast, where I had the good fortune to be born, to the distant, fogbound city of Bogotá, where, from my first visit, I felt more of an outsider than in any other city in the world. As a student I sailed the river eleven times in both directions, traveling on steamboats that came out of the shipyards of the Mississippi already condemned to nostalgia and possessed of a mythic call that no writer could resist.

On the other hand, I was not particularly troubled by the question of historical accuracy, since the last voyage along the river is the least documented period in Bolívar's life. During this time he wrote only three or four letters—a man who must have dictated over ten thousand—and none of his companions left a written memoir of those fourteen calamitous days. Nevertheless, beginning with the first chapter, I had to do occasional research concerning the way he lived, and that research referred me to other sources, and then to more and more until I was overwhelmed. I spent two long years sinking into the quicksands of voluminous, contradictory, and often uncertain documentation, from the thirty-four volumes by Daniel Florencio O'Leary to articles in the most unexpected newspapers. My absolute lack of experience and method in historical research made my days even more arduous.

This book would not have been possible without the help of those who threshed the same ground for a century and a half before me and made my literary audacity easier: I would recount a tyrannically documented life without renouncing the extravagant prerogatives of the novel. But my thanks go in a very special way to a group of friends, old and new, who took as their own affair, and one of the utmost importance, not only my most serious questions, such as the real nature of Bolívar's political thought amid all his flagrant contradictions, but also the most trivial, such as the size of his shoes. Nevertheless, I value most the indulgence of those who, through abominable oversight, do not find themselves included in this grateful accounting.

The Colombian historian Eugenio Gutiérrez Celys, in response to many pages of questions, prepared a card file for me that not only provided surprising information—much of it buried in nineteenth-century Colombian newspapers—but also gave me my first inkling of a method for investigating and ordering facts. Furthermore, his book, *Bolívar Día a Día* [Bolívar Day by Day], coauthored with the historian Fabio Puyo, was a navigational chart while I was writing, which allowed me to move with ease through all the periods in the character's life. This same Fabio Puyo had the ability to soothe my distress with analgesic documents, which he read to me on the telephone from Paris or sent to me with all urgency by telex or telefax, as if they were life-or-death medicines. The Colombian historian Gustavo Vargas, a professor at the Universidad Nacional Autónoma de México, stayed within reach of my telephone to clarify major and minor doubts, above all those related to the political ideas of the period. Vinicio Romero Martínez, the biographer of Bolívar, helped me from Caracas with discoveries that seemed incredible regarding Bolívar's private habits—his vulgar language in particular—and the nature and fate of his entourage and, in the final version, with an implacable review of historical data. To him I owe the providential warning that Bolívar could not eat mangos with the childish delight I had attributed to him, for the simple reason that the mango would not reach the Americas for another few years.

Jorge Eduardo Ritter, Ambassador of Panamá to Colombia and then Foreign Minister of his country, made several urgent plane trips just to bring me books of his that could not be found elsewhere. Don Francisco de Abrisqueta, of Bogotá, was a persevering guide through the intricate and vast Bolivarian bibliography. Ex-President Belisario Betancur clarified doubts throughout an entire year of telephone consultations and established that some verses Bolívar recited from memory were by the Ecuadorian poet José Joaquín Olmedo. With Francisco Pividal in Havana I held the long preliminary conversations that permitted me to form a clear idea of the book I should write. Roberto Cadavid (Argos), the most popular and accommodating linguist in Colombia, did me the favor of investigating the significance and age of various localisms. At my request the geographer Gladstone Oliva and the astronomer Jorge Pérez Doval, of the Academy of Sciences in Cuba, made an inventory of nights when the moon was full during the first thirty years of the last century.

From his Colombian embassy in Puerto Príncipe my old friend Aníbal Noguera Mendoza sent me copies of his personal papers and his generous permission to use them with absolute liberty, although they were notes and first drafts of a study he is writing on the same subject. Moreover, in the first draft of the manuscript, he discovered half a dozen mortal fallacies and suicidal anachronisms that would have cast doubts on the exactitude of this novel.

Finally, Antonio Bolívar Goyanes—a distant relative of the

protagonist and perhaps the last old-fashioned typesetter left in Mexico—had the kindness to revise seven different versions of the manuscript with me in a millimeter-by-millimeter hunt for contradictions, repetitions, irrelevancies, mistakes, and typographical errors, and in a pitiless examination of language and spelling. In this way we surprised in flagrante a soldier who won battles before he was born, a widow who went to Europe with her beloved husband, and an intimate luncheon for Bolívar and Sucre in Bogotá when one was in Caracas and the other in Quito. Nevertheless, I am not very certain I should give thanks for these two final pieces of assistance, for it seems to me that such absurdities might have added a few drops of involuntary—and perhaps desirable—humor to the horror of this book.

G.G.M.

Mexico City, January 1989

Brief Chronology: Simón Bolívar

(PREPARED BY VINICIO ROMERO MARTÍNEZ)

1783   *July 24:* birth of Simón Bolívar.

1786   *January 19:* death of Juan Vicente Bolívar, Simón's father.

1792   *July 6:* death of Doña María de la Concepción Palacios y Blanco, Bolívar's mother.

1795   Bolívar leaves his uncle's house. A lengthy lawsuit is begun, and he is moved to the house of his tutor, Simón Rodríguez. In October he returns to the house of his uncle, Carlos.

1797   The Gual and España conspiracy in Venezuela. Bolívar joins the militia as a cadet in Valles de Aragua.

1797–   Andrés Bellos gives him lessons in grammar and geog-
1798   raphy. At this time he also studies physics and mathematics, both at home and at the academy established by Father Francisco de Andújar.

1799   *January 19:* he travels to Spain, making stops in Mexico and Cuba. In Veracruz he writes his first letter.

1799–   In Madrid he comes into contact with the Marquis de
1800   Ustáriz, the scholar who was his true intellectual mentor.

1801   Between March and December he studies French in Bilbao.

1802   *February 12:* in Amiens, France, he admires Napoleon Bonaparte. He is enraptured by Paris.

May 26: he marries María Teresa Rodríguez del Toro in Madrid.

July 12: he arrives in Venezuela with his wife. He dedicates himself to caring for his estates.

1803   *January 22:* María Teresa dies in Caracas.

October 23: he returns to Spain.

1804   *December 2:* he witnesses the coronation of Napoleon in Paris.

1805   *August 15:* the vow on Monte Sacro, Rome.

December 27: he is initiated as a Mason of the Scottish rite in Paris. In January 1806, he rises to the degree of master.

1807   *January 1:* he lands in Charleston (U.S.A.). He visits several cities in that country, and in June he returns to Caracas.

1810   *April 18:* he is confined to his hacienda at Aragua; for this reason he does not participate in the events of April 19, the first day of the Venezuelan revolution.

June 9: he leaves on a diplomatic mission to London. Here he meets Francisco de Miranda.

December 5: he returns from London. Five days later Miranda arrives in Caracas and is a guest in Simón Bolívar's house.

1811   *March 2:* the first Congress of Venezuela meets.

July 4: Bolívar's speech at the Patriotic Society.

July 5: Declaration of Venezuelan Independence.

July 23: Bolívar fights in Valencia under Miranda's command. It is his first experience of war.

1812   *March 26:* earthquake in Caracas.

July 6: Colonel Simón Bolívar loses the castle at Puerto Cabello as a result of treason.

July 30: together with other officers, he captures Miranda to bring him to military trial, thinking him a traitor for having signed the surrender. Manuel María Casas takes the illustrious prisoner from them and turns him over to the Spanish.

September 1: he arrives in Curaçao, his first exile.

December 15: the Cartagena Manifesto is published in New Granada.

December 24: with the occupation of Tenerife, Bolívar begins the Magdalena River campaign, which will clear the entire region of royalists.

1813   *February 28:* the battle of Cúcuta.

March 1: he occupies San Antonio del Táchira.

March 12: he is promoted to brigadier general of New Granada.

May 14: he begins the Admirable Campaign in Cúcuta.

May 23: he is acclaimed as Liberator in Mérida.

June 15: he issues the Proclamation of War to the Death in Trujillo.

August 6: his triumphant entry into Caracas. End of the Admirable Campaign.

October 14: the Municipal Council of Caracas, in public assembly, acclaims Bolívar as Captain General and Liberator.

December 5: the battle of Araure.

1814   *February 8:* he orders the execution of prisoners in La Guayra.

February 12: the battle of La Victoria.

February 28: the battle of San Mateo.

May 28: the first battle of Carabobo.

July 7: some twenty thousand Caracans, with The Liberator at their head, begin the migration to Oriente.

September 4: Ribas and Piar, who have proscribed Bolívar and Mariño, order their arrest in Carúpano.

September 7: Bolívar issues his Carúpano Manifesto and, ignoring the arrest order, sails the next day for Cartagena.

November 27: the government of New Granada promotes him to General in Chief, with the responsibility for reconquering the State of Cundinamarca. He undertakes the campaign that ends with the fall of Bogotá.

December 12: he establishes a government in Bogotá.

1815   *May 10:* in his attempt to liberate Venezuela, invading through Cartagena, he encounters serious opposition from the city's authorities and decides to sail for Jamaica in voluntary exile.

September 6: he publishes the celebrated *Jamaica Letter*.

December 24: he lands in Los Cayos, Haiti, where he meets with his friend Luis Brión, a mariner from Curaçao. In Haiti he has an interview with President Pétion, who will offer him invaluable cooperation.

1816   *March 31:* the so-called Los Cayos expedition leaves Haiti. Luis Brión is with them.

June 2: he decrees the emancipation of the slaves in Carúpano.

1817   *February 9:* Bolívar and Bermúdez are reconciled and embrace on the bridge over the Neveri River (Barcelona).

April 11: the battle of San Félix, which is liberated by Piar. The liberation of Angostura, the control of the Orinoco River, and the definitive stabilization of the (Third) Republic are achieved.

May 8: a congress convened by Canon José Cortés Madariaga meets in Cariaco. This insignificant Cariaco Congress ends in failure, although two of its decrees are still in effect: the seven stars in the national flag and the name Estado Nueva Esparta [State of New Sparta] for the island of Margarita.

May 12: he promotes Piar to General in Chief.

June 19: he writes to Piar in a conciliatory tone: "General, I prefer combat with the Spanish to these disagreements between patriots."

July 4: in Casacoima Lagoon, hiding in water up to his neck to escape a royalist ambush, he begins a discourse to his astonished officers in which he predicts what he will do from the conquest of Angostura to the liberation of Perú.

October 16: the execution by firing squad of General Piar in Angostura. Luis Brión presides over the court-martial.

1818 *January 30:* his first meeting with Páez, the leader of Los Llanos, in the hut at Cañafístula, Apure.

February 12: Bolívar defeats Morillo at Calabozo.

June 27: he founds the Orinoco mail service in Angostura.

1819 *February 15:* he installs the Congress of Angostura and gives the celebrated speech of that name. He is elected President of Venezuela. He immediately begins the campaign for the liberation of New Granada.

August 7: the battle of Boyacá.

December 17: Bolívar creates the Republic of Colombia, divided into three departments: Venezuela, Cundinamarca, and Quito. The Congress elects him President of Colombia.

1820 *January 11:* in San Juan de Payara, Apure.

March 5: in Bogotá.

April 19: in San Cristóbal he celebrates the tenth anniversary of the beginning of the revolution.

November 27: he meets with Pablo Morillo in Santa Ana, Trujillo. The previous day he ratifies the armistice and the treaty regularizing the war.

1821 *January 5:* in Bogotá, planning the campaign of the south, which he will entrust to Sucre.

February 14: he congratulates Rafael Urdaneta for having declared the independence of Maracaibo, although he expresses the fear that Spain may consider it an act of bad faith, to the detriment of the armistice.

April 17: in a proclamation, he announces the breaking of the armistice and the beginning of a "holy war": "The battle will be to disarm the adversary, not to destroy him."

April 28: hostilities break out again.

June 27: Bolívar defeats La Torre at Carabobo. Although it is not the final battle, at Carabobo he assures the independence of Venezuela.

1822 *April 7:* the battle of Bombóna.

May 24: the battle of Pichincha.

June 16: he meets Manuelita Sáenz in Quito when he makes his triumphal entry into the city at the side of Sucre.

July 11: Bolívar arrives in Guayaquil. Two days later he declares its incorporation into Colombia.

July 26–27: Bolívar and San Martín meet in Guayaquil.

October 13: he writes "Mi delirio sobre el Chimborazo" [My Rapture at El Chimborazo] in Loja, near Cuenca, Ecuador.

1823   *March 1:* Riva Agüero, the President of Perú, asks The Liberator for four thousand soldiers and the assistance of Colombia to achieve independence. Bolívar sends the first contingent of three thousand men on March 17 and another three thousand on April 12.

May 14: the Congress of Perú issues a decree in which it calls on The Liberator to end the civil war.

September 1: Bolívar arrives in Lima, Perú. The Congress authorizes him to subdue Riva Agüero, who has rebelled in favor of the Spanish.

1824   *January 1:* he is ill when he arrives in Pativilca.

January 12: he decrees the death penalty for anyone robbing the public treasury of more than ten pesos.

January 19: a beautiful letter to his tutor, Simón Rodríguez: "You educated my heart to liberty, to justice, to greatness, to beauty."

February 10: the Congress of Perú names him dictator so he can save the Republic, which is in ruins.

August 6: the battle of Junín.

December 5: Bolívar liberates Lima.

December 7: he convokes the Congress of Panamá.

December 9: Sucre's victory at Ayacucho. All of Spanish America is free.

1825   England recognizes the independence of the new American states.

February 12: the Congress of Perú, in gratitude, decrees honors for The Liberator: a medal, an equestrian statue, a million pesos for him and another million for the liberating army. Bolívar refuses the money offered him by the Congress but accepts the sum intended for his soldiers.

February 18: the Congress of Perú does not accept his renunciation of the presidency with unlimited powers.

August 6: an assembly, meeting in Chuquisaca, Alto Perú, decides to create the Republic of Bolivia.

October 26: in Cerro de Potosí.

December 25: in Chuquisaca he decrees the planting of a million trees, "wherever there is greatest need for them."

1826   *May 25:* from Lima he informs Sucre that Perú has recognized the Republic of Bolivia. At the same time he sends him his plan for the Bolivian Constitution.

June 22: the Congress of Panamá is installed.

December 16: he arrives in Maracaibo, where he makes the offer to Venezuela to convoke the great convention.

December 31: he arrives in Puerto Cabello in search of Páez.

1827   *January 1:* he decrees amnesty for those responsible for La Cosiata. He ratifies Páez as supreme commander of Venezuela.

January 1: he writes to Páez from Puerto Cabello: "I cannot divide the Republic; but I want you for the good of Venezuela, and it will be done in the general assembly if that is Venezuela's desire."

January 4: in Naguanagua, near Valencia, he meets with Páez and offers his support. Previously he had told the Congress of Bogotá that it had "the right to resist injustice with justice, and the abuse of power with disobedience." This angers Santander, who nurtures his dissatisfaction with The Liberator.

January 12: he arrives in Caracas with Páez, to the cheers of the people.

February 5: from Caracas he sends the Congress of Bogotá another renunciation of the presidency, with a dramatic exposition of his reasons, which ends: "With these feelings I renounce the presidency of the republic once, a thousand, a million times . . ."

March 16: he breaks definitively with Santander: "Do not write to me again, because I do not wish to answer you or call you friend."

June 6: the Congress of Colombia rejects Bolívar's renunciation and demands that he go to Bogotá to take the oath of office.

July 5: he leaves Caracas for Bogotá. He will not visit his native city again.

September 10: he arrives in Bogotá and takes the oath of office as President of the Republic, facing fierce political opposition.

September 11: letter to Tomás de Heres: "Yesterday I entered this capital and am now in possession of the presidency. This was necessary: many evils are avoided in exchange for infinite difficulties."

1828   *April 10:* in Bucaramanga during the Ocaña Convention, where the Bolivarist and Santanderist parties are clearly defined. Bolívar registers his protest to the convention at the "expression of gratitude directed to General Padilla for his assassination attempts in Cartagena."

June 9: he leaves Bucaramanga with the idea of going to Venezuela. He intends to live on the estate at Anauco owned by the Marquis del Toro.

June 11: the Ocaña Convention is dissolved.

June 24: his plans changed, he returns to Bogotá, to great acclaim.

July 15: in a proclamation issued in Valencia, Páez calls Bolívar "the singular genius of the nineteenth century . . . the man who for eighteen years has suffered sacrifice after sacrifice for your happiness, and has made the greatest one that could be demanded of his heart: the supreme command that he has renounced a thousand times, but which in the present state of the Republic he is obliged to exercise."

August 27: the decree of institutional dictatorship, imposed as a result of the rivalries at the Ocaña Convention. Bolívar abolishes the vice-presidency, thereby eliminating Santander from the government. The Liberator offers him the post of Colombian Ambassador to the United States. Santander accepts, but defers the trip for a period of time. It is possible that the elimination of Santander's office has an influence on the assassination attempt against Bolívar.

September 21: Páez recognizes Bolívar as supreme commander and swears, before Archbishop Ramón Ignacio Méndez and a crowd gathered in the Plaza Mayor of Caracas: ". . . and I promise under oath to obey, keep, and execute the decrees issued as laws of the Republic. Heaven, which is witness to my oath, will reward the fidelity with which I keep my promise."

September 25: an assassination attempt against Bolívar in Bogotá. Manuelita Sáenz saves him. Santander is among those implicated. Urdaneta, as judge at the trial, condemns him to death. Bolívar commutes the death penalty to exile.

1829   *January 1:* in Purificación. His presence in Ecuador is necessary because of conflicts with Perú, which has occupied Guayaquil.

July 21: Colombia regains Guayaquil. The people welcome The Liberator in triumph.

September 13: he writes to O'Leary: "We all know that the reunification of New Granada and Venezuela is bound only by my authority, which must disappear now or later, whenever Providence or men so desire . . ."

September 13: letter from Páez: "I have ordered the publication of a circular inviting all citizens and associations to express their opinions formally and solemnly. Now you can legally urge that the public say whatever it wishes. The point has been reached whereby Venezuela speaks with no concern other than the general welfare. If radical means are adopted for saying what all of you really desire, the reforms will be perfect and the will of the public will be done . . ."

October 20: he returns to Quito.

October 29: he leaves for Bogotá.

December 5: from Popayán he writes to Juan José Flores: "General Sucre will probably be my successor, and it is also probable that all of us will support him; for my part I offer to do so with all my heart and soul."

December 15: he indicates to Páez that he will not accept the presidency of the Republic again and that if the Congress elects Páez President of Colombia, he swears to him on his honor that he will obey his orders with the greatest pleasure.

December 18: he categorically disapproves the plan for a monarchy in Colombia.

1830 *January 15:* once again in Bogotá.

January 20: the Congress of Colombia convenes. A message from Bolívar: he presents his renunciation of the presidency.

January 27: he requests permission from Congress to go to Venezuela. The Congress of Colombia denies him permission.

March 1: he hands over power to Domingo Caicedo, president of the Council of Government, and retires to Fucha.

April 27: in a message to the Admirable Congress he reiterates his decision not to continue in the presidency.

May 4: Joaquín Mosquera is elected President of Colombia.

May 8: Bolívar leaves Bogotá to meet his final destiny.

June 4: Sucre is assassinated in Berruecos. Bolívar learns of it on July 1, at the foot of La Popa Hill, and is profoundly shaken.

September 5: Urdaneta takes over the government of Colombia in the face of an evident lack of civil authority. In Bogotá, Cartagena, and other cities in New Granada there are demonstrations and pronouncements in favor of The Liberator's return to power. Urdaneta, in the meantime, waits for him.

September 18: on learning of the events that placed Urdaneta at the head of the government, he offers himself as citizen and soldier to defend the integrity of the Republic, and he announces that he will march to Bogotá at the head of two thousand men to uphold the existing government; he rejects in part the request that he take power, stating that he would be considered a usurper, but he leaves open the possibility that in the next elections, ". . . legitimacy will shelter me or there will be a new President . . ."; finally, he asks his compatriots to unite around Urdaneta's government.

October 2: in Turbaco.

October 15: in Soledad.

November 8: in Barranquilla.

December 1: he arrives prostrate in Santa Marta.

December 6: he goes to the plantation at San Pedro Alejandrino that belongs to the Spaniard Don Joaquín de Mier.

December 10: he dictates his last will and testament. When the physician insists that he confess and receive the sacraments, Bolívar says: "What does this mean? . . . Can I be so ill that you talk to me of wills and confession? . . . How will I ever get out of this labyrinth!"

December 17: he dies on the plantation at San Pedro Alejandrino in the company of a very few friends.

FOR THE BEST IN PAPERBACKS, LOOK FOR THE 🐧

In every corner of the world, on every subject under the sun, Penguin represents quality and variety – the very best in publishing today.

For complete information about books available from Penguin – including Puffins, Penguin Classics and Arkana – and how to order them, write to us at the appropriate address below. Please note that for copyright reasons the selection of books varies from country to country.

In the United Kingdom: Please write to *Dept E.P., Penguin Books Ltd, Harmondsworth, Middlesex, UB7 0DA.*

If you have any difficulty in obtaining a title, please send your order with the correct money, plus ten per cent for postage and packaging, to *PO Box No 11, West Drayton, Middlesex*

In the United States: Please write to *Dept BA, Penguin, 299 Murray Hill Parkway, East Rutherford, New Jersey 07073*

In Canada: Please write to *Penguin Books Canada Ltd, 2801 John Street, Markham, Ontario L3R 1B4*

In Australia: Please write to the *Marketing Department, Penguin Books Australia Ltd, P.O. Box 257, Ringwood, Victoria 3134*

In New Zealand: Please write to the *Marketing Department, Penguin Books (NZ) Ltd, Private Bag, Takapuna, Auckland 9*

In India: Please write to *Penguin Overseas Ltd, 706 Eros Apartments, 56 Nehru Place, New Delhi, 110019*

In the Netherlands: Please write to *Penguin Books Netherlands B.V., Postbus 195, NL–1380AD Weesp*

In West Germany: Please write to *Penguin Books Ltd, Friedrichstrasse 10–12, D–6000 Frankfurt/Main 1*

In Spain: Please write to *Alhambra Longman S.A., Fernandez de la Hoz 9, E–28010 Madrid*

In Italy: Please write to *Penguin Italia s.r.l., Via Como 4, I-20096 Pioltello (Milano)*

In France: Please write to *Penguin Books Ltd, 39 Rue de Montmorency, F-75003 Paris*

In Japan: Please write to *Longman Penguin Japan Co. Ltd, Yamaguchi Building, 2–12–9 Kanda Jimbocho, Chiyoda-Ku, Tokyo 101*

A CHOICE OF PENGUIN FICTION

The Captain and the Enemy   Graham Greene

The Captain always maintained that he won Jim from his father at a game of backgammon...'It is good to find the best living writer ... still in such first-rate form' – Francis King in the *Spectator*

The Book and the Brotherhood   Iris Murdoch

'Why should we go on supporting a book which we detest?' Rose Curtland asks. 'The brotherhood of Western intellectuals versus the book of history,' Jenkin Riderhood suggests. 'A thoroughly gripping, stimulating and challenging fiction' – *The Times*

The King of the Fields   Isaac Bashevis Singer

His profound and magical excursion into prehistory. '*The King of the Fields* reaps an abundant harvest ... it has a deceptive biblical simplicity and carries the poetry of narrative to rare heights. At eighty-five, Isaac Bashevis Singer has lost none of his incomparable wonder-working power' – *Sunday Times*

The Enigma of Arrival   V. S. Naipaul

'For sheer abundance of talent, there can hardly be a writer alive who surpasses V. S. Naipaul. Whatever we want in a novelist is to be found in his books' – Irving Howe in *The New York Times Book Review*

Lewis Percy   Anita Brookner

'Anita Brookner shines again ... [a] tender and cruel, funny and sad novel about an innocent idealist, whose gentle rearing by his widowed mother causes him to take too gallant a view of women' – *Daily Mail*. 'Vintage Brookner' – *The Times*

A CHOICE OF PENGUIN FICTION

Humboldt's Gift Saul Bellow

Bellow's classic story of the writer's life in America is an exuberant tale of success and failure. 'Sharp, erudite, beautifully measured ... One of the most gifted chroniclers of the Western world alive today' – *The Times*

Incline Our Hearts A. N. Wilson

'An account of an eccentric childhood so moving, so private and personal, and so intensely funny that it bears inescapable comparison with that greatest of childhood novels, *David Copperfield*' – *Daily Telegraph*

The Lyre of Orpheus Robertson Davies

'The lyre of Orpheus opens the door of the underworld', wrote E. T. A. Hoffmann; and his spirit, languishing in limbo, watches over, and comments on, the efforts of the Cornish Foundation as its Trustees decide to produce an opera. 'A marvellous finale' (*Sunday Times*) to Robertson Davies's Cornish Trilogy.

The New Confessions William Boyd

The outrageous, hilarious autobiography of John James Todd, a Scotsman born in 1899 and one of the great self-appointed (and failed) geniuses of the twentieth century. 'Brilliant ... a Citizen Kane of a novel' – *Daily Telegraph*

The Blue Gate of Babylon Paul Pickering

'Like Ian Fleming gone berserk, the writing is of supreme quality, the humour a taste instantly acquired' – *Mail on Sunday*. 'Brilliantly exploits the fluently headlong manner of Evelyn Waugh's early black farces' – *Sunday Times*

A CHOICE OF PENGUIN FICTION

A Far Cry From Kensington   Muriel Spark

'Pure delight' – Claire Tomalin in the *Independent*. 'A 1950s Kensington of shabby-genteel bedsitters, espresso bars and A-line dresses ... irradiated with sudden glows of lyricism she can so beautifully effect' – Peter Kemp in the *Sunday Times*

Love in the Time of Cholera   Gabriel García Márquez

The Number One international bestseller. 'Admirers of *One Hundred Years of Solitude* may find it hard to believe that García Márquez can have written an even better novel. But that's what he's done' – *Newsweek*

Enchantment   Monica Dickens

The need to escape, play games, fantasize, is universal. But for some people it is everything. To this compassionate story of real lives Monica Dickens brings her unparalleled warmth, insight and perception. 'One of the tenderest souls in English fiction' – *Sunday Times*

My Secret History   Paul Theroux

'André Parent saunters into the book, aged fifteen ... a creature of naked and unquenchable ego, greedy for sex, money, experience, *another life* ... read it warily; read it twice, and more; it is darker and deeper than it looks' – *Observer*. 'On his best form since *The Mosquito Coast*' – *Time Out*

Decline and Fall   Evelyn Waugh

A comic yet curiously touching account of an innocent plunged into the sham, brittle world of high society. Evelyn Waugh's first novel brought him immediate public acclaim and remains a classic of its kind.

A CHOICE OF PENGUIN FICTION

A Natural Curiosity Margaret Drabble

Moving effortlessly from black comedy to acute social observation, Margaret Drabble picks up the thread of the characters and stories of *The Radiant Way*, as her engrossing panorama of the way we are today shifts to the north of England. 'Confident and marvellously accomplished' – *London Review of Books*

Summer's Lease John Mortimer

'It's high summer, high comedy too, when Molly drags her amiably bickering family to a rented Tuscan villa for the hols ... With a cosy fluency of wit, Mortimer charms us into his urbane tangle of clues...' – *Mail on Sunday*. 'Superb' – Ruth Rendell

Nice Work David Lodge

'The campus novel meets the industrial novel ... compulsive reading' – David Profumo in the *Daily Telegraph*. 'A work of immense intelligence, informative, disturbing and diverting ... one of the best novelists of his generation' – Anthony Burgess in the *Observer*

S. John Updike

'John Updike's very funny satire not only pierces the occluded hocus-pocus of Lego religion which exploits the gullible and self-deluded ... but probes more deeply and seriously the inadequacies on which superstitious skulduggery battens' – *The Times*

The Counterlife Philip Roth

'Roth has now surpassed himself' – *Washington Post*. 'A breathtaking *tour de force* of wit, wisdom, ingenuity and sharply-honed malice' – *The Times*

FOR THE BEST IN PAPERBACKS, LOOK FOR THE

PENGUIN INTERNATIONAL WRITERS

Gamal Al-Ghitany	**Zayni Barakat**
Wang Anyi	**Baotown**
Joseph Brodsky	**Marbles: A Play in Three Acts**
Shusaku Endo	**The Samurai**
	Scandal
	Wonderful Fool
Ida Fink	**A Scrap of Time**
Miklós Haraszti	**The Velvet Prison**
Ivan Klíma	**My First Loves**
	A Summer Affair
Jean Levi	**The Chinese Emperor**
Harry Mulisch	**Last Call**
Cees Nooteboom	**A Song of Truth and Semblance**
Luise Rinser	**Prison Journal**
Anton Shammas	**Arabesques**
Josef Škvorecký	**The Cowards**
Tatyana Tolstoya	**On the Golden Porch and Other Stories**
Elie Wiesel	**Twilight**
Zhang Xianliang	**Half of Man is Woman**

FOR THE BEST IN PAPERBACKS, LOOK FOR THE

PENGUIN INTERNATIONAL WRITERS

Baotown Wang Anyi

One of China's foremost young writers draws on the stories and characters of the remote village where she was exiled during the Cultural Revolution, portraying peasant life with the vividness of a Chinese Gorky. 'This is an immemorial China of superstition, starvation and subsistence ... Here we have some of the same studied parochialism as in [Jane] Austen' – *Literary Review*

Marbles: A Play in Three Acts Joseph Brodsky

Imprisoned in a mighty steel tower, where yesterday is the same as today and tomorrow, Publius and Tullius consider freedom, the nature of reality and illusion and the permanence of literature versus the transience of politics. In a Platonic dialogue set 'two centuries after our era' in ancient Rome, Nobel prizewinner Joseph Brodsky takes us beyond the farthest reaches of the theatre of the absurd.

Scandal Shusaku Endo

'Spine-chilling, erotic, cruel ... it's very powerful' – *Sunday Telegraph*. '*Scandal* addresses the great questions of our age. How can we straddle the gulf between faith and modernity? How can humankind be so tender, and yet so cruel? Endo's superb novel offers only an unforgettable bafflement for an answer' – *Observer*

A Summer Affair Ivan Klíma

David Krempa, a biologist in Prague, and married, lives for his work. Iva, young and crazy, lives only for the moment. Their affair was madness, but once it had begun there was no going back. 'Short and sharp ... it leaves one breathless' – *Literary Review*

A Scrap of Time Ida Fink

'A powerful, terrifying story, an almost unbearable witness to unspeakable anguish,' wrote the *New Yorker* of the title story in Ida Fink's award-winning collection. Herself a survivor, she portrays Poland during the Holocaust, the lives of ordinary people in hiding as they resist, submit, hope, betray, remember. 'A masterpiece ... we are brought as close to the Holocaust as it is possible for literature to take us' – Alan Sillitoe

FOR THE BEST IN PAPERBACKS, LOOK FOR THE

PENGUIN INTERNATIONAL WRITERS

On the Golden Porch and Other Stories Tatyana Tolstaya

'There are thirteen stories in this collection and every one's an absolute gem of emotion ... It's not hard to see why quite so much fuss is being made over Tatyana Tolstaya' – *Time Out*. 'With one collection ... she has established herself as a new and original force in Russian literature in her own right' – *Mail on Sunday*

A Song of Truth and Semblance Cees Nooteboom

Two writers meet in an Amsterdam arts club, drink wine, skirt nervously around any talk of their own work and argue about the nature of fiction. For one of them, a floating pair of epaulettes is on the point of fleshing into Georgiev, a nineteenth-century Bulgarian colonel. The banal and irritating phrase 'the colonel falls in love with the doctor's wife' itches at the back of his mind...

Half of Man is Woman Zhang Xianliang

'The gulag literature of the Soviet Union is world-famous, but China's equivalent is almost unknown. *Half of Man is Woman* is exceptional not only for belonging to this genre but also – in China – for daring to make sexuality its theme, together with politics, freedom and identity' – *Observer*

The Velvet Prison Artists Under State Socialism Miklós Haraszti

'A fascinating account of totalitarian aesthetics ... he describes a culture where the traditional antagonism between censor and artist has been replaced with a strange form of collusion. In this new relationship all censors and most artists are entangled in a mutual embrace. This is the "velvet prison"' – *Guardian*

Last Call Harry Mulisch

'Intricately rewarding ... Uli Bouwmeester, an obscure former vaudeville actor, wartime collaborator and member of a famous stage family, is unearthed to play Prospero in a version of *The Tempest* that is also a play-within-a-play about the swansong of a famous actor ... who nurses a guilty secret like the old man playing him...' – *Guardian*

BY THE SAME AUTHOR

Love in the Time of Cholera

'A powerful, poetic and comic long-distance love story set on the Caribbean coast. For fifty years a breath-taking beauty, now old and just widowed, has recoiled in pride and guilt from her secret lover. His desolate obsession has led him into an enigmatic existence in spite of his renown in business. One Pentecost, love found a new tongue with which to speak. Unique Márquez magic of the sadness and funniness of humanity' – *The Times*

'The book is rich and brilliant with emotion – an extraordinary poeticisation of old age. It brings everything close: the disabling heat, the presence of the sea, the storms ... the great coastal swamps behind which García Márquez was born in 1928, the civil wars in the background as regular as the seasons. It suggests that true love is not blind, but sees all the faults and does not mind' – *Observer*

and published in Granta Books

Clandestine in Chile

In 1973, a portly, dark-haired, bearded film director fled Chile after the military coup. Twelve years later he returned, slim, fair, clean-shaven, bringing with him a false passport, a false name, a false past and a false wife.

What kind of man trades his own identity for an invented one? What compels an exile to return to the country where he is on the wanted list?

This is the story of Miguel Littín, who risked his freedom to bring the world a truer picture of life under Pinochet. From eighteen hours of taped interviews, Gabriel García Márquez's prestige and force of expression achieve something still more important. Littín's underground adventure, far from appropriating a starring role for the director – portrayed as a notably incompetent, almost Clouseau-like clandestine – contrives to represent and dramatize the heroic resistance of countless other Chileans, some successful, many others tortured or disappeared, over the past fifteen years' – *Guardian*